EMPIRES

FALL

SHERRYL D. HANCOCK

Published by Vulpine Press in the United Kingdom in 2017

ISBN 978-1-83919-247-0

Cover by Claire Wood

www.vulpine-press.com

These books are for romance readers everywhere. Growing up watching movies and reading books about romance there were two things that bothered me. First, there were never enough strong, independent female characters. Second, the characters spent the whole movie/book trying to get together and at the very last scene/page they do, we never saw how they are together. We never see how they act, talk, handle problems together. I always wanted to know, what happens after "they lived happily ever after." I've written my books to change that, I hope you all like that change!

CHAPTER 1

"Rick," Midnight said incredulously, "he's gone. Joe's gone ..."

"Who's gone?" Rick asked, thinking she was talking about Robbins getting away.

"Joe!" she said miserably, turning her face into his body as she cried.

Putting his finger on her cheek, he turned her back to face him. "Babe," he said, looking at her to make sure she was paying attention. "Joe is fine, he woke up about two hours ago. He's okay."

Midnight's eyes grew wide. "But Robbins said he called the hospital."

"He did," Rick said, nodding, his tone serious, "and they told Robbins exactly what we told them to ... that he had died a half hour before."

"Oh thank God!" Midnight cried, so relieved that it brought tears to Rick's eyes.

"I'm going to get you to a hospital, now," Rick said.

He took off his jacket and draped it around her shoulders. Then he picked her up and carried her to her Corvette. He put her in the passenger's seat and told the police officer he was taking her to the hospital.

She watched him as he drove her car. He glanced over at her a couple of times, concern written all over his face.

"So … your girlfriend, huh?" she asked when they were halfway to the hospital.

Rick smiled then looked over at her seriously. "Yeah."

Midnight nodded and leaned back against the seat, sighing. "Joe's really okay?" she asked again, worried that he was just trying to keep her from freaking out.

"Yes, Midnight, he's fine. He's going to be in the hospital for a while, but they say that he has come out of it surprisingly well."

"Oh God, you can't imagine how it felt, hearing that he was dead. Rick, he was laughing about it."

"I know it was real hard on you. I had a feeling that's why he wanted to know, so he could use it against you, but we couldn't take a chance of him sending someone to finish Joe off either."

Midnight nodded. "Good thinking. How did you find me?"

"We started searching all the houses that Tim had given us. We had practically the entire force out there looking for you," Rick said.

"Wow," Midnight said. She was surprised that she'd meant enough to the department to turn out in numbers to find her.

At the hospital, Rick paused before getting out of the car. He touched her face gently. She was bruised and bleeding, but to him she still looked incredible. When he had realized she'd been taken by

Robbins, he knew he had to get her back, even if it meant his life. He loved her and no matter what he was going to protect her. He didn't know what all had happened to her but he found out an hour later when the doctor who had examined her came out. It was a female doctor and it was obvious she was not happy with what she had found.

"Doc, is she going to be okay?" Rick asked, his eyes very worried.

The doctor looked up at him. "Are you her husband?" Rick shook his head, but it was obvious to the doctor that he was very worried about her. "Boyfriend?" she asked then, and after a moment's hesitation Rick nodded.

"Well Ms. Chevalier basically went through hell and she will have to be handled very carefully for a while."

"What aren't you telling me, doc?"

"Mr.?"

"Debenshire, Rick"

"Rick, your girlfriend was brutally raped. She's surprisingly calm about it though. Whoever did this, hated her very much …" Her voice trailed off as she looked at Rick, wondering who would hate a woman like that so much.

"Yeah, he hates her alright, and thanks to me he's still out there," Rick said, looking very morose.

"Well from the looks of it, you didn't exactly come away from the day's events clean," the doctor said, gesturing to his shoulder and the cuts on his face. She knew about Joe Sinclair, and she knew that Midnight Chevalier was related to the whole thing. She had seen

Randy Curtis just a few hours before in Joe's room. These four were an interesting group, with some dangerous enemies.

"I'm going to release her," the doctor said sighing, "but that's only because she has already informed me that she won't stay even if I try to keep her. I've told her she can see Sinclair when she wants to. Ms. Curtis is already there with him."

"Thanks, doc," Rick said smiling at her. She returned his smile, thinking remotely that Midnight Chevalier was lucky to have a man like this to worry about her. He was handsome, charming, very intense, and obviously very much in love with her.

****

Randy had been sitting in Joe's room since the doctors had told her she could. Things were very tense for the first few hours. He was still in critical condition. She had watched him lying there so still, and cried. She held his hand, touching his ring, thinking of the night they'd made love. It was so long ago, and yet she had relived it so many times, remembering his touch, his kiss, and the look in his eyes. He'd told her he loved her, now here she was just praying that he would live through the night.

Rick had come in two hours into her vigil, and told her that Robbins had Midnight and that he was working on a plan to get her back. At that point, they were still looking for her, but they had lots of manpower doing so.

Randy had been sitting at his bedside for five hours when Joe moved the first time. She had her head down on the bed, still holding his hand. She was almost asleep when Joe's hand twitched. At first, she thought she had imagined it, but then she saw him move his head slightly. She held her breath, praying that he would wake up. He opened his eyes slowly, and Randy smiled through her tears. He looked at her for a few minutes, his eyes mere slits, then slowly he smiled. It was a small smile but a smile all the same. Randy felt like jumping up and down and screaming with joy. She realized that this didn't mean he was out of the woods, but it was a good sign.

She reached over and rang for the nurse. "Yes?" she answered.

"He's awake," Randy said, joyfully, "call the doctor!"

Joe's eyes watched her. She held his hand tightly. His eyes moved to her hand in his, and then looked back at her. He hadn't spoken, but Randy didn't care, she was just glad that he was alive. The doctor came in a few minutes later. He checked Joe's pulse and flashed a light in his eyes, and then he looked at Joe's chart.

Randy squeezed Joe's hand and stood to follow the doctor out of the room. She held her hands tightly as she waited for the doctor to speak.

"He's doing much better now. His blood pressure is stabilizing, and he seems stronger. This is a good start." He looked down at Randy and she smiled.

"He's going to make it, doctor, I know it. He has too many people who love him here to leave us."

"If he's a fighter, he just might make it after all," the doctor said.

"He is, believe me!" Randy said happily. When she went back into the room, Joe's eyes were closed again but when she took his hand, they opened.

"The doctor says you're doing great," Randy told him. The smile twitched at his lips again.

"Good," he said, his voice sounding gravelly.

"I told that doctor you were a fighter," she said, smiling.

He nodded slowly then, but it was obvious it hurt him to do so.

"Are you in pain?" Randy asked worriedly. "If you are, I can call the nurse." He shook his head and squeezed her hand.

"Just stay here," he said, his voice quiet and halting.

"I'm not going anywhere," Randy answered him, as she brushed a lock of hair off his forehead.

London, England, 1980

A week after the accident, Joe woke in the hospital. He'd been in and out of consciousness, but this time he stayed awake longer. He didn't say anything at first. With his head turned slightly on the pillow, he just watched Rick, who was asleep in the chair next to the bed. Rick woke to find Joe watching him. He smiled at his lifelong friend.

"Hey," Rick said, his voice jovial, "you keepin' tabs on me?"

Joe's lips twitched in a small smile in response. "So ... " Joe said, his voice gravelly. "How am I?"

Rick shrugged. *"You have seven broken ribs, a punctured lung, a severe concussion and a broken arm ..."* Then canting his head to the side comically he said, *"Basically you're a jigsaw puzzle."*

Rick could see the sorrow in Joe's eyes. He wasn't sure if it was just the idea of the accident or if he knew.

He had his answer a minute later when Joe said, *"They're ... dead ... aren't ... they?"* His eyes begging Rick to deny it.

Joe's eyes begged Rick to tell him he was wrong. Rick didn't say anything at first, not sure whether or not he should lie to him. Rick realized that there was no way he could lie to him, he couldn't give him false hope. Taking a deep breath, Rick nodded miserably as he exhaled. Joe turned his face back to the ceiling, and as Rick watched with tears in his eyes, he saw silent tears slide from Joe's eyes. Joe's good hand was clenched in a fist at his side. He glanced at Rick, another thought taking over. *"When ... did ... they ..."* His voice trailed off, he was unable to say the words.

"The funeral was three days ago," Rick answered knowing what Joe was asking. *"You've been out for over a week."* Joe nodded as he turned his eyes heavenward again. After a few minutes, Joe's eyes closed and he was mercifully unconscious again.

It was later that week when Scotland Yard had made their appearance, accusing him of killing his parents for their money. They'd brought up Joseph Sinclair Senior's will, and that he'd had an appointment with his lawyer, Robert Debenshire, to change it, writing Joe out if he didn't marry Roslynn Ellington. Unbeknownst to Joe, the appointment had been scheduled for the day after they were killed. It had been damning evidence.

****

The memories came back too fast, and Joe closed his eyes against them, falling unconscious again, fortunately. When he woke again, he seemed to search the room.

"Night and Rick?" Joe asked. Randy just looked at him. She knew she couldn't tell him what was happening. She wouldn't even know what to say.

Randy had just been told a few minutes earlier that Rick was headed over to Robbins' hide out to rescue her. She prayed everything would be okay, and that Midnight would still be alive. Rick had been sure that they were planning to kill her, just as they thought they had killed Joe.

"Rick's fine, Joe. He got some cuts, but he's okay." She tried to distract him by giving him information on Rick. But his eyes bore into hers, and he knew something was wrong.

"What's going on, Randy?" he asked. She could feel him tensing, and she knew from the look on his face that it was causing him pain to do so.

"Okay, okay, I'll tell, you, but you have to relax, everything is under control, and twisting yourself into a knot and worsening your condition is not going to help, okay? Joe?" she asked sternly. Joe had never heard her use that tone of voice before.

After a few moments he nodded and relaxed.

"Okay," Randy said, still not sure that she should tell him, but it was obvious that what he was imagining was probably worse. "Joe,

Robbins has Midnight." She squeezed his hand tightly as she saw him tense, his eyes narrow with anger at his present situation that forbade him going to the aide of his partner. "It's okay, Rick knows where, and he's gone to get her back. It's okay!"

"He'll kill her," Joe said, his tone grave.

His thoughts instantly turning back to his parents, and how he'd been unable to help them, to save them. Not again, he thought, his mind reeling.

"Rick's gone to get her back, it'll be okay, Joe. It's got to be." Her voice was begging him to agree. Joe swallowed the fear climbing up his throat and squeezed her hand reassuringly.

"Rick knows what he's, doing he'll get her back." His voice was very quiet and hesitant, and he was breathing heavily when he finished saying it. Randy rang for the nurse; he was definitely in pain now. The nurse dosed him with morphine and he drifted back into unconsciousness.

When Joe woke again, he looked around to find an empty room and he was instantly worried. Randy wasn't there, neither was anyone else. After a few panicked moments, Randy came in the room and walked over to the bed. She stood looking down at him for a few minutes. He was afraid of what she was going to tell him. But then she smiled. "Joe, Midnight is okay, she's here at the hospital, and she'll come see you as soon as the doctor checks her over. Okay?"

"She's okay though?" he asked, his words still halting.

"Yes," Randy said, nodding. She sat down, taking his hand in hers, giving him a reassuring look. "You should rest some more though, so you can talk to them when they get here."

Joe nodded and closed his eyes, more relieved than he could have ever voiced. It was an hour later when Midnight and Rick came into the room. Randy was shocked by Midnight's appearance. She had never seen Midnight looking so disheveled. Midnight had assorted bruises on her cheek, jaw line and forehead, as well as a nasty cut, and bruises on her throat. From the look in her eyes, the blond leader of FORS was exhausted and damaged. Randy just hoped that Midnight could use her usual strength and determination to get through this latest assault on their group, and she hoped Rick would be there for Midnight while she did.

Midnight walked over to stand beside Randy. She looked at Joe with sad eyes. She reached out, touching his cheek, tracing her finger down his jaw line. Joe stirred, and after a few moments opened his eyes. He looked up at Midnight, his eyes pained at the bruises on her face, but Midnight smiled at him.

"I look worse than I feel," she said, trying to make her voice upbeat, Joe wasn't fooled. "Night ..." Joe said, his voice full of the pain he felt for her state.

Midnight stepped forward, with tears in her eyes. She leaned down and kissed his cheek. Then, with her lips still very close to his face, she stared into his eyes. "I'm okay, Joe. I will be." She straightened, looking down at him. "I'm worried about you though, and I want you to concentrate on getting better. Okay?"

Joe was looking up at her, the pained look in his eyes only growing deeper at her bravado.

"Hey!" Midnight said, her tears running over, knowing he was feeling guilt at not having been there for her. "Joe, you couldn't be there, I know that babe. You almost died. In fact they lost you at one point so please don't tear yourself up about me. I'm fine okay?" Her eyes begged him to listen to her words. "The important thing right now is that you get better and that's what I want you to do, you hear me?" she said, her voice taking on her commanding Lieutenant tone.

Joe smiled and nodded, unshed tears still in his eyes.

Joe noticed the cuts on Rick's face and his arm in a sling. He raised an eyebrow at Rick, a sardonic grin pulling at his lips.

"I hope the other guy looks worse."

"I wish," Rick said, his voice tight. He kept his eyes on Midnight.

Joe looked at Midnight, his eyes narrowing. "He's still out there?" he asked, his voice deep and threatening.

Midnight looked at Rick, her eyes pained at the look on Rick's face. He felt tremendously guilty for letting Robbins get away. Then Midnight looked down at Joe.

"Rick had no choice. Robbins would have killed me but we'll get him, the four of us." Her voice was determined, as she looked at Rick and then at Randy.

Midnight walked back over to Rick, reaching a hand up and touching his cheek. She hugged him tight. Rick bent his head to her and closed his eyes. When they parted, Rick looked at Joe, and Joe nodded at him. He understood that Rick had had to sacrifice getting Robbins to save Midnight and it had been a more than even exchange.

"I'm going to get her home now," Rick said, looking down at Midnight. She still stood in the circle of his arms but was now facing Joe. She was leaning against Rick, and he could tell she was tired. "Night?" he said, his good arm squeezing her waist.

Midnight nodded, glancing up at him. She walked over and leaned down, kissing Joe tenderly on the lips.

"You take it easy, okay?" she said, eyeing him seriously. He nodded, grinning.

"You too, love," he replied, giving her an equally serious look. It was obvious he was still worried about her.

****

When Rick pulled up in front of Midnight's house, Midnight was asleep snuggled under his jacket. He sat and watched her for a few minutes, thinking of the evening's events.

Earlier that night, after dropping Midnight off at her house, Rick had asked that an officer be assigned to drive by her house to check on her. The officer had found her front door wide open. Upon further investigation, the officer had found blood on the carpet where she had fallen when Robbins had hit her. The officer had called the hospital immediately. Rick had felt absolutely sick, knowing that Robbins had not stopped with him and Joe, and had moved on to Midnight.

Rick had steeled himself against the terror that had threatened to overwhelm him and had gotten together with some of the people from the police department, one of whom had been Mike Harlow, who was still in the hospital from his accident. They had decided that Robbins was trying to extinguish FORS. They had tried to kill Joe and were now planning to kill Midnight. The fact that they hadn't found Midnight's body indicated that Robbins still wanted something from her. Again, Rick had to clamp down on his own fears for Midnight so he could think clearly.

Now looking down at her, he cursed himself for not being faster. The thought of Daniel Robbins raping her made him sick, and filled him with rage. He was overwhelmed with the desire to protect her and keep her safe from anything like that happening to her ever again.

He reached out and touched her cheek, and she stirred. She looked around realizing they were in front of her house. She sat up and opened the door. Rick got out and ran around to help her out of the car, but she shook her head, as she stood. She slipped her arms into his jacket, shivering. She walked up to her front door and then turned to him.

"Keys," she said, her brows furrowing as she tried to remember what had happened to them.

Rick put his hand inside the pocket of the jacket she wore, and pulled out her keys. "The police officer who discovered you were gone found them on the floor." Rick's voice was pained at the thought of her dropping them as Robbins hit her.

Midnight nodded, her eyes wide as she took them from him. She turned to the door and unlocked it. Once inside she noticed that the alarm wasn't on and it occurred to her then that Robbins must have cut something to keep it from going off when he had gotten inside. She made a mental note to herself to have it checked and repaired later.

Rick watched her, knowing she was running through a list of things she needed to do, and he was once again amazed at her inner strength. She had just been through hell and yet she was already moving on, planning for the next confrontation. Rick grabbed her hand and pulled her back to him. He leaned against the door, and held her against him. She seemed to melt against him. They stayed that way for a few minutes, but Midnight realized that they better lay down soon before they fell down.

"Come on," she said softly, taking his hand and leading him down to her bedroom.

She let go of his hand and walked into her room. He leaned against the doorjamb watching her. She kicked off her boots, and shrugged out of his jacket, laying it gently over a chair. She was wearing her bloodied shirt, and some sweatpants that Rick had found in her car. She looked very disheveled, but still beautiful to him.

"I'm going to take a shower," Midnight told him.

"Okay," Rick replied. "I'll be here."

Midnight smiled softly. She knew it was his way of telling her that he'd keep watch. Part of her knew that she needed that, but the independent part of her wanted to rebel against needing a man to protect her. Regardless, she walked into the bathroom and closed the door.

She emerged from the bathroom a half an hour later. She'd spent most of that time simply letting the water run over her, trying to remove all evidence of Daniel Robbins. She wore a dark blue bathrobe, her hair wet but pulled up into a ponytail. Her mind continually veered away from remembering what had happened. Instead, she focused on finding him again, and taking him down.

To her surprise Rick was sitting in a chair; she'd expected him to be lying on the bed. They were both exhausted.

Midnight looked at him. "Come here," she said, beckoning to him.

He walked over to her. She reached up and removed his bloodied shirt. She softly pressed her lips to some of the cuts on his chest. He closed his eyes in response.

"Night," he said softly.

"It's okay," she said looking up at him, her green eyes shining in the darkened room. It was her way of telling him that she didn't want to talk.

She led him over to the bed. He lay down, pulling her down with him. She rested her head on his chest, his good arm holding her against him. She moved so she could look up at him. Her hand reached up to touch a cut on his cheek. He closed his eyes slowly at her touch and opened them when she moved her hand away. She snuggled closer to him, and his arm tightened around her shoulders protectively. They fell asleep soon after.

The next morning Midnight was up with the sun, and gone before Rick even woke. When he did wake up, he was alarmed to find her gone. Then he saw the note she had taped to the face of her computer that read, "Gone to FORS." Rick couldn't believe that she had actually gone to work, so he called her office number.

"'Lo," she answered, sounding distracted.

"Night, what are you doing there?" he asked, looking at the clock. It was only seven thirty.

"Working, what do you think?" she answered simply.

"Babe, don't you think you should take it easy for a little while?" he asked, his voice concerned.

"Rick, I'm not like Joe, I didn't get shot or anything. I mean, the doc released me and everything." Her voice sounded a little short.

"Yes, but she said to take it easy."

"Well, I promise I won't do any calisthenics at my desk."

"Well, I guess if you're feeling up to it," Rick said reluctantly, knowing that she wanted to catch Robbins in the worst way. "I think I'll head in too," he said, wanting to be around to keep an eye on her.

"Oh no, Mr. Debenshire, you are hurt and you do need rest. Just rest, and I'll be home before you know it," she said lightly, but Rick could tell it was forced.

Midnight did not come home until seven o'clock that night, and she brought lots of reports home with her. Rick chastised her for overdoing it, but she just shrugged him off. She told him that she had gone to see Joe, but they were keeping him sedated so he could heal better.

"Randy was still there, as steadfast as ever," Midnight said, glad that Randy was so loyal to Joe. Randy loved him and that made it easier for her to leave him in Randy's care.

"Yeah, I know," Rick said, sitting down on the couch next to Midnight. "I went to see him too." He looked at her, trying to decide if he should talk to her about what had happened to her, but he figured she'd talk to him about it when she wanted to. He didn't want to push. "Randy's been great through all this," he said.

"Yeah, she has." Midnight nodded. "And I think she's in love with him, which is good." She looked at Rick, seeing the look of longing in his eyes, but trying to avoid it. She knew that Rick wanted her to be in love with him, but she just couldn't handle it at that point.

She felt very cold and closed up. She didn't want to be close to anyone right now, but she was glad he was there. She knew she was once again being unfair to him, but she couldn't help but want someone around after what had happened last time she was alone in her house.

"Yeah, well I think the feeling is mutual," Rick said, smiling, happy that things might work out for Joe.

He was especially happy that Joe was still alive so things could work out for him. He knew that things could have gone very differently. Rick could see from the look on Midnight's face that she didn't want to talk about them, or anything of that nature right now, and Rick forced himself to drop the subject. They spent the rest of the evening in the living room sitting on the couch. Midnight read reports and Rick watched television, and Midnight out of the corner of his eye.

He was worried about her working so hard already, but he figured she knew her own body, and if she needed to rest, she would. Rick started to doze off by eleven o'clock. After securing a promise that Midnight would follow shortly, he went to bed. When Rick felt her crawl into bed beside him, he glanced at the clock and saw that it was

17

almost four thirty in the morning. He turned over and found her back to him. He put his arm around her waist but felt her stiffen. He kissed the side of her head, and felt her relax against him. Midnight moved her head so that he could slide his arm under her neck, and she snuggled back against him. Rick fell asleep with his arms wrapped protectively around her, his body curved to fit hers.

Midnight stared into the darkness, feeling Rick's breathing become even, as he fell asleep. She was glad that he wasn't pushing her, but she knew that it wouldn't last. She knew he'd want to talk sometime, and she dreaded it. She didn't want to talk about what had happened to her, she just wanted to forget it. By six thirty she was up and gone again, leaving the same note on the computer.

Again, she didn't return to the house until seven that evening. When Rick tried to talk to her about the rigorous schedule she was keeping, her eyes flashed angrily at him and he backed off quickly.

Two weeks passed with the same routine. Rick was terribly worried about Midnight. She wouldn't talk to him. He tried to get her to, but most of the time he just left her alone, not wanting her to get to the point of asking him to leave.

The day before Joe was to be released from the hospital, Rick went to see him. Joe looked a lot better, but he knew that the doctor was only releasing him because Joe had threatened to check himself out if the doctor didn't.

"Hey, man," Joe said, smiling at Rick when he walked in. His smile faded as he saw the worry clear on Rick's face. "What's going on?" he asked, his brow furrowing.

"It's Night," Rick said, sitting down in the chair next to Joe's bed.

"What's wrong?" Joe asked.

"I don't know, Joe, she won't talk to me. She's been working her-self to death. I swear she can't have had more than ten hours' worth of sleep in the last two weeks. She isn't eating, she just works all the time. I don't know what to do." Rick looked at Joe and was dismayed to find that Joe was also worried. Rick had half hoped that Joe would tell him that this was the way Midnight dealt with things, but that didn't seem to be the case.

"That's probably why I haven't seen much of her lately, and that explains why she only comes by at night. It's usually dark in here by then and I can't see her as well. Rick something is going on in that head of hers and you need to find out what it is before she makes herself sick." Joe's voice was very tense. Again, he wasn't going to be able to be there for her and it bothered him immensely.

Rick shook his head miserably. "She won't talk to me, I've tried. She just closes up."

"Well, you're just going to have to make her talk to you, there's no other way to find out where her head's at."

Rick nodded solemnly, knowing that Joe was right, but dreading a confrontation with Midnight. He had found over the last couple of months that she was a very tough adversary, and he liked being on her good side a lot better than on her bad side. Being on Midnight Chevalier's bad side was like being in Siberia, and he wasn't looking forward to being there. But he cared about her, and if it would help her in some way, then he'd risk it.

That night he waited for her to come home. She finally did at nine thirty. Rick watched her as she sat on the living room couch. He could see that she was exhausted; she had lost weight, and there were dark circles under her usually bright eyes. He knew she had been living on caffeine and sugar for the past couple of weeks, and he could see it taking its toll. Her hands shook when she tried to hold something; she would have to put the paper down on the couch and lean down to it to read. Seeing her so disheveled strengthened his resolve to talk to her.

"Midnight," he said, his voice strong and sure, "we need to talk."

Irritation flashed in her eyes as she looked up at him. "Not now, okay, I have a lot of things I want to do tonight." She got up from the couch and went to the bedroom.

Rick waited a few minutes to gather his resolve; he knew this was not going to be easy. Then he got up from the couch and walked toward the bedroom. When he entered the bedroom, he saw Midnight sitting on her bed. She had her feet up on the sideboards, with her arms resting on her knees and her head rested on her arms.

Rick walked over to her, and stood looking down at her. She became aware of his presence after a few moments, and her head snapped up. Her eyes were narrow, as if she suspected him of something. "I thought we weren't going to do this now," she said, her voice cool.

"Well, you thought wrong," Rick said, his voice equally cool.

"Fine," she said rolling her eyes, "what is it?" Her tone became businesslike on the last part.

Rick looked down at her for a few moments. She didn't seem like herself at all. He reached out to touch her cheek, as if to reassure himself that it was really her. She pulled away sharply, her eyes flashing in anger.

"Midnight!" he all but yelled. "What is going on with you?" His voice was harsher than he had meant it to be, but her reaction to his touch had alarmed and angered him. He knelt in front of her, his eyes searching her face. "Babe," his voice was softer now, "talk to me."

Midnight looked down at him, her eyes cold. "About what?"

"About anything!" he said, doggedly trying to hold on to his patience, but he knew she was being difficult on purpose.

"Rick," she said, sighing. "I don't have time for this, do we really have to do this now?"

Rick stood, his eyes flashing. "I see, what is it you have to do tonight, Midnight?" he said, his voice become harsh again as his anger increased. He wasn't getting anywhere with her, and it was frustrating him. "What is it you have to do, that'll keep you from sleeping again tonight?"

She was obviously taken back by the anger in his voice. She looked up at him, her eyes wide. But then they narrowed. "Back off, Rick," she said, her voice low and threatening. "I don't answer to anyone."

It was Rick's turn to be taken back; he hadn't expected her to respond with so much venom.

"Well, you're going to talk to me if I have to make you!" Rick said, raising his voice in anger.

"Yeah?" she responded with just as much anger. "And what are you going to do?" She laughed then, her face a mask of cynicism. "What the hell do you think you can do to me that hasn't already been done?"

Rick drew a sharp breath at the ice in her tone, as well as her words. It took all the anger out of him.

"Midnight." His voice was soft, but she was already standing to leave, her face set in a cold mask.

He reached out, taking her by the shoulders. Lightning fast, Midnight brought her arm up and through his, knocking his hands away from her. She turned again to leave, but Rick wasn't giving up that easily. He grabbed her upper arm, and had to catch her other hand as it came up to slap him. As he held that hand aloft, he saw that she balled it into a fist.

"Midnight!" he yelled. He was losing control of this situation and was trying desperately to get through to her. She looked up at him, her eyes boring into him. Her insolent look made him angry again. Without realizing it, he tightened his grip on her arm, to the point where she cried out. When he loosened the grip, she wrenched her arm away.

"Well, why don't you just go ahead and do it?" she snapped. She sounded totally foreign to him suddenly.

He looked down at her as if he didn't know who she was.

"Do what, Midnight?" he asked finally.

"What men do when they have no control over a woman," she spat at him.

"And what is that?" he asked keeping his voice cool, but his eyes were looking for some sign of what was going on in her head.

She looked at him for a long moment. "Oh just go to hell!" she said and turned away from him.

Rick stood looking at her back for a few moments, then he moved around her so that he faced her. She kept her head down. He touched her under the chin with his index finger, lifting her face to him. She was crying now, and he knew that this was related to what had happened to her.

"Babe ..." he said then, his voice a soft caress.

She expelled her breath in a sob and he pulled her to him. He stood holding her for a long time. She cried tears of sorrow and anger.

After a while, Rick moved to sit on the bed, pulling Midnight down with him so that she was sitting on his lap. Her head was buried against his shoulder, her arms up around his neck.

"Night," he said eventually, keeping his voice as gentle as he could. "Babe, talk to me. Tell me what you're thinking, what you're feeling, please."

Midnight shook her head, but after a few minutes she looked up at him. "I don't think I ever thanked you." Her voice was a soft whisper.

"For what?"

"For coming for me …" Her voice trailed off as she looked away from him.

He brought her face back to his with a gentle finger. "Midnight, you don't have to thank me. I came for you because I love you." Seeing the protesting look she gave him, he rushed on. "Look, I know that you don't feel the same, and I don't expect you to, but …" His look bordered on miserable. "It's true."

Midnight looked at him for a full minute before she shook her head. "But how? Why?"

Rick shook his head at her. "What do you mean why? Midnight, you are the most incredible woman I have ever met. You're beautiful, intelligent, and feisty as hell. You're everything. Why?" He repeated her question in disbelief.

"But why now?" she asked, her brow furrowed.

"You mean, as compared to the last time we were together?" he asked.

She nodded.

"I don't know, really," he said. "I think you were too hard for me to take before, because I hadn't seen you vulnerable. But when all that shit with Joe happened, and then Tim, I found myself wanting to drop everything for you. Believe me, it was a totally new feeling for me. Usually when a woman gets needy I run in the other direction."

He stared down at her face. He could see that she was confused and upset, but he knew that he needed to tell her. He didn't want her to think that he was hanging around waiting until he could jump in the sack with her again. Besides, he thought to himself, she had the right to know that he loved her.

"You know, when they had me," she said, sounding very far away, "I think the thing that I hated the most was that I had no control over what was happening to me." She looked up at him then, her eyes haunted.

"I know, and I promise I'll never let anything like that happen to you again."

Midnight shook her head. "Rick, you can't protect me from everything. I just don't like feeling vulnerable, I don't like feeling out of control you know?" She looked up at him, pleading with him to understand.

"Yeah, I know, but babe, you've got to let someone in sometime."

"Do I?" she asked, doubtful.

"Midnight, no one can survive in a vacuum, not even you." He smiled at her then.

"I've done a pretty good job so far," she said, a smile tugging at her lips.

He looked at her for a long moment, hoping that he was in some way getting through to her. She reached up, touching his cheek, her eyes worried.

"What is it, babe?" he asked.

"I, well," she stammered, "I just hope you understand."

"Understand what?" he asked softly.

"That, loving someone isn't in the cards for me right now. I'm just not capable of it. I'm sorry ..." Her voice trailed off, her eyes looking pained.

"Midnight," Rick said, his eyes searching hers. "I told you, I don't expect you to love me back. I know that's too much to ask from you, especially right now. It's okay, I just hope you'll let me be here for you." He smiled. "Even though I had the nerve to go and fall in love with you."

She laughed, then her look turned serious. "I want you here with me, I guess that's what makes it worse, the fact that I'm using you and now ..." She shrugged helplessly.

"You're not using me, Midnight. I want to be here, I'm glad you're willing to lean on me." He shook his head in wonder. "It's probably really dumb, but I feel pretty damn lucky."

"Lucky?" Midnight repeated, her tone mockingly cynical.

Rick laughed, nodding his head. "How many guys have you let this close to you?"

"Two," Midnight said, her look somewhat sad, "unless you count Thomas, then three."

"Joe and Tom Ryan?" Rick asked.

"You got it," Midnight said, nodding.

"That's why I feel lucky," he said, smiling softly.

To his complete surprise, she reached her hand up to touch his cheek and then kissed him. Her lips were soft against his and her hand moved through his hair. Rick's arms tightened around her as they continued to kiss with increasing passion. Her hands started to unbutton his shirt. When her hands touched his chest he groaned against her lips. She smiled, moving her hands over his chest and inciting more response from him. Rick's hands caressed her back, touching her gently, but with the intensity born of the passion they were sharing. Midnight pulled away from his lips to kiss his neck.

"Make love to me," she whispered into his ear, her voice deepened by passion.

Rick pulled away, looking down at her, concern clear in his eyes. "Are you sure?"

She touched his face at the temple with her fingertips, and traced them down his cheek to his lips, her eyes staring into his. "Rick, you can't erase what he did to me," she said softly, "but you can give me something to put it farther away." She kissed his lips softly. "Please, make love to me."

He kissed her, his lips were soft and gentle, as were his hands as they touched her. They made love, but it wasn't with the usual fervor of their past love making. Rick took his time, touching her as if it were her first time, and Midnight found herself responding as if it were. He kissed her and caressed her, stroking her skin with gentle hands, treating her as if she were fragile, because as far as he was concerned she was. There was no pain when his body moved into hers, and she was grateful to him for the care he had taken to make this a beautiful contrast to the horror of the rape.

Afterwards, she lay in his arms, feeling very safe and comfortable. It did bother her that he said he loved her; she didn't want to hurt him, but she knew she just couldn't love him back. Not right now, maybe not ever. She didn't want to think about that, she was feeling too good just then. She hadn't known how sweet and gentle Rick could be

27

during lovemaking until that night. This side of him surprised her, although she realized that it shouldn't. He had been so gentle with her during the fight with Joe and after Tim's death. But they hadn't made love then. She figured that a man made love the way he did, no matter what the situation, but tonight had been almost a complete contrast to their previous times. It was something to think about.

Midnight looked up at him, seeing that he was staring down at her. He leaned down and kissed her forehead.

She smiled, looking at him for a few long moments, then laying her hand on his cheek softly she said, "Thank you."

Her eyes saying everything her words didn't.

"Anything for you," he replied, his eyes staring into hers.

She laid her head on his shoulder, closing her eyes, a smile still on her face. She fell asleep and slept until late the next day. The cycle of working herself half-sick was broken.

CHAPTER 2

When Joe was released from the hospital, Randy went home with him. She was staying at his house to keep an eye on him. She'd had to make a deal with Joe's doctor, since Joe was threatening to leave either way. Joe was doing a lot better, but the doctor would not release him unless he had someone with him twenty-four hours a day to keep an eye on him.

Shortly after getting back to Joe's house, Midnight and Rick came by to check on him. Randy busied herself getting Joe settled, while Midnight, Rick, and Joe visited. They made a point of keeping it short, because Midnight was still tired. Rick wanted to get her home so she could rest more. Her body had been craving sleep for the last week and a half, and now it was demanding it. When Midnight left the room for a few minutes to talk to Randy, Joe took the opportunity to talk to Rick about Midnight.

"Obviously you talked to her," Joe said, smiling.

"Yeah, it wasn't fun but I think she's okay now. I'm going to keep a close eye on her though, just to make sure," Rick said. "So far she's letting me."

"You told her, didn't you?" Joe said, sensing it without Rick having said anything pertaining to his feelings for Midnight.

Rick looked at Joe for a long moment, then he nodded, looking chagrinned.

"What'd she say?" Joe asked.

"Well, she said that she couldn't love me back right now."

"And that felt, how?" Joe asked.

Rick shrugged. "What choice do I have, man? I love her. I can't just stop, but at least I told her." Rick looked unhappy. "Joe, she means too damn much to me."

"Yeah, I know where you're coming from, but don't push her, it's like backing a cat into a corner, she'll come out fighting."

"Yeah, I know, I'm not pushing. She said she felt guilty for using me though." Rick shook his head once again at the thought.

"She's used to only using me for that," Joe said, his smile slightly melancholy.

"Joe," Rick said, looking at Joe with concern, "you're not mad that ..." Rick made a gesture to indicate himself and Midnight.

Joe shook his head, waving his hand. "No, man, I'm not mad. I love her too, and I want her to be happy. I can't do that for her. I just wish she'd wise up and grab you while she can."

Rick grinned as Midnight came into the room, looking at both men suspiciously.

"Grab who while who can?" she asked, her eyes narrowing at Joe.

"Nothing," Joe said, trying to look innocent and only partially succeeding.

"I see," Midnight said. She walked over and stood in front of Rick, leaning back against him.

He put his arms around her, hugging her to him, and kissing the top of her head.

Randy walked in, seeing Rick's arms around Midnight, and smiled. She was glad that things seemed to have smoothed out for them. She had been worried about Midnight. Unlike Joe, Randy had realized that Midnight was overdoing it. She had seen her in the lighted corridor outside of Joe's room a couple of times, and Midnight hadn't looked good at all. She had lost weight and looked exhausted. Now as she looked at Midnight, she saw that the dark closed look was gone from her eyes, and she looked content.

After Rick and Midnight left, Randy and Joe watched some TV. Joe slept off and on, but Randy stayed in the room to keep an eye on him. She cooked them dinner, but could see that Joe was still too tired to really eat. He took a few bites and lay back down. He was lying mostly on his side to keep his weight off his still-healing back.

In the end, Randy ended up sleeping behind him, keeping a foot of distance between them, so as not to put pressure on the mattress under him. Her hand was on his shoulder so she could keep contact with him. All in all, the first day home had been easy.

The next morning, Randy woke to feel a hand on her cheek. Opening her eyes, she was staring into Joe's light blue eyes.

"Good morning," she said, smiling.

Joe smiled tiredly.

"You're awake early," she said, "are you okay? Do you need anything?" she asked, worried suddenly that he was in pain.

"No," he said, shaking his head. "I don't need anything." He grinned. "'Cept maybe you."

Randy looked back at him for a long moment, then smiled at the sweet comment.

"Thank you for being here," he told her, his tone sincere. "I don't know what I would have done if I'd had to stay in that place much longer."

"You don't like hospitals much, do you?" she asked, her eyes searching his.

"Spent too much time in one … after the accident."

Randy nodded, having guessed it had to do with the accident.

"Well, I'm glad you're letting me take care of you," she said, reaching out to touch his cheek.

Joe smiled in response, closing his eyes again.

****

Later that day they were watching a movie when Joe's doorbell rang. Randy got up to answer it. She was stunned to see Taylor standing there.

"I," Randy stammered, not even sure what to say to the other woman. "What are you doing here?" she finally asked, knowing how rude it sounded, but not caring.

Taylor stared back at Randy as if she'd just come upon a trespasser in Joe's house. "I could ask the same of you," Taylor said, brushing by Randy as if she lived there. "I understand my nephew has been shot," she went on, her manicured hands grasping elegant silk driving gloves. "I'm here to see him." She said the last looking at Randy challengingly.

Randy stared back at the woman, unable to formulate a reply. Since she said nothing, Taylor took that as acquiescence and headed back toward Joe's room. Suddenly regaining her sense, Randy hurried after Taylor, wanting to say the right thing to stop her, but it was too late.

"I see I was right," Taylor announced to Joe as she walked into his room.

Joe glanced at her, shock written on his features. "What the—" he began, but Taylor steamrolled him too.

"You simply must come back to England now," she said, her tone no nonsense. "It's obvious to me that you're only going to languish in this atrocious place if I don't insist."

"Taylor—" Joe began, only to be cut off once again.

"Joseph Michael, it's for the best, I've arranged for you to fly back with me. I can't have this," she said, gesturing to Randy, her look condescending, "be what you come to."

"Okay, that's fucking it," Joe snapped, levering himself up from the bed. He moved too quickly and a shooting pain ran up his back. He gasped at the sudden intense pain.

That was when Randy had it.

"Joe!" Randy exclaimed, moving to his side instantly. "Stay down," she ordered him. "I'll take care of this," she said, looking at Taylor with fire in her eyes. "I don't care what you say about me Taylor, because it's obvious to me that you have absolutely no sense whatsoever. But I will not have you coming in here and upsetting Joe again. You've done enough damage with your condescension and accusations. Now," she said, once Joe was settled back on the bed. She moved toward Taylor with menace. "You get out of here! Out!" she said, pointing toward the door, her eyes shooting sparks, "or I swear to God, I'll call San Diego PD, who by the way think Joseph Michael Sinclair is the best cop they've ever known, and they'll haul your sorry ass downtown and throw you into jail for trespassing! You got that, you heinous bitch?"

Taylor stood stock still, unable to believe she what she was hearing. Randy stood waiting for Taylor to do or say something else. Taylor glanced to Joe, who was lying watching the scene unfold with a most puzzled smile on his face.

"You heard her," Joe said simply to Taylor. "Go."

Taylor drew in a deep breath, drawing herself up, then turned and walked out of the room with as much dignity as she could muster. Joe and Randy heard the front door slam shortly after that.

Randy turned back to Joe, half-afraid of what he would say now.

"That," he said, pointing at the spot where Taylor had stood moments before, "was incredible."

"Incredible?" Randy repeated, her tone unsure.

"Yeah," Joe said, smiling brilliantly, "you were incredible. I've never seen anyone talk to Taylor like that."

Randy grimaced.

Joe held his hand out to her. "Come here."

Randy moved to kneel next to the bed, putting her on eye level with him.

"I love you," he told her sincerely.

"I love you too," she said, smiling finally.

"Remind me never to get you riled up," Joe said, grinning then.

"Oh stop," she said, swatting his hand.

It turned out to be a good day.

Later that night, they watched movies. Joe's head lay in Randy's lap, her hands stroking his hair. She was amazed at how comfortable she felt with him. It amazed her constantly that this handsome, charismatic man loved her. She'd never have believed that this could happen to her.

When she thought back to the time before her parents left, she remembered the feeling of being worthless. She'd heard it so often from her parents when they were fighting. "They're draining us dry!" her father would scream whenever they needed new shoes, or clothes.

"Darrell is trying to get a job," her mother would say. "He can help out then."

"He'll just spend all his money on booze and women," her father would snap. "And the other two will be worthless for years to come yet!"

That was the term Randy had held onto for years. "Worthless." She was worthless to her own parents. Having someone as incredible as Joe Sinclair love her, meant more than she could ever tell him. She had no words to describe the wonder of it.

At one point, she got up to get his pain meds, and when she turned around, she saw that he was watching her. She smiled self-consciously.

"You don't like people to stare at you do you?" Joe asked. Randy shook her head, sitting back down on the bed next to him. Joe moved his head back into her lap, and looked up at her.

"Why?" he asked.

"I don't know," Randy said, shrugging. "I guess I always wonder why they're staring, and think that something is wrong with me."

"Couldn't it just be that you're beautiful, and people tend to stare at a beautiful woman?" Joe said, looking up at her.

Randy was blushing, averting her eyes from his. He reached up and turned her face back to his. "You are beautiful, Randy, but you don't believe that do you?"

Randy shook her head, trying to avert her eyes, but Joe's hand cupped her chin, keeping her facing him.

"Well, you are." He touched her check softly, his eyes looking into hers. After a few long moments, he smiled at her. He could see he was embarrassing the poor girl. He took her hand again and rested it on his chest, with his hand covering hers.

Later that night, they'd both gone to sleep. Randy was lying facing him on the bed. She was jarred awake by the sound of him gasping for breath. She opened her eyes and sat up to see that Joe was awake, but he looked like he was trying to calm down.

"Joe?" she queried, worried. "Are you okay?"

Joe swallowed a few times, closing his eyes and trying to slow his breathing. He nodded, but Randy wasn't convinced.

She lay back down, reaching over to touch his cheek.

"Was it a nightmare?" she asked.

Joe closed his eyes again, nodding slowly.

"About the shooting?"

He shook his head. "My parents," he answered, sounding pained.

"Joe," Randy said. She wasn't sure if she should ask the questions she wanted to. But she thought she might understand him better if she knew the answers. "What happened?"

He knew of course what she was asking about, and for once he didn't feel the reluctance to tell the story.

"It started with this gang leader from a rival gang. He apparently took the gang thing very seriously, whereas I was just playing at it," he began. His voice was distant almost as if he could tell the story from a remote location where it wouldn't hurt as much. His eyes were focused on the wall behind Randy as he remembered. "Unfortunately, for me, I didn't realize how serious he was. We'd fought a few days before the accident. He'd confronted me, and I'd kicked his ass in front of his own gang. Apparently, that didn't go over well. To get back at me, he decided to cut the brake lines in all the cars in my parents' garage, including my Porsche."

"Oh my God," Randy said, closing her eyes.

Joe nodded, his look grave. "My parents had a party to go to, my dad sucked at driving at night, so I offered to drive them," he said, his voice breaking. Randy reached out touching his cheek, her eyes reflecting sympathy. "We went over a cliff. I was pinned against the wheel. I lay there for hours. I kept listening for some sound from them, praying that they were just unconscious. I never knew if they died on impact or if they laid there and died, and I couldn't …" His voice broke again and he closed his eyes, willing his own tears back.

"You couldn't get to them, right?" Randy asked, her voice shaking a little.

Joe shook his head in response.

"And you still feel guilty about that, don't you?" she said. It was more of a statement than a question.

He made a noise in the back of his throat, kind of a sardonic laugh. "Yeah."

"But why, Joe?"

"Why? What do you mean why?" He was shocked; he couldn't believe she had just heard the story and still wanted to know why he felt guilty.

"Why do you feel guilty, Joe? Do you really think you should have known that gang leader would do that? That you could have changed anything?" she asked, her eyes searching his.

"Yeah, I could have changed something" he said, his eyes flashing with anger, but the anger wasn't directed at Randy, it was directed inward. "I could have never started the fucking gang in the first place, then it wouldn't have happened. There wouldn't have been someone like Jake who would want to hurt me or my family. I could have done a lot Randy. I could have tried harder to get to them. I might have been able to save them, something! Damn it!" Randy could see him tensing and it wasn't good for his back or him.

"Joe!" she exclaimed, trying to get through to him. "You couldn't have done anything. Nothing, except maybe have died in that accident like he meant you to. How were you supposed to know that anyone would be such a bastard? And besides, if it wasn't for your affiliation with your gang, you wouldn't be here, and you wouldn't have done all the good you've done here. Doesn't that count for anything, Joe? All you've done here? The lives you've saved? I know that they're not your parents, but they're lives and if it wasn't for you where would those people be?"

Randy's eyes flashed angrily. She felt that if she couldn't make him understand and agree with what she was saying, it would negate everything. Everything that she felt for him was because of who he was right then, who he had become after the accident, his determination, his drive, his passion, everything. Joe understanding how important he was in her life, and how much being with him meant to her, was key to everything. He'd changed her world, like he'd changed others and she needed to make him understand that.

"Damn it, Joe! You mean a lot to a lot of people and you've changed lives and made them better. You can't hold on to the past forever. Did you ever think that there was a reason for all of this to happen? If your parents hadn't been killed, or had died because of something else, you may never have come here. You wouldn't have been so mad about the whole gang thing that you joined something like FORS to do some good. Would you have done all you have, would you be who you are? Doesn't that matter to you?" Randy's voice pleaded with him. He had to understand; he had to agree with her.

She felt like her heart was in a vice and what he said would either tighten the vice and kill her or loosen it and save her. As she stared down at him, her eyes were filled with tears.

Joe must have seen the hurt in her eyes, because suddenly he was looking at her, seeing her. He was no longer in England with that haunting memory. For a few moments, he just looked into her eyes, then suddenly his breath caught in his throat and the tears that he'd been holding back came flooding out. All the years of guilt and anger. He had always felt so cheated and hated by the fates, but she was right. If his life hadn't taken such a dramatic turn, he wouldn't be here now, he wouldn't have met Midnight and all the members of FORS, and most importantly he wouldn't have met Randy. Joe found himself hugging her to him, holding on to her as if he were drowning. She was holding him too with her head bent next to his, stroking his hair and rocking him back and forth as he cried.

She cried too, praying that she understood what was happening, and that he had really just come to grips with his parents' death, and his role in it. Joe could feel that she was crying, and he realized that she was crying for him. Suddenly, like some blinding flash of light, his life was restored to him. It was his again, not haunted by some terrible shadow of a memory. He felt the weight of years of guilt drop off his shoulders. And it was Randy's words that had done it.

"I love you," he told her. He felt exhausted by what they'd just gone through, but he needed to tell her.

"I love you," Randy repeated, touching his cheek. She, too, felt drained.

They fell into an exhausted sleep. Joe hadn't slept better in years.

The following day, Joe slept in late. The guilt being off his shoulders seemed to lighten everything and let him rest finally. Randy let him sleep, knowing he probably needed it. She busied herself straightening up his house, and even decided to run out to the market to buy the makings for dinner that night. She borrowed the keys to Joe's Jaguar, and left a note on the nightstand in the event that Joe woke before she got back.

She was driving up the driveway, returning to Joe's house, when she saw Darrell's Camaro.

"Oh God," she said out loud, terrified of what might have transpired while she was gone.

She wasn't sure if she had more reason to be relieved or nervous when she saw Darrell just getting out of his car. He stood gawking at his sister as she drove up in the late model black Jaguar.

"Where the hell did you get this?" Darrell asked, narrowing his eyes at Randy. "Did Sinclair buy it?" He didn't like the idea of Sinclair buying his sister anything.

"Yes, Darrell he bought it," Randy said, her voice flip and casual. "About four years ago, for himself. God! What kind of man do you think he is? You thought he bought it for me, you thought he was trying to buy me didn't you?" Her voice was angry, and harsh.

Darrell looked at her for a long minute. She looked different, but he couldn't tell what was different about her. Now here she was getting pissed at him because he had made what he considered a natural assumption.

"Yeah, that's what I thought, so what?" he answered her, as he straightened, automatically moving to help her with the groceries she was taking out of the trunk.

Much to Randy's dismay, they were inside Joe's house before she realized that Darrell was still with her. She was brought back to reality when Darrell stood stock still staring wide-eyed at Joe's house.

"Jesus, this guy is really loaded, isn't he?" he asked in awe.

"Darrell," Randy warned. "Please don't fucking start," she said tiredly.

"Nice, you learn that from Sinclair?" Darrell asked angrily.

"No I learned words like that from your friends, Darrell. I also learned pussy, bitch, cunt, and a few other choice phrases, would you like to hear them?" Randy's eyes blazed at him now.

"I see," Darrell said, his eyes blazing right back at her. "You're telling me that cop doesn't say anything crude in front of you? Bullshit!"

"Yeah, Darrell? Well you don't know him like I do. He says nice things to me, things like how beautiful I am, and he's nice to me but you wouldn't understand that."

Darrell's grin was malicious. "Yeah, I bet he'll say anything to get you into bed."

"Well, I have news for you, Darrell," Randy said, her face a mask of superiority. "He's already gotten me into bed, and before you say anything"—she held her hands up in a defensive angry gesture—"I wanted him to. I asked him. In fact, he didn't want to because he wanted me to be totally sure. But you know what, Darrell? I was sure, because I love him." Her breath was coming in quick short gasps by the end of her tirade.

She hadn't meant to tell Darrell what had happened between her and Joe, but she had gotten so angry at his insinuations that her temper had gotten the better of her. Darrell was staring at her in total shock. After a few moments, Darrell's eyes grew wary and doubtful.

"Yeah, and he probably told you how he loves you too, and he'll marry you if you'll just go to bed with him," his voice was full of derision.

"As a matter of fact, Darrell," Randy said, her hands on her hips, her eyes staring directly into his, "he did tell me he loves me, but it wasn't until after we had made love, so I guess that screws up your little theory doesn't it?"

Once again, she had stunned Darrell into silence.

Randy was busying herself putting things away in the refrigerator, so she didn't notice Joe walk in. Darrell did.

All Randy heard was, "Son of a bitch!" She turned in time to see Darrell lunge at Joe.

Joe wasn't as fast as he usually would have been, so he didn't side step quickly enough and Darrell slammed into him. They hit the wall together. Randy screamed.

Joe recovered quickly enough to shove Darrell away from him. Darrell went to punch Joe in the face, but Joe was faster, blocking the punch, and hitting Darrell in the stomach. Darrell stumbled back, his eyes blazing. Randy put herself between Darrell and Joe, facing her brother.

"Darrell, stop it!" she screamed as he pushed her out of the way.

Once again, Joe was faster. He grabbed Randy by the waist, taking her out of Darrell's path, in time to catch Darrell's head in his midsection. Both men fell to the floor. Joe managed to get from under Darrell, shoving him back with his foot. Darrell got to his feet, swinging at Joe, but not connecting. Joe's swing, however, connected solidly, stunning Darrell with its force.

"Stop it!" Randy screamed, seeing that Joe was bleeding, and wincing in pain when he moved.

"He's just using you like any other piece of ass—"Darrell began.

Joe didn't wait for the rest, he lunged at Darrell again, catching him in the stomach and knocking him back against the wall.

"Joe!" Randy screamed. "Please!" she pleaded, grabbing his arm.

Joe stopped instantly, afraid he'd hurt Randy by mistake.

She pulled him away from Darrell, eyeing her brother nastily.

"Just leave, Darrell," Randy said.

"I don't know what you're fantasizing about, Randy," Darrell said, his voice derisive, his breath coming in gasps. "But don't be dreaming of wedding bells or anything. Don't get your hopes up. And when he's done using you, don't think you can just come back home, I'm warning you."

Joe stood breathing heavily, his light blue eyes watching Darrell. To Randy's surprise, he smiled.

"Guess you don't know everything, do ya?" Joe said sarcastically to Darrell.

Darrell just stared back at Joe. His mouth dropped open as Joe went down to one knee in front of Randy and took her hand.

"I was gonna wait," he said, still sounding slightly out of breath, "till I could get something a little more official but," he said, taking off his signet ring, "this'll have to do for now." With that, he slid it onto Randy's left ring finger. "Will you marry me, Randy?"

Randy stood staring at him for a full minute, her mouth open in shock.

"Silence is not an appropriate response to this type of question, you know," Joe said, his smile growing wider. He stood up still holding her hands.

"I … I," Randy stammered. "I don't know what to say."

"Well, 'yes' suits me perfectly," Joe said, his eyes still on hers.

"Can't disappoint the boss, can I?" Randy said finally regaining her wits. "Yes," she said then, her eyes glowing with happiness.

He kissed her, while Darrell stared at them in shock. They didn't even notice when he walked out of the house. Neither of them cared.

Later, when Randy had gotten Joe painkillers and settled him back in bed she couldn't help but ask about the proposal.

"When did you decide to ask me to marry you?"

Joe grinned, wondering when that question would come up. "I dunno," he said, "somewhere between you telling Taylor off and last night when you saved my life."

"I didn't save your life," she said, shaking her head.

"Yes, Randy, you did," he told her. "You gave me back my life."

"But," Randy began, looking confused, "why me? I mean, I'm just," she said, shaking her head and shrugging, "plain."

"You're far from plain, Randy," Joe said, his look shocked. "Why are you so down on yourself?" He pulled her closer to him.

"I'm not, I'm just realistic. I mean, people like you don't fall in love with people like me, no one loves me like that ..." Her voice trailed off, as she looked down.

"Randy, this is about your parents isn't it?" he asked gently.

"No," she said, not sounding very convincing.

"I think it is," he said, his voice sure. "I think that you think that if your own parents didn't love you enough to stick around, then there must be something wrong with you." He brought her face back to his with his hand.

She looked at him for a long moment, as if trying to figure out how he knew that. She had never even really admitted it to herself, but here he was telling her what her deepest darkest fear was. She knew he was right, that was what she thought.

"Isn't that true though?" she asked, her voice taking on a harsh tone. "I mean your parents are supposed to love you unconditionally." She laughed a short harsh laugh. "Mine didn't even bother to look back." She looked devastated and Joe pulled her into a tight embrace, kissing the top of her head. "Doesn't that mean that there's something wrong with the kids?" she asked. Her voice was muffled because her face was against his chest.

"No, Randy, that means there's something wrong with the parents," Joe said then. His voice was a little sharp as he tried to get through to her. "There's nothing wrong with you, Randy. You are a fantastic person, who had shits for parents. I'm surprised you didn't end up in a gang like Midnight, her parents are no winners either. But you didn't, you hung in there, and you're stronger for it." His voice was very sure.

He looked down at her. He sincerely hoped that he was getting through. He had meant what he had said about her saving his life, and he wanted to do the same for her, if she'd only let him.

"I'm just not strong like Midnight. She's accomplished so much, overcome such odds."

"So have you, Randy," Joe said, his voice strident. "You've taken care of things at home, you've stayed straight, you went to school and even to college. Midnight's life is different, but you think she would have done so much, if her brother hadn't been killed? She wouldn't have. But just like you pointed out to me last night, everything has its meaning. Maybe if your parents hadn't left, you wouldn't be so shy, maybe you wouldn't have this vulnerability about you that drew me to you. I fell in love with that, Randy, and your sincerity, your loyalty, your faith in me. Everything that you are now, Randy. You may not have been that if your parents had been around." His eyes were watching her, and he could see her mind working over what he was saying.

After a few minutes she nodded, and looked up at him.

"My words are coming back to haunt me," she said smiling.

"Yeah, I know that feeling," Joe said, smiling back.

Randy began to believe that maybe he was right. Maybe she'd believed people who weren't worth believing. It was definitely something to think about.

It was another week before Joe was ready to go back to the office. By the time he returned, Midnight had already been in touch with another department, the Department of Justice to work with them on the case. In her absence, Spider had found out about a unit called the Violence Suppression Unit that DOJ had to track parolees. Although Daniel Robbins wasn't a parolee, many of the members of the Scorpions were. So it was hopeful they'd find Robbins via the connection with DOJ.

Things between Rick and Midnight were smooth. Rick knew she wasn't in love with him, but he was holding out that she at least cared about him.

Joe, on the other hand was on top of the world when he walked into the office, his hand in Randy's. He walked over to Rick's desk first, kicking the desk to get Rick's attention. Rick looked up, and was surprised to see that Joe was back.

"Hey, man!" Rick said, standing up and putting his hand out to Joe. "You're back this soon?"

"Probably too soon," Randy said, rolling her eyes.

"Uh-huh," Rick said, grinning.

"Come into Midnight's office with me," Joe said, nodding his head toward Midnight's office.

"Okay," Rick said, looking mystified.

He followed Joe and Randy into Midnight's office. Midnight looked up from her desk, shocked by Joe being there, and also by the elated smile on his face.

"What's going on?" she asked as Joe closed the door behind Rick.

"Not much," Joe said, sitting in the chair in front of Midnight's desk. He pulled Randy down on his lap.

Rick caught the glint of the diamonds on Randy's left hand, and stepped closer to examine the ring. He looked at Joe then, recognizing the ring well.

"You didn't ..." Rick began.

"Didn't what?" Midnight asked, trying to catch up.

Rick just looked back at Joe, his smile widening.

"Didn't what?" Midnight repeated.

Joe looked at Midnight, smiling. "Randy and I are engaged," he told her.

Midnight stared at him openmouthed for a long moment, then shook her head. "Wow," she said, sounding as stunned as she looked.

"Uh-huh," Joe said, grinning.

"Congratulations," Midnight said, still sounding shocked.

Joe nodded, knowing he was catching her by surprise.

Midnight stood up to hug Joe and Randy.

"Wow," she said, again, shaking her head, not sure how to respond.

She'd known Joe and Randy were together, but she hadn't expected this. It was great, she told herself, but so sudden.

"I want to celebrate," Joe said, "tonight."

"Where?" Midnight asked.

"I dunno, maybe dinner and Park Place."

"Park Place is a bar, isn't it?" Randy asked.

"Yeah," Joe said, grinning, "don't remind me again how young you are."

Randy laughed softly.

"Sounds good to me," Rick said, looking over at Midnight to see her response. He detected she was reeling a bit from Joe's announcement.

"Yeah, sure, sounds good," Midnight said, nodding.

That night at dinner Joe glanced over at Midnight a few times, wishing that she would be as happy with Rick as he was with Randy. It was clear she was not fully ready for him to get married. He wasn't sure what to do with that.

Rick could sense Midnight's tension too. He felt a cold hard knot start in his stomach, knowing that all the progress he thought he had made with Midnight had just been wiped away with her reaction to Joe's pending marriage. He didn't know how long he could take it and he wondered if he would ever be in her heart like Joe was. He wondered if there was room.

It was obvious to both Rick and Midnight that Joe was very much in love with Randy, and she with him.

Midnight was glad for Joe. She knew that Randy was probably what he had always needed, but she was sad for herself, in a way she couldn't put her finger on. She just felt a terrible sense of loss that she couldn't shake. She could also feel the tension from Rick. She knew that she was hurting him, but she couldn't explain what she was feeling to him, because she didn't understand it herself. She knew trying to explain would only make it worse. So she was silent, which was always her way of dealing with things she didn't understand.

After dinner, they all went to Park Place where Midnight proceeded to drink three shots of Southern Comfort in a row. Joe and Rick jokingly followed her up by drinking shots of tequila. Randy didn't drink, she just watched. She'd never seen Joe in a social situation. He was different, but she liked it. He smiled more, and seemed more outgoing, less brooding. She didn't know that it had a lot to do with her.

Joe felt like a huge weight had lifted from him since he and Randy had gotten together. The only damper was Midnight, but after a few drinks he could see that she was lightening up. What he didn't know was that Midnight was making a point of being cheerful for him, knowing that she was putting a downer on his mood.

Joe and Midnight knew the band that was playing that night, so during the breaks they had a few drinks with them. The guitarist for the band, Danny, had always had his eye on Midnight, and flirted with her outrageously. Midnight just laughed and flirted back, but Rick was ever present in case the guy actually decided to make a move. Joe was talking to the lead singer with his hand clasped in Randy's the whole time. A couple of times during the conversation, he would lean over and kiss her on the top of the head, or nuzzle her hair. Randy felt very special, being there with him. She could see other girls in the bar looking at Joe and they looked at Randy with envy, as they saw his hand in hers.

At one point, during the band's first break, Joe stepped away for a minute and the bassist had started to talk to her. Joe had reappeared suddenly and put his arm around her possessively. He had looked at the bassist with a sardonic grin and said, "Forget it, Steve, she's mine."

Randy hadn't been interested in the bassist. He was cute, but in her opinion, Joe was by far the best-looking man in the whole bar. She felt an incredible sense of comfort at Joe's reaction to another man giving her attention.

It was a little after eleven thirty and the band had just gone back on for their penultimate set of the night. Randy saw Midnight slip out the side door. She had noticed Midnight's mood earlier and wanted to talk to her, so she followed. Joe had gone off to talk to someone at the other end of the bar, and Randy figured he wouldn't notice if she was gone for a few minutes. She walked outside, looking around for Midnight, not sure where she could have gone. She was almost to the corner of the building when she saw her. Midnight's back was to her; she was standing with her legs apart, her arms down at her sides, but away from her body. She was looking at something, or someone. Randy felt a cold knot tighten in her stomach. She edged her face around the building, and saw the stocky man that faced Midnight. He was holding a nasty looking knife and grinning evilly. Randy turned and ran back into the bar, searching frantically for Joe. She spotted him and Rick at the other end of the bar. She pushed her way through the crowd, screaming for Joe. His head snapped up the second he heard her voice. He and Rick came pushing through the crowd toward her.

"Randy! What is it?" Joe yelled, over the din of the crowd.

"It's Midnight, come quick!" She half-dragged Joe through the crowd, with Rick close on his heels.

When they got outside all three broke into a dead run. They skidded around the corner. The man with the knife looked up, Midnight didn't. She recognized the sound of Joe's boots on the pavement and knew her reinforcement was there now.

"Joe! There are three of them!" she yelled, not taking her eyes off the guy with the knife.

The guy jumped at her, but Rick was there, almost as if by magic. He grabbed the guy's arm and twisted it, making him drop the knife. The guy brought his fist up, cuffing Rick on the side of the head, but Rick didn't go down. Midnight launched at kick at the back of the assailant's knee. She could see the second man, who had stood in the shadows, starting to move toward them. He had a knife too.

"Rick!" she yelled pointing to the second attacker, but he was too busy with the first.

She glanced over and saw Joe standing in front of Randy, keeping her out of danger from a man that was advancing on him. Midnight decided she had to take out the second guy. She moved toward him, but he was fast, and he lunged at her, catching her off guard. He caught her upper arm with the blade. She cried out, but she didn't look at the cut, she kept her eyes on him.

Joe was watching a blade of his own The shorter man was advancing on him, but Joe knew that Randy was right behind him, so he couldn't move aside if the guy lunged at him. He knew he had to be careful. Joe decided then that he'd have to attack first to avoid the chance that Randy would get caught by the knife. Joe took two quick strides, bringing his foot up, trying to kick the knife from the guy's hands, but the other man was fast and agile. Instead of backing away from Joe's advance, he stepped into it, and caught Joe in the midsection with the blade, sticking it halfway into Joe side. Randy screamed Joe's name when she saw the blade go in.

Feeling the searing pain of the blade, Joe shifted back, knowing that if he gave the other man the chance, he'd move it around plenty to do extra damage. He brought his arm down, knowing he was risking another slice, but wanting to end this fight quickly. The knife cut through the leather jacket sleeve, but barely scratched Joe as it was dislodged from the man's hand. Joe brought his other fist up, punching the man in the face, knocking him out cold.

Joe turned and to his horror saw another man holding a knife to Randy's throat, his eyes locked on Joe. Joe had to still his breathing. He shuddered at the thought of what the man could do to Randy in one easy stroke. Closing his eyes for a moment, Joe forcibly calmed his nerves. He opened his eyes, reached under his jacket and calmly drew his gun, pointing it at the man's head. Midnight and Rick had managed to dispatch the two they'd been fighting and came up to flank Joe.

"Drop the knife!" Joe said, his voice cold steel.

"Fuck you, Sinclair. You put the gun down or I'll kill her!"

Randy's eyes were on Joe. She was calm; she had complete faith in him. She knew he wouldn't let anything happen to her. She had been terrified when the man had grabbed her, when Joe was still fighting the other man, but when Joe had turned around, Randy had watched him as he closed his eyes. She had almost felt him centering himself. Randy felt calmed by that, she trusted Joe implicitly.

"Man, I'm warning you, you even twitch like you're going to hurt her, and I'll drop you right here. Didn't they tell you that I'm a top ranked marksman," Joe said conversationally. "I can hit a target from a mile out, and you're certainly a lot closer than that."

"He's good," Midnight said, standing beside and just behind Joe, "believe it."

"He'll kill you, man," Rick said, his voice certain.

Joe had his finger on the trigger; he had the guy in his sights. If Randy was hurt … But he wouldn't let himself think it, he'd kill the guy first.

The man holding Randy stood ten yards from them, but Joe could sense his indecision from where he stood. He narrowed his eyes at the other man, settling his finger on the trigger of his gun. The guy swallowed convulsively, his eyes on Joe's trigger finger.

"Just let her go, and you walk," Joe said. He could see the guy was getting nervous. Joe was half-afraid he'd cut Randy by mistake with a hand shaking from fear.

"You think I believe that, Sinclair?" the knife wielder yelled back, his voice breaking nervously on Joe's surname.

When Joe's eyes met Randy's, he could read complete trust in them and he felt his nerves grow totally calm. He knew that if the kid holding the knife to her throat did twitch, he could nail him. Randy believed it, and because of it, so did Joe.

"You don't have a choice punk, you either let her go, or I'll drop your ass. It's as simple as that." Joe's voice was calm and rational.

The man knew he was screwed, but he thought he'd make a ditch effort to get away. He didn't care what Robbins said, there was no way he was going to risk cutting this woman he held hostage. Sinclair was too good, he'd kill him in a heartbeat. Hell, the chick wasn't even shaking, she must know how good her boyfriend was. That's what scared him the most. She wasn't afraid.

In a blinding flash, he pulled the knife away from her throat and shoved her as hard as he could toward Sinclair. He had time to see Sinclair pull the gun up and lung forward to catch Randy, before he turned to run. Suddenly a five foot five blond woman tackled him.

Midnight had taken off after the guy, as soon as she saw that Randy was clear of the knife. She tackled the kid, and as she turned, saw Rick coming up right behind. She handcuffed the young man, and Rick hauled him to his feet. Midnight gave Rick a lopsided grin as he chuckled. He knew the man he was holding was likely to be mortified at being run down by a woman.

Joe was holding Randy against him, he was shaking, but she surprisingly wasn't.

"Randy, are you okay?" he said, looking down at her.

"I'm fine," she said, her voice perfectly calm.

Joe shook his head at her. "You're amazing," he said then.

"Why?"

"Most women would be a little on the hysterical side right now. He could have killed you, you know, that's probably what he was sent to do ..." Joe's voice trailed off, as he watched Rick haul the kid to his feet.

"But you were here—oh God, Joe you're bleeding!" she said, her voice growing upset. Her hand had touched his side and she had felt the sticky warmth.

Joe laughed. "Great, you're not worried about your own neck, but I'm bleeding a little and you go crazy."

"A little! No, Joe, you're bleeding a lot. We've got to get you to a hospital or something." Randy's voice was on the edge of becoming hysterical now.

Joe took her by the shoulders, looking straight into her eyes. "Randy! I'm okay, it's just a little cut. Calm down."

"Hey, you okay?" Midnight asked, coming up to him.

"Yeah," Joe answered, rolling his eyes.

"You're bleeding ya know," Midnight said, smiling at him.

"I know," Joe said calmly.

Randy seemed to take comfort in Midnight's casual attitude, and Joe felt her relax. He was grateful to Midnight. All four turned then to realize that a crowd had gathered from inside the bar to watch the proceedings. Midnight and Joe held up their badges. Joe's arm was around Randy's shoulders. Rick had handcuffed the kid to nearby water pipe. He put his arm around Midnight, and the crowd applauded and cheered. The four of them laughed.

Later, the black and white showed up to take the Scorpions into custody, and the paramedics arrived to check out Midnight and Joe.

"We seem to be pretty popular," Joe said later. The bar was closed for the evening and the band was breaking down for the night. The owner of the bar had offered them any drinks they wanted on the house. Joe and Rick had opted for Tequila as usual, Midnight went for Red Hot shooter, and had even managed to talk Randy into one. They had a good laugh at Randy's reaction to the alcohol and the fiery effect of the drink. Randy laughed too, once she could get her eyes to stop watering. Joe and Rick were both working on beers now. Midnight had switched to a Bailey's and coffee and was trying to get Randy to try that but she was expectedly gun shy this time.

Danny wandered over and put his arm around Midnight, and took a sip of her drink. Midnight laughed and swatted at him.

"So when are you going to teach me some of those moves you used out there?" Danny asked, his eyes looking down at her suggestively.

"Which ones?" she asked, grinning at him.

"Well the tackling part looked fun," Danny replied, his voice full of innuendo.

"I wouldn't want you to get hurt," Midnight said then, smiling up at him.

"Neither would I," Rick put in, his eyes boring into Danny's. He kept his voice even but you couldn't miss the threat.

Midnight looked over at Rick, surprise clear in her eyes, but she laughed. After a couple of tense moments, Danny laughed too.

Steve wandered over and sat down at the table, right across from Randy. He put his elbow on the table and rested his head on his hand. He gave Randy a sad-eyed puppy dog look. Joe watched with an amused grin on his face.

"If you ever get tired of the tough, good looking, rich, English cop type, will you give me a call?" Steve said, his voice was melodramatically sad. Everyone at the table laughed.

"You'll never win, Steve," Joe said, his smile wide. He leaned over to kiss Randy on the lips. Their kiss lasted an extra few moments and Steve sighed dramatically as he watched. Randy and Joe broke into laughter.

Rick, Midnight, Joe, and Randy stayed at the bar until well after four o'clock in the morning. Finally, they left when the owner told them he had to close or risk getting into trouble with "the cops." They laughed, knowing he knew that they were "cops."

They left good naturedly, in a surprisingly good mood for a group who had just had their lives threatened yet again by a gang that was out to end FORS. They all knew what it meant but none of them wanted to be the one to bring it up, so no one did. But they were all thinking it. Robbins had just sent them a message.

This wasn't over yet.

CHAPTER 3

After spending two days relaxing, for the most part in Rick's arms, Midnight was itching to get back to work. Rick could sense her agitation. It was eleven o'clock in the morning, they were in Midnight's living room with the stereo was on. Rick had discovered that the stereo was usually on a lot more than the television. Midnight had just gotten up to change the disk on the CD player. She put on the soundtrack to The Bodyguard. Rick had also figured out that she was very into soundtracks from movies, especially dance movies. He found that she liked to dance, and that she did so very well. Now watching her, the song "Queen of the Night" came on, and she began to move. She looked at him as she danced seductively. Rick enjoyed the show and Midnight very obviously enjoyed performing for him.

As the song played on, Rick stood and walked over to her. He held her by the waist, and she continued to moved, her eyes looking up into his, as she repeated the chorus of the song. The phrase about how she could bring a man to his knees had him grinning.

"You do, and I am," Rick said smiling down at her.

"On your knees?" she asked then.

"Figuratively speaking," Rick said, laughing.

"I see …" Midnight said, reaching up to kiss him. Rick's arms moved to her back, holding her against him as they kissed. After a couple of minutes, he looked down at her.

"Why don't we go in today?" he said.

Midnight looked at him, surprised. She thought she'd have to drag him to the office. She'd been thinking about a way to broach the subject.

"You mean the office?" she said.

"Yeah, I can tell you're getting ready to climb the walls." Then, putting his index finger on her collarbone, he looked at her seriously. "But, you have to take things slow. I don't want you getting back into that cycle of overworking yourself again. I've just gotten you back to normal, okay?" His eyes bore into hers, indicating how serious he was.

"Yes, I promise," Midnight said, a mischievous grin on her face, as she looked up at him like a naughty schoolgirl.

Rick laughed at the look she gave him. "Go on!" he said then, giving her a gentle shove toward the bedroom. "Get dressed and I'll wait for you."

Midnight went into the bedroom and threw on her jeans. She reached into her closet for a shirt, and pulled out one of Rick's, a black oxford. She shrugged into it and then sat down to pull on her boots. She ran a brush through her hair, still damp from the shower she had taken earlier. She put on a touch of mascara, and a little bit of blush, and she was ready to go. She walked back into the living room, ten minutes after she had left. Rick could never get used to how quickly she could be ready to leave. She was very different from the prima donnas he'd dated in England.

After Joe had left England, he had fallen into the habit of doing what his parents wanted him to, which was date the debutantes that his status afforded him. The girls he dated were very proper in appearance, although he had found that many of them could get down and dirty with the best street walkers in London, in private. He'd spent a lot of time, getting very jaded on the whole scene, the parties, the openings, the balls … that had been one of the reasons he had left England and come to see Joe. That and a certain woman … but that was history now too. Rick was devoted to Midnight now, even if it was a hopeless venture.

As he looked at her, he was pleased to realize the shirt she was wearing was his. It was big on her, but it made her look even more attractive to him. She looked like a waif, wearing anything to be clothed. The shirt hung halfway to her knees, her jeans were tapered, so her shapely legs were outlined by them. She looked sexy even in that and it amazed him over and over how she could look incredible even in the most casual of outfits. There was nothing fake about her, she was genuine; no nose jobs, no lifts, no tucks, no boob jobs, she was the real thing, and it made her a glaringly difference from the women he had been trying to get away from in England.

****

When they got to the office, Spider was sitting in Joe's office. He had become the person to keep things running while Midnight and Joe were out of the game. Midnight was very happy that he'd worked out so well. In fact, she had recently recommended both him and Tiny to the police academy, and the chief had just signed off on the request. When Spider saw Midnight and Rick enter the office, he stood and walked out to them.

"Hey," he said, looking down at his boss, "how you feelin'?"

"Oh, I'm okay, Spider. What's goin' on here?" Midnight responded, moving toward her office. Spider and Rick followed. Midnight sat down at her desk, gesturing for Spider to sit down.

"As a matter of fact," Spider said, sitting in the second chair in front of Midnight's desk. Rick took up a position on the low credenza behind Midnight's desk, next to the window. "I've just been talking to BNE ..."

"BNE?" Midnight asked.

"The Bureau of Narcotic Enforcement ..." Spider supplied. "Yeah, it seems that they have a new program that might help us out some."

Midnight looked skeptical. "Narcotic enforcement? What's that got to do with FORS?"

"Well, normally not a lot, other than the drug dealing aspect of it, but it seems that BNE has just started a new unit called the Illegal Weapons and Violence Suppression Program. They call it VSU. Anyway, they target violent repeat offenders, and one of those main targets is gang members, and especially parolees ..." He waited for the impact of what he had said to sink in. He watched with a smile on his face as Midnight's eyes widened slightly.

"You mean ... they can get info on the Scorpions?"

"Yep, and as luck would have it, I talked to one of their Criminal Intelligence Specialists just today, and she said that the unit can keep an eye open for our boy too, as well as the rest of the Scorpions."

Midnight was nodding, her eyes alight with the desire to catch Robbins. "What's their main thing though? I mean VSU, how are they going to spot Robbins?"

"Well, their main thing is getting illegal weapons off the street and out of the hands of parolees, gang members, and the like. But they do a lot of hits on houses like the one we hit, when I took one …" His voice trailed off as he remembered the day he'd been shot. His recovery had been long and painful, but Tammy had been there for him the whole time.

"Shit …" Midnight said. Her mind worked through the assistance this VSU could be to them. "Spider, do you realize how much that increases the odds … this is great! But hey, what can we do for them?" she said then, always wanting to return the favor when it came to working with other agencies.

"Well, I'd say we have the biggest handle on the gangs in this area, we could give them all the info on that. I was thinking it might be a good idea to meet with their special agent in charge down at their office, it's downtown here too. We could offer our information and formally ask for their assistance … What d' ya think?" Spider asked, not wanting to take too much for granted. Midnight was still the leader, no matter how much she'd been through recently.

"Yeah, Spider that sounds good, let's get that set up. I'll go, and I want you there with me, since you're the one who seems to know about this new unit of theirs."

"You don't want to wait for Sinclair?" Spider asked, happy that she was willing to let him stand in for Joe, but unsure if he felt comfortable about it.

"Joe's gonna be down for a while longer. I want him back full strength, so … no I don't think we should wait. I think this is too important, we need to get the ball rolling. Can we try to set it up for today?"

"I can see," Spider said, standing up and turning to leave her office.

"Great!" Midnight said. "Hey," she called, causing Spider to turn back around.

"Thanks, Spider ... if it wasn't for you ... you kept things goin' and I appreciate it," Midnight said, smiling at him.

"For you, boss, anytime," Spider said, smiling back. Then he turned to Rick who nodded to him, appreciating his loyalty to Midnight.

Midnight turned to Rick, putting her booted feet up on the credenza. "This might just work yet," she said, her eyes bright.

"You love your work, don't you?" Rick said, smiling down at her.

"Ah, yes, I do. Give me a gun and a raid to go on and I'm a happy camper," she said, turning to her computer. She turned it on and as it was warming up, she starting going through some of the stuff on her desk. After hovering around her office for a bit, Rick finally headed over to his desk and checked out things there.

Spider came back a half hour later saying that they could meet with the SAC at BNE at three o'clock. "Perfect," Midnight said, then turned back to her work.

A few hours later, Spider went into her office to retrieve her for the meeting. As they walked by Rick's desk, Midnight stopped and said, "Why don't you come too." He looked up at her questioningly. "Moral support," she said smiling. He stood, stretched, and pulled his jacket off the back of his chair. Midnight watched him as he did. He was wearing jeans and a navy-blue shirt. She thought how gorgeous he was, for the millionth time since she'd met him. He was tall and lean, leaner than Joe, and his face had finer bones than Joe's. She shook her head, thinking how fate was a nasty character, having not created him for her.

"What?" Rick said, seeing her shake her head.

"Nothing," she answered, smiling at him. "Come on."

They drove over to the BNE office in Rick's Mustang. They parked in the lot below the building and went up to the third floor in an elevator. When they got to the reception area, Midnight showed her badge to the receptionist. The receptionist noticed that Spider and Rick seemed to be standing guard behind this blond woman who identified herself as a police officer. A couple of minutes later, the special agent in charge came out to greet them. He was a handsome man, with short dark hair, that was graying at the temples, and blue eyes. He introduced himself as Jim Griffin and shook all their hands warmly. He escorted them back to his office and introduced them to one of his special agent supervisors, Mike Buffington.

"Mike's one of our best, and he's running the Violence Suppression Unit out of this office," Griffin said.

Mike shook hands with the three members of FORS, but didn't say anything.

"So, I've heard a lot about your unit," Griffin said, sitting down at his desk, and gesturing for them to sit too. "You've done a lot of good work."

Midnight nodded. "Thank you." Then she leaned forward, her eyes on Griffin. "I'm sure you've heard about what happened to my partner, just recently …"

Griffin nodded. "I hear he's doing okay now though, is that right?"

"Yes, that's true, but the guy that did it, got away, and I want him back," Midnight said seriously.

Griffin looked at this small woman, amazed at her size, and her appearance; she didn't quite fit the image he had of her. He had heard about the highly intelligent, highly efficient, rough-edged, ex-gang leader turned leader of FORS. He hadn't quite expected this small, beautiful woman that sat in front of him now. But there she was, and he could see from the look in her eyes that she wanted this guy that had "gotten away" really badly. Griffin had also heard what the leader of the Scorpions had done to Lieutenant Chevalier, and looking at her now, he couldn't believe that this woman had been through all that, and had bounced back so quickly. It hadn't even been two weeks since the incident. Griffin's respect for Lieutenant Chevalier doubled in that moment.

"Well, I think we can help you," he said to Midnight. Then he looked at Mike. "Mike, why don't you tell Lieutenant Chevalier what it is your unit will be doing, and let's see if we can come to some sort of agreement."

Mike nodded to his supervisor, and then turned to Midnight. "Well, you see, Lieutenant, we plan to gather information on violent repeat offenders using some of the computer programs we already have online here at BNE, as well other Department of Justice online systems. When we have a hit on some of these people carrying illegal weapons, or in the case of parolees, any weapon, then we'll arrest them and off they go back to jail, keeping the streets safe for women and children again."

Midnight nodded excitedly, then she looked over at Rick and Spider. "Yeah, and you'll probably put us out of business."

Mike laughed, surprising Midnight, he seemed so sedate otherwise. "Well, we hope so."

"So … " Midnight said, looking between Griffin and Mike. "Since one of your targets is parolees, you don't have to have warrants to search … but my guy isn't a parolee. What do we do now?"

"Yeah, but most of his members are, right?" Mike said, warming to the subject.

"Yeah …" Midnight said, not sure where he was headed.

"So we track him through them," Mike shrugged. "It's a start."

"Yeah," Midnight said, working it all over in her mind. She looked over at Spider again, then back at Mike. "We may be able to help you guys out some too, maybe give you some info on whereabouts, and the like. Maybe tip you off on some of our guys …" She gestured to Spider to take over there, and he did. He and Mike talked about the computer system that FORS had set up, and how they could supply BNE with all the information it needed. As Midnight listened to Spider and Mike talk, something kept nagging at her, something that was just on the edge of her mind, but she couldn't think of it. Rick watched her, as did Griffin. Midnight knew it had something to do with Robbins, but she just couldn't grab it. Slowly, carefully she started to go over their last meeting. She closed her eyes, trying to mentally step around the rape, and get to what he had said to her, but even those were painful memories. She felt someone touch her hand, and she opened her eyes. It was Rick looking concerned.

"Night, what is it?" he asked softly. All talk in the room had stopped and all eyes were on her.

She shook her head slowly. "Something …" She closed her eyes again, and felt Rick's grip tighten on her, as he realized what she was thinking of. She sat holding his hand tightly, as she remembered that night. She thought about waking up in that dark room, the pain in her head, the light on under the doorway, the terror she felt when Robbins had walked in and she had recognized him. She thought of what he said then. He had admitted to trying to kill Joe, and also trying to kill Rick … He had said that FORS was becoming a bother to him … Then she remembered!

"Wait!" she said as her eyes flew open She saw that Griffin was staring at her, concern etched on his face. "They're working with the cartel," she said, her voice strong and sure, "the Riveras. They're working with the Riveras. You guys have to have an open case on them, they're one of the biggest Columbian families working San Diego and the border!"

Griffin was nodding excitedly. "Hell yeah, we've got an open case on them, and you say this guy is working with them? That's pretty high-level for a gang … These guys are well connected."

"Tell me about it, they've tried to kill three cops so far, as well as having killed two kids, and trying to kill one of my members here." She gestured to Rick. Griffin's look went to Rick. He had seen the love and worry in Rick's eyes a few minutes before, it was obvious these two were a couple, but they'd try to kill him too? This gang was dangerous, Griffin thought, he hadn't realized just how dangerous.

"Well, in that case, I guess we have a new priority," Griffin said, looking over at Mike. Mike nodded.

"We'll give you everything we can," Griffin said to Midnight, his eyes looking directly into hers.

"Thank you," Midnight responded, her eyes shining with determination as she stood.

"I'll have to run it by the deputy chief at HQ, but he's real pro-interagency cooperation, so I don't think it'll be a problem. I hope your partner gets better fast, Lieutenant Chevalier. And I hope we can help you get this guy quickly, before he has a chance to do anymore damage to this community," Griffin said. Midnight's battle had just become his and his Bureau's now too.

Midnight left the BNE office feeling very good, she was sure they'd catch Robbins now. It was only a matter of time, with an agency as big as the Department of Justice, Bureau of Narcotic Enforcement on board with the investigation and on her side.

"I think that went well," Spider said, grinning as they took the elevator down to the parking garage.

"I'd say so," Rick said, grinning too.

"Oh you two ... *well*, is a major understatement, it went fucking great!" Midnight said, laughing.

They went back to the office. Midnight worked for a couple more hours, then Rick went to her office and leaned against the doorjamb watching her.

She looked up at him. "What?"

He looked pointedly at his watch. She looked up at the clock to see it was almost six o'clock.

"Oops," she said, smiling at him.

"Oops nothin' young lady," Rick said, wagging a finger at her. "You promised, so let's go."

Midnight looked chagrinned for a moment, then a slow grin started on her lips. She rolled her eyes. "Okay! You win, I'll go ... but ..." Her smile widened and her eyes sparkled mischievously.

"But?" he asked, smiling at her, glad that she wasn't angry at his insistence that she not overdo it.

"You have to take me to dinner," she said then, her eyes on him, her smile wide.

"I think I can handle that," he said, walking over to her desk. He held a hand out to her, and she stood, taking it, and smiling up at him. She reached into her desk drawer and pulled out her gun, putting it into its usual place.

"Oh good, I'll have protection too," Rick said, smiling down at her.

"Oh shit, that reminds me," she said, looking around on her desk, "I need your signature on this." She retrieved a piece of paper from one of the piles on her desk.

"What's this?" he asked, as he signed it.

"It's your CCW paperwork."

"CCW?" Rick repeated, handing her the paper back.

"Yeah," she said, turning to her desk and rummaging through a drawer. She turned back and handed him a card and a gun. Rick looked at her perplexed.

"Permit to carry a concealed weapon. Rick, you're legal now."

"Oh," he said, looking at the gun.

"Department issue, but you can buy your own if you want," Midnight said, smiling at him.

"I have my own, thank you," Rick said, handing her back the gun.

Midnight looked at him, furrowing her brows. She watched as he pulled a gun out from under his shirt. He was carrying his gun in the same place she carried hers.

She clicked her tongue at him. "Richard Debenshire, that's illegal."

"Yeah, so is assaulting a cop," Rick replied, his voice dead serious, his eyes searching hers. "I wasn't takin' any chances."

Midnight looked at him for a long moment, knowing that she should give him a hard time for carrying a concealed weapons without a permit, but what the hell. She figured it was only a misdemeanor anyway, and he had the permit now. Besides, her mind qualified, he was doing it to protect her. She smiled at him.

"You win," she said, putting her hands up in a surrendering gesture.

"Come on, love," Rick said then, putting his arm around her, and escorting her out of her office. They went to dinner at a small Mexican restaurant in Mission Beach. Rick noticed that even though she seemed to know everyone in the restaurant, including the owner, she still picked a table where she could see everything that was going on, and sat with her back to a wall. Hazards of being a cop, Rick thought to himself. They ate in companionable silence, the food having come quickly, brought by the owner who doted on Midnight. He said the "señorita" never ate enough, that's why she was "muy poquito," indicating that she was very little. Midnight laughed good-naturedly with the owner, surprising Rick with the fact that she knew Spanish. She spoke to the owner in Spanish as well as some of the waiters that seemed to find it necessary to come by. Rick watched it all, his eyes on Midnight, seeing yet another side to her. She was being social. The owner's wife came over at one point, looking at Rick appreciatively, elbowing Midnight companionably.

"Como te Llama?" she asked Midnight, still looking at Rick.

"Ricardo," Midnight answered in a perfect Spanish accent.

"Es muy guapo," the older woman said, telling her that Rick was very handsome. Midnight nodded laughing. Rick looked at them both, not knowing what the older lady had said.

"Rosa," Midnight said, gesturing to the woman, a wide smile on her face, "says you're very handsome."

Rick laughed, and looking at the older woman, he said, "Thank you." The lady looked at him confused.

"Gracias," Midnight told Rick.

"Gracias," Rick repeated, the Spanish word sounding strange with his English accent. Rosa was still looking at him, she canted her head to the side, her eyes studying him.

"Amigo es el Ingles," Midnight told Rosa, when Rosa looked at her, confusion still clear on her face. "Britain," Midnight said to clarify.

"Ah, si," Rosa said then, nodding.

When they left the restaurant, Rick sat behind the wheel of his Mustang looking at Midnight.

"What?" Midnight said, noticing that he wasn't starting the car.

Rick shook his head, his eyes still on her. "Every time I turn around there's a new side of you that I've never seen."

"Oh, and I suppose I've seen all there is to you?" Midnight said, laughing.

Rick considered her words, knowing she was right. "Okay, you win," he said conceding early on, knowing he'd lose eventually.

Later that night, they were in bed. They had just made love and she still lay in his arms. She looked up at him. "So tell me about Richard Debenshire."

"What d'ya want to know?" he asked, looking down at her.

"Let's see … what about your family? Do you have any brothers and sisters, or are you an only child like Joe?"

"No, I have four sisters."

"Older?"

"All older but one."

"I see … and I'll just bet they are super protective of you aren't they?" Midnight said, smiling at him. She sat up, looking down at him.

"Why do you say that?" he asked, reaching his hand out and touching her leg, not wanting to lose all contact with her.

"Well," she said, stroking his hand that rested on her leg. "I know I was protective of Thomas when it came to girls. He was already trying to make it with one of my members, at sixteen!" Her voice showed her surprise at such outrageous a thought.

"Sixteen? You think that's young?" Rick said, raising an eyebrow at her.

"Well, yeah I do …" she said. Then her eyes took on a mock suspicious look. "Why, how old were you when you slept with your first girl?"

Rick laughed then. "Oh no, I'm not tellin' you, you'll probably try to arrest me or somethin'."

"Only if she was jail bait … or were you?" Her face was composed in a half-surprised half suspicious look.

"She wasn't," Rick said, smiling again. "I was …"

"Oh really, Mr. Debenshire ... how old was she?"

"I think about thirty."

"Oh my God," Midnight said, in mock horror, laughing. "And how old were you?"

"Fourteen," he answered simply, his eyes watching her, an embarrassed smile on his face.

"Good Lord, they start you guys early over there, don't they?"

"Didn't seem early to me," Rick answered.

"So who was she?" Midnight asked then. Her hand moving to touch his chest and her finger lazily traced a pattern on it as she looked at him.

Now he looked really embarrassed. "Well ..." he said, his voice trailing off as he smiled.

"Come on."

"Well, who was your first? How old were you?" Rick said, trying to avoid answering.

"I asked you first," Midnight said, laughing.

"Okay, okay ... she was ... my little sister's nanny."

"Oh, my God!" Midnight said, laughing uproariously. "Remind me never to leave my kid with her!"

"She wasn't *my* nanny ..." Rick said, a smile still on his face.

"So what did she do? Seduce you? Are we talking Mrs. Robinson time here?"

"More or less," he said. "Besides she wasn't only my first ..." She knew he was baiting her.

"Who's else?" she asked curiously. Then it occurred to her, some-how she just knew. "Joe?" she said then her eyes wide.

Rick nodded, his lips twisting in a sardonic grin, his grin wicked.

Midnight laughed so hard then she fell over on the bed next to him. Then she sat up, putting her hand on his chest again. "I guess she must have been something, if she got both of you."

"She was … nice …" Rick said, nodding, his voice indicating she was a lot more than that.

"Yikes!" Midnight said, still laughing. "So that would have made Joe sixteen?" she said doing the quick calculation.

"Yep," Rick said, looking intently at her. "So …"

"So what?" Midnight said, her face showing nothing.

"Who was your first?"

"Well … I wasn't as young as you two perverts," she said, smiling at him.

"Okay, so how old were you?" Rick asked. He was really curious, he wanted to know everything about her, including this.

"I was nineteen," she said, her eyes giving nothing away.

"And who was the lucky man?" he asked, thinking that the man had indeed been lucky.

Midnight averted her eyes from his then, smiling a shy smile, then she looked back at him "He was … um …" she stammered.

"Come on, I told you," Rick prompted.

"Okay, okay," she said, laughing. Then she took a deep breath. "He was one of my professors at UCSD."

"Oh my …" Rick said, his eyes widening dramatically. "What subject?"

"Pre-law," she answered simply, her grin wide.

"Midnight, Midnight, Midnight …" he said, shaking his head. "You probably ruined him for life with other women," he said, his eyes on her.

"I doubt that! Every girl in the class was after him."

"Including you?" he asked.

"Actually, no, " she said, her face serious. "He kind of zeroed in on me, because I was the only one that didn't throw herself at him … I think he felt sorry for me … I wasn't quite as outgoing back them as I am now."

"Felt sorry for you?" Rick said, shaking his head. "Midnight, if you were even half as beautiful then as you are now, you probably blew every other girl in the class out of the water. I doubt it was sympathy that drew him to you, babe."

Midnight looked at him for a long moment then sighed. "Well, he was a prosecutor for the city at the time. I think he found out about my past, and he made a point of trying to help me. He really did … and one night … after class, he asked me to dinner. I had never been on a real date before, so I accepted. We went out for about two months before he ever even kissed me. I guess he could tell I was a little gun shy. Well, eventually one thing lead to another …" She shrugged then, looking at Rick. He had been watching her as she told the story. He found himself wishing he had been there for her back then, that he'd been her first. But he couldn't even imagine what she'd been like then. That would have been right after she'd gotten out of the gang, after her brother had been killed. She was probably totally different then than she was now.

"So what happened to him?" Rick asked then.

She shrugged. "I moved on, so did he. It wasn't true love or anything …" she said, her voice trailing off. She looked at him then. "Joe's the closest thing I've ever come to that."

Rick looked at her, seeing from the look in her eyes that she wasn't trying to hurt him, she was just trying to be honest with him. It did rankle him though, that Joe was the only man she had come close to loving. But he suppressed that thought.

"Does that bother you?" she asked, as if reading his mind.

Rick didn't answer at first, his hand reaching up to touch her hand that was still on his chest. He covered her hand with his, pressing her hand flat against his chest, his eyes not leaving hers. "Yes," he answered simply. His voice was quiet, his eyes searching hers, but there was no anger in his voice, no accusations in his eyes, only honesty.

Midnight leaned down, moving her hand, and kissing his chest where it had lain, her eyes watching him. She saw him close his eyes slowly in response to the touch of her lips. His hand touched her head, moving to caress the base of her neck. She kissed his neck, and made her way up to his lips. She kissed his lips softly, her eyes watching him the whole time, he had opened his eyes and was staring back at her.

"So …" she whispered, her eyes taking on an alluring look, "was the nanny pretty?" she asked, her lips almost against his. Rick's breathing had grown heavier, and she knew what effect she was having on him, and it gave her a thrill.

"She … " he started to say, but his voice hardly came out. "She wasn't half as beautiful as you," he said then, his voice still hoarse. His hand was still at the base of her neck, and he put pressure on it to bring her lips back into contact with his.

They kissed for a few minutes, her hands entwining themselves in his hair. He groaned in response. Midnight laid her body against his as they kissed. She pressed against him, enjoying the closeness and the warmth his body exuded. It made her feel safe. They made love, his body, his hands, and his lips bringing her to new heights of passion. She was forever astounded by her body's response to him. She had never felt this way with any man, not even Joe. The thought didn't seem to jab at her as much this time, but she didn't take the time to wonder at it. She was too busy enjoying Rick's body and his lovemaking.

****

The next morning Joe woke up before Randy. He lay next to her watching her sleep, reflecting on the incident the night before. It had terrified him to see the man holding Randy like he had, the cold fear still clutched at his heart like an icy hand. He knew that Robbins wasn't done with FORS yet, and Joe knew that Robbins knew about Randy now. The thought sent a shudder through him. He had to warn Randy, he had to make her understand what Robbins was capable of. He had to protect her at all costs. He was afraid for her, she was now caught up in a game that she knew nothing about, she didn't know the rules. Joe knew the rules, and the rules were that there were none. Robbins had declared war on FORS, and he wouldn't stop until either he was dead, or FORS was.

Randy stirred and her eyes opened. She looked up at him and saw the worry in his eyes. She touched his cheek, he closed his eyes, bringing his hand up to cover hers, pressing her hand to his face. He turned his head, kissing her fingers.

"Are you okay?" she asked, seeing the tension on his face. She could tell that he was worried about her, but she wasn't sure she understood why.

He shook his head. "No, I'm not ... Randy ... listen, this is important." He pulled her up to a sitting position, and he sat with his hands on her shoulders. "I want you to be very careful for a while, okay? I don't want you goin' anywhere without me, okay?" he said seriously.

"Okay ... but why?" Her eyes reflected worry. She could see that he was afraid, and she didn't like seeing him that way.

"Randy, last night ... that was a warning ... Robbins is still out there, and he still wants us dead ... he's not finished." Joe's voice held a desperate note. He wanted her to understand, they were all in danger, but he was worried about her because she couldn't really defend herself.

Randy nodded, closing her eyes. When she opened them, he could see that she was trying to control her fear. "That's what I was thinking, but ... I was hoping ..." She shook her head then, dismissing what she was going to say.

"Randy, what scares me the most is he knows about you now, and he knows you're important to me. That makes you a prime target. If he can't manage to kill me, but if he can manage to get to you, and hurt you or ... worse." He took her hands, holding them tight. "Baby, I can't let anything happen to you, if something did ..." He shook his head indicating that he didn't know what he'd do.

"Nothing is going to happen to me, Joe," Randy said, her voice sure. "You're here and you'll protect me." Her eyes looked up into his. He could see that she honestly believed what she was saying.

"And I will protect you, but you need to be careful, okay?"

"Okay," she said, her voice as serious as his.

He kissed her, holding her against him.

"Joe ..." Randy said, glancing up at him.

"What?" he asked, looking down at her, his arms still around her.

"Midnight isn't happy about us, is she?" Randy asked, her eyes shadowed with concern.

Joe considered his answer carefully. He knew Randy had a great deal of respect for Midnight, and therefore for her opinion. He didn't want Midnight's unsettling reaction to their engagement to take away from Randy's happiness. Seeing no other way out though, he finally shook his head.

"Why do you think?" she asked then.

"To tell you the truth, Randy, I don't really know ..." Joe said, his voice trailing off as he thought more about the situation.

Randy put her hand on his chest, looking up at him seriously. "Is it possible ..." Her eyes searched his as she hesitated for a moment. "That she loves you more than you realize ... that maybe she wanted to marry you?" Randy's voice held concern, not jealously.

Joe shook his head. "No, that's not it."

"Are you sure? Because ... I know how close you two have always been, and you said that she's not serious about Rick. Maybe she is about you … but you just haven't known …" She leaned her head against his chest. "If you wanted her … I'd understand." Her voice was very quiet, but dignified.

"Randy!" Joe said, sounding shocked. He brought her face up to his, and looked straight into her eyes. "Baby, if it was Midnight I wanted, I would have married her a long time ago. If it was me she wanted, she would have grabbed me a long time ago. But it's not Midnight I want, it's you … I love you." His tone was strong and sure. After a few moments, he smiled. "Besides … you'd give me up that easy?" His voice held humor, and Randy couldn't help but smile at his words.

"No …" Then her eyes grew serious again. "I just want you to be happy …"

"I am happy, with you," Joe said then, the tone of his voice brooking no argument.

"Okay," she said smiling. "So why do you think Midnight's upset?" she asked.

"I don't know, Randy, but I'm gonna talk to her about it, it's not like her … you know?"

They resolved that Joe would try to talk to Midnight, but he told Randy that Midnight was probably the only female he had ever met who didn't like to talk about how she was feeling about something.

They went to the office later that morning. Joe went in to see Midnight an hour after they got in. She was working at her desk, but stood when he walked in. She could see from the look on his face that he wanted to talk to her and she was sure she knew what it was about.

"How's the side?" she asked smiling.

"Fine, how's the arm?" he replied.

"Just wonderful … so what's up?" she asked, trying to get straight to the point.

"Babe, we need to talk …" Joe said, his eyes watching her. She nodded as she walked over to the couch in the office and sat down. She looked up at him, and he sat down next to her.

"So, you're very obviously not happy about me and Randy …" Joe started out.

"No!" Midnight said, shaking her head. "I am happy." She reached out and took his hand, holding it tightly in hers. "I'm happy for you, I really am."

"Then what is it, babe? I know something's wrong," Joe said, his eyes staring directly into hers.

"If I was sure, I'd tell you, but I'm not really …" she said, her voice showing her own confusion over her feelings.

"What do you think it is?" Joe asked, wanting to get to the heart of the matter.

"I don't know, I guess I feel this sense of loss … like I'm losing you." Her eyes begged him to help her understand.

"Losing me? You mean like our off and on stuff? I thought you didn't want that anymore either …" His voice trailed off as Randy's words of that morning came back to him, but he knew that wasn't it, not totally.

"No, well, maybe, I don't know. You've always been my security blanket. I don't know if I'm ready to give that up … kinda like Linus on Peanuts," she said then, smiling.

"Are you comparing me to that ugly tattered blue thing he always carried? Gee, thanks!" They both laughed.

83

"Night …" Joe said then, his eyes concerned. He didn't know what he could say that would make her feel better.

"Joe, you have to live your life, and I have to live mine. If they don't always parallel then, maybe it's just meant to be that way … it's okay. I'm just not adjusting to it as fast as you have. I think Randy is perfect for you, and she obviously loves you, so I'm happy for you. I guess I'm just not happy for me, ya know?" Again, her eyes pleaded with him, this time asking him to understand her.

His face was still drawn with concern, but he nodded.

"I'm losing my partner …" she said, her eyes inexplicably filling with tears.

"Oh, babe …" Joe said then, pulling her into an embrace. "You're not losing me." He kissed the top of her head, as he murmured, "I'll always be here for you, always, no matter what."

She was nodding against his chest, her tears were still flowing. She knew it would never be the same between them, and she guessed that was alright, but she just couldn't bear the pain of separation right now, not when she didn't have someone like he did. He had found his right match, but she hadn't yet, and she knew that was part of the problem. She wondered if she would ever find her match. She was terrified she wouldn't.

After a while, she sat up brushing almost irritably at her tears. "I'm sorry, I'm not making this very easy on you, am I?"

He grinned at her. "You're not supposed to, you're supposed to give me a hard time, and make my life difficult, it's your job."

"And I do it so well," she said, laughing at him.

"I love you, babe," he said seriously, his eyes staring directly into hers.

"I love you too," she said, her eyes staring right back at him.

"And I want you to be happy."

"I will be ... someday."

"Night ..."

"Joe, it's not something you can *make* happen, either it does or it doesn't, and it hasn't yet. I can live with that."

"Can you?"

"Yes."

He looked at her for a long moment, then he shook his head resolutely. He couldn't live her life for her, or make her fall in love with who he wanted for her. They conversation moved onto other things then. The air had been cleared and Joe was glad about it, but he was still worried about his partner. He wondered if she would ever fall in love, or if she'd just wait around for the rest of her life for "Mr. Right" to find her.

The rest of the day was rather uneventful. Everyone was out working on the Scorpions case, following up leads. The trail had gone somewhat cold.

Joe and Randy left the office around five o'clock that evening. They were both very tired from the night before, and they wanted to spend a quiet night at home. Rick and Midnight stayed behind working on more reports.

Rick was still feeling very put off by Midnight's reaction to Joe and Randy's engagement, but he was trying to put it behind him. It made him realize again how far away she kept him. They were close only when she needed him. Since she had gotten back on her feet from the rape, she had distanced herself again. She was at a friendly distance from him all the time, except when they made love, then she was there, she was his. Those times were what kept him hanging on, hoping.

"I'm tired, babe," Rick said, standing and stretching. It was now seven o'clock. "Can't we go now?"

Midnight looked up at him, stifling a yawn. "Yeah, I suppose we could, I'm pretty beat myself."

They left the office and went back to Midnight's house.

CHAPTER 4

Joe and Randy were halfway to Joe's house when his cell phone rang. He answered expecting it to be Midnight.

"Yeah?" he said.

"Sinclair?" an unfamiliar voice said.

"Yeah, this is Sinclair, who's this?"

"This is Sergeant Dickerson. Look I talked to Lieutenant Chevalier and she said to call you … I've got one of your people down here, and he needs one of you two down here to authorize a search."

"Damn …" Joe said, knowing his quiet evening with Randy was blown. "Down where?"

"San Ysidro. Right off five near the factory stores, you can't miss us. You'll see the black and white," Sergeant Dickerson answered.

"Well, I'm almost to PB, so it'll be a little while. Tell him to hang on. Who is it anyway?"

"Uh … Dibbins … I think."

"Alright, I'll be there as soon as I can," Joe said, looking over at Randy. "I can drop you off …" he said, clearly disappointed they weren't able to spend some time together.

"Maybe I could just go with you, and when you're done, we could have the rest of our evening," Randy said, smiling over at him.

"Well, that'll work," he said. He got off on the next freeway exit, and turned around to head south.

They got off the freeway at the exit Dickerson had indicated. He saw the black and white. The police car was off one of the side streets next to an open field. There were apartments on the other side of the fence next to the squad car. Joe pulled up behind the squad car, and got out. He looked around and thought he saw some movement to his left, in the field. He turned toward it, his hand automatically reaching for his weapon. He heard Randy scream, and as he drew his gun and turned, he was hit in the head with something hard. He fell, his eyes going unfocused. He could see that someone had Randy, but he couldn't make out faces. He blacked out shortly after that with his gun next to him on the dirt road.

****

Joe woke in a room. The first thing he sensed was how damp it was. The musty smell was overwhelming. He decided he was most likely in a basement. The room was dark, but as he looked around he could he could make out faint shapes. There was a mattress under him, but feeling around he could tell it was just a mattress on a floor. The floor was ice cold. His head was pounding, and he suddenly remembered that Randy had been with him.

"Randy?" he said, his voice barely coming out at all, but the response was instant.

"Joe!" Her voice was off to his left. He looked in that direction, but the moonlight coming from right above him was dim, and he couldn't see her. He tried to sit up, but his head was pounding so hard he had to lay back or risk blacking out again.

"Baby, are you okay?" he asked.

"Yes ..." she said, her voice uncertain. "But, where are we, what's happening, is this Robbins?"

Joe closed his eyes, knowing it was. He was terrified because Randy had been taken too. "Yes, it is, I'm sure of it. Randy whatever you do, don't give him a reason to hurt you. I'll do everything I can to get us out of this."

Someone turned on the light. It was dim, but Joe could see Randy. She was tied to the furnace. It was indeed a basement.

"Well, well, well, Sinclair," came a voice from the shadows. Then Daniel Robbins stepped out into the light, his evil sneer directed at Joe. "It's about time we meet, wouldn't you say?"

"What the fuck do you want, Robbins?" Joe spat.

"What I want, Sinclair," Robbins said, standing above Joe, "is to kill you slowly and painfully." Then he looked over at Randy, his face becoming a leering mask. "And meanwhile, I want to fuck your latest ... she's a real piece, Sinclair. How do you do it?"

"You leave her out of this, Robbins. This is between you and me."

"That's where you're wrong, Sinclair. This is between you and me and Midnight, and your buddy Rick, and the Riveras, and none of us are real happy with none of you, and since nobody even knows you're gone yet ... I'd say you're screwed, Sinclair."

Robbins walked over to Randy and knelt down next to her. She looked up at him with wide terrified eyes. She knew this was the man who had raped Midnight, and she couldn't control the fear that was rising in her. He reached out and grabbed her by a handful of hair. She shrunk from his touch, but he yanked her head toward him, his lips came down on hers in a bruising lustful kiss.

"Robbins!" Joe roared. He had sat up, but his vision was already swimming. He tried to get up, but his vision darkened instantly, threatening to go totally dark on him.

Having kissed Randy, Robbins stood up, looking down at her. She was rubbing her face against her shirt, trying to get all traces of him off her. He started to move toward her, to teach her a lesson she wouldn't soon forget.

"Robbins!" a voice called then from somewhere above them.

"What?" Robbins answered, clearly irritated by the interruption.

"I need ya."

Robbins turned to Randy. "Try not to think about me too much while I'm gone." He winked at her and walked away. He stopped looking down at Joe, who was staring at him with narrowed eyes.

"What's a matter, Sinclair, don't you like to share?" His voice was leering and sarcastic.

"You touch her again, Robbins, and I'll kill ya," Joe replied, his voice cold steel.

"Yeah, yeah," Robbins said. Then without warning, he launched a kick at Joe's ribs. Randy cried out as Joe doubled in pain. "Don't fuckin' threaten me, Sinclair, it's me that's gonna kill you, and don't forget it," Robbins said as he left.

"Joe?" she said, her voice hesitant and terrified.

"I'm okay, babe ... tough ribs ..." He tried to smile at her, but he couldn't manage it.

He knew they were in the worst possible situation. Midnight would have no idea they were gone until they didn't show up at the office the next day. When they had left the office, Joe had told Midnight that he'd kill her if she called him that night. She had promised she wouldn't. So he knew that he and Randy were on their own, at least until morning, and he didn't know if they'd be still alive by then. The thought of Robbins getting his hands on Randy made him almost physically ill. He knew he couldn't let that happen.

He must have slept for a while, because when the light came on again, he was surprised to see Robbins was standing under the light, his eyes watching Joe. When he knew Joe was awake, he walked over to Randy and touched her hair. He clicked his tongue at her when she tried to pull away from him. "Now, Randy. Is that any way to be?" He looked at Joe. "So how is she, Sinclair? You broken her in for me?"

"Robbins ..." Joe said, his voice holding a steel edge. "I'll kill you."

"Yeah, Sinclair, you already said that ... but ya know, I just gotta ask, who's better? Midnight or Randy? I mean you fucked 'em both, right?"

"Yes he did," came a vaguely familiar voice.

When a woman stepped out of the shadows, Joe recognized her immediately, but he wasn't sure what she could have to do with all of this.

San Diego, California, 1988

One night, a year and a half after the beginning of FORS, Midnight and Joe were taking an official, but rare, night off. They were sitting companionably in Joe's living room on his sofa watching TV.

"Hey turn that back!" Midnight said, as Joe flipped through the channels.

"What?" he said, grinning over at her, as he changed the channel again.

"Joseph!" she said, lunging for the remote. He held it above his head so she couldn't reach. She leaned over too far and ended up in his lap. They both laughed, as Midnight grabbed the remote and changed the TV back to the channel she wanted.

"Spoiled," Joe said, and Midnight laughed evilly.

A little while later, there was a muffled ring. Midnight immediately looked embarrassed.

"You're not supposed to have that bloody thing," Joe said, his voice a little edgy.

That was the deal they always made on their nights off: no cell phones, no pagers, and instructions to the staff that they were only to be called at Joe's in case of the direst emergency.

"I know, I know," Midnight said, reaching to her FORS jacket that was lying of the back of the couch. "But I've been waiting for this one call." She pulled out her cell phone, glancing at Joe, and smiled as she flipped it open.

"Yes?" she said into the phone. "Yes this is Midnight Chevalier ... you do? Great! Yes, well I'm at my second's house. He's at ... oh ... you do? I see." She looked at Joe. She was clearly surprised by what the person on the other end had said. "Okay ... well I guess I'll see you soon, thanks." She hung up, but Joe could see she was still discomfited.

"What the fuck was that about?" Joe asked, his voice low. He hadn't liked the sound of the conversation.

"That was Tasha Wood," she said, still a sounding confounded. "She's bringing over a file I've been waiting on. She said she had your address." She put her phone back in her jacket pocket as she looked over at him. "You ever date her?"

"I don't even know her," he said, his eyes narrowing suspiciously.

"Well," Midnight said, shrugging to dismiss the strangeness of the situation, "she does deal with our confidential DMV files. She's like the supervisor of the section that handles them. Maybe she just came across it today while getting my information together or something." She shrugged again.

She had no reason to be suspicious of Tasha. She had been nothing but helpful from the first time Midnight had dealt with her.

"Yeah," Joe said, not totally convinced.

The doorbell rang a few minutes later. They looked at each other. Joe's eyebrow lifted at her. "That didn't take long," he said wryly.

He stood up and walked to the front door. He opened it and stood holding the door, staring down at the woman standing there.

Tasha stood looking at Joe for a full minute. She had heard that he was good looking, but she had never actually met him before. He was wearing faded jeans, white high top tennis shoes, and a white cotton oxford-style shirt that he hadn't bothered to button. With his tan and his light blue eyes, he was very handsome indeed.

Joe looked Tasha over too. She was a petite woman, about the same height as Midnight, but a complete contrast to Midnight. Tasha had auburn hair that was just past her shoulders and blue eyes. Joe found her attractive, maybe it wouldn't be such a bad thing, this woman having his address. But he was still curious as to what had prompted her to look it up.

"Hi," Tasha said, feeling uncomfortable at the silence. "You must be Joe." Her voice almost cracked on his name.

Joe's lips curled in a sardonic smile. "I must be."

He stood back, indicating that she should enter. She stepped inside promptly stumbling on the slightly raised threshold. Joe reached out, catching her before she actually fell. Once she was steady again, he made a point of looking at the three inch heels she wore. "Those things'll kill you."

Before she could respond, he started off down the hall. She could do nothing but follow him, feeling foolish. She was a bit taken back by his attitude. She usually made a more definite impression on men, but Joe had barely feigned interest. 'Well,' she thought to herself shrugging inwardly, 'that's why I'm after him, because he isn't like most men.'

She had dressed with care that night, choosing a black silk straight skirt and a sapphire-blue jacket that made her eyes stand out. She had also worn silk stockings and black leather pumps to emphasize her nice legs, and all he'd had to say was, 'Those things'll kill you.' He was definitely going to be tough.

Joe continued through the house with Tasha trailing behind him. When he reached the living room entryway, he stood aside and gestured for her to precede him. He moved to the nearest wall and leaned indolently against it, observing Tasha as she talked to Midnight.

"Midnight," Tasha said smiling at the leader of FORS. Midnight stood, extending her hand to the other woman.

Tasha and Midnight were a contrast in many ways, Joe reflected. Tasha was dressed to the nines and obviously well pampered in terms of her nails, skin, and hair. There wasn't a hair out of place, and she smelled strongly of Opium perfume. Whereas Midnight was wearing faded jeans, a black tank top, and black boots. She wore no makeup, her nails were never painted, and she only wore musk if she wore anything at all. Midnight's copper-blond hair was in its usual shaggy, unruly mane. As he watched them, he became aware how incredibly beautiful Midnight was once again, in her natural way without all those extras. Tasha was beautiful too, but because she seemed to have to work at it, Joe didn't feel that it counted as much. The eyes of the two women were a major contrast as well. Midnight's were not always warm, but they were always direct, whereas Tasha's had a cold calculating look to them.

"Tasha, it's nice to finally meet you," Midnight said, shaking Tasha's hand. They'd spoken on the phone frequently over the past few weeks, but hadn't actually met in person before now.

She noticed that Tasha's hand was very cold, not unlike the look in her eyes. Midnight wondered at that. Tasha had been very friendly on the phone, but you never knew about someone until you looked into their eyes.

"Yes, you too," Tasha was saying, her gaze drifting over to Joe.

"Oh," Midnight said, her glance touching on her second, "have you met Joe?"

Tasha turned to look at Joe then giving him a brilliant smile. Her eyes lost the cold look, but the calculation remained. "Yes, I believe I have," she said, her voice almost breathless.

Midnight raised an eyebrow at Joe, and Joe had to stifle a laugh. Tasha knew something was going on, but she was determined to keep her cool.

Joe nodded in acknowledgment keeping his eyes on Tasha's. She returned his steady gaze. She wasn't shy, this one, Joe decided. She could be interesting.

****

Joe stared at Tasha. He remembered where she'd worked, but it also occurred to him that she must not have been connected with the Scorpions for long since Robbins still didn't have all the confidential information he'd been looking for. Tasha worked for the confidential section of the Department of Motor Vehicles (DMV). It was a section that handled peace officer information such as their home address and vehicle information. When an officer was registered with the DMV their information was kept confidential and only other officers were able to access the information and then only with authorization.

He and Tasha had begun a short but volatile relationship after their first meeting. It had lasted no more than six months. Tasha had been extremely jealous of Midnight and had expected Joe to cut Midnight out of his personal life completely. Further, she'd fully expected Joe to ask her to marry him, within that short timeframe. He'd laughed in her face. Neither thing was something that Joe had considered doing for even a moment and it had rubbed Tasha completely the wrong way. Their break up had been a colossal battle, because Tasha had been drunk at the time. Joe had also suspected that she'd been on drugs, but hadn't bothered to worry about it once she'd slammed out of his house.

It was, however, still hard to take that she was apparently in this with the Scorpions now. It meant that she was willing to endanger the lives of police officers with her betrayal.

"Yeah, and I fucked her too," Joe said, looking at Tasha, a knowing leer on his face.

Tasha looked at him, her eyes traveling provocatively down his body. "Yes you did," she said then, a hint of nostalgia in her voice.

Robbins walked over to Tasha and grabbed her by the waist. "Just remember who you're fucking now," he said angrily.

Tasha looked at Robbins, a slow smile starting on her face. "Yeah, I remember …" She kissed him passionately. After a few minutes, Robbins was obviously excited and he led her from the room.

Joe looked over at Randy then. "Randy …"

"I know, Joe, I know … it's okay …" She knew he'd been trying to keep the focus off of her and she was grateful to him. The thought of having Robbins rape her made her stomach turn over. She'd rather have him kill her.

Robbins came back a few hours later. Joe wasn't even sure how long they'd been there by that time. It was getting light out though so he knew it was morning. Robbins walked over to Joe this time, and stood looking down at him. "So, Sinclair … how you feeling?"

Joe looked up at him for a long moment. He was sitting up, his head feeling a little better. He had found the bloody cut on the back of his head a little earlier. As Joe watched, Robbins pulled out Joe's own gun, much as he had with Midnight's almost a month before.

"Now, Sinclair, there's some information I never got from your partner … and I want it now." He leveled the gun at Joe. "I want the addresses of all the members of FORS, and you're going to give them to me or I'm going to take you apart piece by piece, you got it?"

"Go to hell, Robbins," Joe said, his voice calm and clear.

Without a word, Robbins fired a single shot into Joe's shoulder. Joe cried out involuntarily, his cry echoing in the room. Randy screamed Joe's name.

"Now that you know I'm not kidding …" Robbins said, his voice icy. "Start talking, Sinclair."

"What the hell are you doing!" Tasha's voice came from above them. She descended the stairs two at a time.

"Trying to get our friend here to talk," Robbins said, looking over at her.

"Oh Jesus!" Tasha said, seeing the blood flowing from Joe's shoulder. She grabbed a nearby towel and walked toward the bed. Robbins' hand stopped her.

"What the fuck do you think you're doing?" he asked, his voice angry again.

Tasha looked at him, and then down at Joe, who was looking up at her through pain-clouded eyes.

"If he bleeds to death, Daniel, you won't get anything from him." She moved around Robbins and knelt next to Joe. She pressed the towel to his shoulder. Joe jumped at the pain it caused.

"I'm sorry," Tasha whispered to him.

"Well, if I can't get anything from Sinclair …" Robbins said as he backed toward Randy. His intention was clear as he put the gun down on a nearby table.

Joe could see that Randy was in tears, and she was shaking. He noticed that Robbins was still focused on him and Tasha. Tasha was leaning over him. She was on his right side, and the gunshot wound was in his left shoulder, so she leaned across him.

He made a quick decision. "So …" he said, his voice soft, but loud enough for Robbins to hear. "This is what happened to you?"

"Shut up, Sinclair," Tasha said, pressing the towel harder into his shoulder, causing him to wince in pain and let his breath out in a hiss.

"It's just a shame … ya know … we had somethin' good goin'. The sex was always great …" he said, his voice trailing off as if he really missed it.

"She doesn't want you anymore, Sinclair," came Robbins' voice. He had taken a few steps forward away from Randy, in his urge to protect what he considered his property now.

"No?" Joe said, his eyes looking up at Tasha.

"No, she doesn't," Robbins answered for her. "Tell him, Tash."

Tasha looked down at Joe, her eyes giving her away. She did still want him, but there was still the glint of hate and anger in her eyes too. Joe knew he was playing a dangerous game, but it was worth it if it kept Robbins away from Randy.

"Yeah," he said seductively, "tell me, Tash …"

His right hand touched her waist and he felt her sharp intake of breath. She leaned down then and kissed him, her mouth all but devouring his, he had to force himself to kiss her back. Her hand touched his face and trailed down to his neck. Her nails were as long and manicured as ever, and they raked a bloody path down his throat from his ear when Robbins dragged her away from him and carried her from the room.

Joe looked over at Randy when they were gone. He could see trust in her eyes, there was no accusing look. Once again, she had faith in him. He felt strengthened by her devotion to him, and he knew if they were going to make it through this, he would have to continue to draw on that faith.

He got up from the mattress, feeling a little lightheaded from the pain in his shoulder, but knowing that this may be his only opportunity to check around. He walked over to Randy first and kneeled in front of her. She had a slight bruise on her cheek, but she looked otherwise unharmed.

"Joe …" she said, her voice agonized. She couldn't touch him because her hands were tied. Her eyes were on his shoulder that was still bleeding. Then they trailed to the bloody welts that Tasha's nails had left on his throat.

"It's alright, babe," he told her.

"Who is she?" Randy asked.

"Her name is Tasha Wood. I dated her a while back."

"Was it serious?" Randy asked.

"Not as serious as she wanted," Joe said wryly.

"What does that mean?"

"She wanted me to stop seeing Midnight. I refused and it pissed her off. The scary thing is that she works for the confidential records section of DMV. It's probably how Robbins got Midnight's address."

He said, grimacing as he did. "Look, I'm gonna look around. I don't know when or if the cavalry will arrive and I don't want to take any chances of us losing this round." His words were light, but the look in his eyes told her that he was afraid for both of them.

He touched her cheek, and leaned over to kiss her. When he pulled back, her eyes were watching him and he could see that she was afraid.

"We'll get out of this ... somehow," he said, trying to make his voice sound confident.

She nodded, her eyes wide. He stood and walked around the room. He walked over to the stairs that led down from the main part of the house, then he checked the walls to see if there were any other doors. There was one, but it was locked. He tried a couple of times to force it, but to no avail. He walked back over to the mattress and checked the window there. It was locked but there were no bars. It wasn't very wide though, he didn't think even Randy could fit through it. He looked over at her, and he saw that she was watching him still.

He walked back over to her and kneeled down. He put his uninjured arm around her and hugged her to him as best he could.

"It'll be okay, babe ... we just have to hold on for a while longer ... " He looked down at her, her eyes were filled with tears. "Don't do that, babe please ..." He hugged her to him again.

He wanted to stay near her, but he knew he shouldn't. He didn't know if Robbins knew how serious he was about Randy, but he knew that any extra affection shown right now, would tip that. Robbins would be doubly interested in raping Randy if he knew that Joe was in love with her and that they were engaged.

He suddenly remembered the ring. "Randy, the ring … do you have it on?" He looked at her hands and saw that she did. It had taken some work to make it fit her small finger temporarily, but she wanted to wear it. It was his. "Shit, Randy you have to take it off … " he said, reaching for her hand. "Robbins won't know that ring, but Tasha will, and if she sees it …"

"Sees what?" came Tasha's voice from behind him. It was a casual drawl, but when he turned, he saw that she was staring down at him.

She was standing twenty feet away. Joe's body still blocked Randy so he made a quick ditch effort to try to pull the ring off and pocket it, but he couldn't manage. He stood, looking down at Randy, his eyes going to the ring again. Then he turned and walked over to the mattress, easing himself down in a sitting position, his eyes watching Tasha.

"Sees what?" Tasha repeated, her hands on her hips. She was looking from Joe to Randy.

"Nothin'," Joe said, his eyes showing indifference.

"Bullshit, Sinclair," Tasha said angrily. "What don't you want me to see?" She looked at Randy then, her eyes trailing over the younger girl. She started to walk toward her.

"Tasha," Joe said. His voice stopped her, and she turned to him, her eyes wary.

She walked over to him, and got down on her knees in front of him. She traced her fingers down the marks she had left on him earlier. Then her hand moved to his wounded shoulder. Her eyes turned to ice as she pressed her hand against it, causing him to gasp in pain.

"What are you hiding from me, Sinclair?" she asked, her voice as cold as her eyes.

When he only returned her look she pressed harder into his shoulder. He cried out then, the pain was excruciating.

"Tasha!" Randy yelled. "Leave him alone!"

Tasha's head snapped around and she narrowed her eyes at Randy. She stood, and walked over to her. Joe was half-unconscious from the pain and had been close to passing out when Randy had yelled to Tasha. He watched Tasha cross the floor to Randy. Tasha stood over Randy in a very threatening manner. Randy looked up at Tasha, her eyes shooting sparks of anger at the older woman.

"I know you weren't talking to me, *little girl*," Tasha said, her voice cold and hard. Randy continued to stare up at her, her eyes narrowed. "'Cause what you don't realize here is that I have all the power, you have nothing, you got that?" Her voice grew strident on the last part as Randy shook her head.

"You're wrong," Randy said, her voice surprisingly calm. "Robbins has the power; you're just a pawn to him, an easy one."

Tasha's hand whipped back and slapped Randy so hard the younger woman's head snapped back. But Randy didn't cry out, she turned her face back to Tasha and gave her a knowing look, shaking her head again.

"You bitch!" Tasha screamed, slapping Randy again.

"Tasha!" Joe yelled, starting to get up. But Tasha whirled around producing a gun, and pointed it at Joe.

"Don't fucking do it, Sinclair!" she said, her voice sounding harsh and partially hysterical. "I'll kill you, I swear!"

The look in her eyes told Joe that she meant it. He stayed where he was, afraid to anger her further, lest she turn on Randy with the gun. He had been surprised at Randy's courage; her interruption had given him the opportunity to regain his strength. But he couldn't let Tasha continue to slap Randy. Tasha backed up, keeping Joe in her sight, but getting behind Randy.

"You think you're so smart, little girl, you think you got Joe? You don't, he doesn't commit to anyone. He just fucks 'em and leaves 'em, don't you Joe?" Her voice was derisive.

When he didn't answer, she drew the gun back threatening to hit Randy with it.

"Yeah, okay, yeah!" Joe said, putting his hand out in a halting gesture.

Tasha smiled, enjoying having power over Joe again.

"So, Randy," she said then, her voice making a nasty word out of her name. "He'll be doing the same to you … no matter what he told you … he lies you know, don't you Joe?"

Again, she looked at him, her hand moving back in the same gesture.

"Yeah, Tasha, I do," Joe said keeping his voice calm, even amiable. He wanted to get her away from Randy, as fast as possible, before she saw the ring. He was willing to admit to anything to make that happen.

He wanted her to think that Randy was just a passing thing, then maybe she wouldn't want to kill Randy so much. He knew if she saw the ring, that was it for her. Glancing at Randy's hands, he noticed she had crossed her right hand over her left, covering his ring. *Good girl!* he thought to himself. His eyes went back to Tasha. She was still watching him with the gun pointed at him, he read both indecision and longing on her face.

"You lied to me, didn't you Joe?" Tasha said then, her voice touched with ice.

Joe didn't answer, he wasn't sure what she expected him to say.

"Didn't you, you bastard!" Tasha screamed hysterically.

Joe tensed as he saw her finger tighten on the trigger. She walked over to him again, staring accusingly up at him. She stayed just out of his arm's length, not taking the chance of getting close enough for him to be able to grab the gun.

Her eyes grew unfocused as she started to talk. "You lied to me, you let me into your world, you gave me your lips, your hands, your body, but you wouldn't give me your heart … why Joe? Wasn't I right for you? Didn't I do everything that you wanted, and more? I gave you my heart … my soul, but you didn't want it … why?" Her eyes grew wintery again. "Was it Midnight? That bitch always got in the way, I should have taken her out myself … but Robbins wanted to do it his way." Her voice was derisive of Robbins' methods, and she shook her head in confusion. "What does Midnight do for you, Joe? What could she possibly do?"

"Love me," Joe said simply, trying to draw her in closer so he could grab the gun.

Her eyes flashed with anger then. "You fucking bastard, I loved you! Don't you know that? I loved you and you didn't want me, you didn't want me!"

She brought the gun up, aiming it at his head, but she had taken a step closer and his hand whipped out grabbing the gun from her grasp. Joe heard a click, right next to his ear. He turned his head slightly, and saw the muzzle of a gun pointed directly at his head. It was Robbins. He had come in during Tasha's tirade, and Joe hadn't heard him. Now Robbins stood with a gun to his head. Joe held the gun he had grabbed from Tasha up with his fingertips.

"Take it, Tash!" Robbins yelled.

Tasha didn't move, her eyes averted from Joe's.

"Sinclair," Robbins said then, his voice sounded tired, "you're really starting to get on my nerves, ya know?"

Joe felt the barrel of the gun pressed to the side of his head. He closed his eyes, not sure if this was it or not. He opened them and saw Randy, her eyes were wide with terror. Tears were flowing down her face, and she was shaking her head, denying that this was all happening. Randy was shaking from head to foot, she was terrified that Robbins was going to kill Joe, shoot him in the head, right then.

There was a sudden crash above them and they all looked up. Joe took the opportunity to dive out of the way of Robbins' aim, but he landed on his wounded shoulder, which made him drop the gun he still had in his possession. It dropped with a clatter behind him on the cement floor.

"Goddamn it, Sinclair!" Robbins yelled pointing the gun at Joe. But as he fired, Joe threw himself to the side.

"Hold it, Robbins!" came Midnight's voice from the stairs.

Joe was almost faint with relief at seeing her and Rick on the stairs. Midnight was pointing her gun at Robbins. Rick had his back to them checking the other side of the stairs. Midnight descended the stairs keeping her eyes on Robbins the entire time. Rick followed her down and moved to untie Randy and help her up.

"Put the gun down, Robbins." Midnight said sternly.

But Robbins had the gun still pointed at Joe, who still lay on the floor, trying to gather the strength to stand.

"Do it, Robbins!" Midnight yelled. "Put it down!"

"Daniel?" Tasha said, her voice showing her uncertainty.

She was standing between Midnight and Joe facing Robbins. Robbins looked at her and Joe used his distraction to reach for the gun behind him. He shoved it into the small of his back. He turned and saw that Randy was watching him. He gave her a lopsided grin, and then moved to stand, slowly. Robbins looked at him again, the gun he held still trained on Joe.

"Get your hands up, Sinclair, let me see 'em!" Robbins yelled, his eyes trying to keep track of everyone.

Rick walked over to them. Randy moved to stand behind and to the left of Joe. Rick was holding a shotgun with it trained on Robbins.

"Do what the lady says, Robbins," Rick said.

Tasha started to back up, and Midnight took her eyes off Robbins to keep an eye on Tasha.

"Don't move, Tasha!" Midnight said, but Tasha continued to back up, her eyes on Joe.

Robbins lifted the gun slightly, and Rick could see that his finger was tightening on the trigger.

"Robbins!" Rick yelled then, stepping forward.

Without warning, Robbins turned the gun on Rick and shot him. Rick stumbled back with the force of the shot and dropped to the floor.

"Rick!" Midnight screamed, training her gun back on Robbins. "You fucking bastard, if he's dead … so are you!" Robbins was smiling evilly.

Midnight moved to Rick's side, he had been hit in the chest. Midnight couldn't stop the tears that started when she saw all the blood.

"Now you put down the gun, lady," came a voice from behind all of them. One of Robbins' men came out from the shadows.

Joe noticed that the door that he had tried earlier, stood open now. Midnight looked up, her hand tightening on her weapon, but she could see that the guy already had a pistol trained at her head. She looked at Joe who was watching Robbins, his hands at his side, but his fingers were working, like a gunfighter before a fight.

"Do it, bitch!" the same man yelled at her.

Midnight held up her hands, her gun swinging from the bottom of the trigger guard.

"Now this I'm gonna enjoy," Robbins said, lifting the gun to Joe's head again. "Goodbye Sinclair," he said, as his finger tightened on the trigger.

"Wait!" Tasha yelled, moving to stand between Joe and Robbins.

She faced Robbins. "Don't kill him yet," she said, her voice persuasive.

"Why?" Robbins asked derisively. "And keep your hands up, Sinclair!" he said, seeing that Joe was dropping his hands. "Why?" he asked Tasha again. He'd been thrown by her statement.

"I want him to get a taste of what he'll be missing in the next life," she said, and turned to Joe, looked at him seductively. "You still want me don't you Joe, you don't want to, but you do."

Joe looked down at her for a long moment. She had moved to stand right in front of him and her hands reached up to touch his chest. He pursed his lips, as if trying to decide.

"You don't know?" Tasha said then, her eyes gazing up at him in alluring way. "Well I can make you, you know." She pulled him toward her.

They kissed, her hands gliding through his hair as she pressed her body against his. Joe caressed her back then he moved one hand slowly to the back of her head. Without warning, his hand tightened on a handful of her hair and he spun her around, twisting his hold on her hair even tighter. She cried out. Joe kept her in front of him as a human shield, and he backed up.

"Now you put it down, Robbins, or I'll snap her fucking neck," Joe said, his tone acidic

Tasha was gasping in pain. Joe's good arm was the one that held her hair. His wounded arm was around her waist, keeping her in front of him. Robbins looked at Joe for a long moment, hatred burning in his eyes. Joe wasn't sure that this would even work, he didn't know if Robbins gave a shit about Tasha. He didn't notice Tasha's hand moving down to her pocket. Joe continued to back up. Glancing behind him, he saw that Randy was standing against the wall about three feet from him.

He took two steps back then stopped. e looked over at Midnight who was still looking up at the man who had the gun trained on her, but he was looking at the scene going on with Joe and Robbins. Midnight's gun rested by her knees and Joe saw her hand moving toward it. He waited until it was on the gun and he knew she was ready. He felt, Randy's hand at his back, she pulled the gun out that he had stuck there. He wasn't sure if he was doing the right thing; he didn't even know if Randy could shoot a gun, but he knew that one of the only reasons that Robbins hadn't shot him yet was because he could still see Joe's hands and didn't consider him much of a threat empty handed and twenty feet away.

Everything happened in a blur; Joe shoved Tasha away but she whirled on him. The knife that she'd kept hidden in her pocket was in her hand now and she drove the knife home, catching him in the chest. She brought it back a second time aiming for his heart, but she was stopped by two bullets in her chest. Joe had time to glance back at Randy and saw that she had fired the gun.

He looked over at Midnight and saw that she had picked up her gun and from a squatting position had fired a shot at the other man. Joe charged Robbins, who was standing in momentary shock. He brought the gun up as Joe charged him, but Joe hit him first, knocking him to the floor. They grappled, Robbins tried to bring the gun up a second time, but Joe grabbed for it. He grabbed Robbins' wrist and twisted it, hearing a crack as Robbins dropped the gun. Midnight had stood and run over to where they were fighting. She stood watching them fight, with her gun trained on them; if Robbins even looked like he was going to win, she would kill him. Robbins hit Joe's wounded shoulder twice, but Joe came back with surprising strength. He was letting his anger flow for all the things that Robbins had done to all of them. Joe let his temper flair, he let it burn hot, and Robbins never had a chance. He beat Robbins until he was unconscious.

Joe was gasping for breath as he stood up. Suddenly the pain hit him. Randy was there instantly supporting his weight against hers. Midnight darted back over to Rick and checked for a pulse. Her hands were shaking so hard she couldn't feel anything. A dark fear was clutching at her heart, and she didn't want to know …

"Rick?" she said desperately. "Rick!"

He didn't move. "Oh, God, no … " Midnight said, tears flowing down her cheeks, "not you Rick, not you … come on … please … "

Randy had led Joe over to the stairs and sat him down. His head rested on her shoulder, his eyes closed. She was watching Midnight over his head. Neither one of them saw Robbins stir.

Midnight was looking down at Rick, trying once again to feel for a pulse, her hand clutching as his arm. She caught his hand twitching out of the corner of her eye. Then she noticed Robbins. When she turned her head, she could see that he was watching her with an evil smile holding a gun. Midnight screamed like a banshee warrior as she dove for her gun that lay a foot away.

She heard Robbins' first shot, and she ducked her head before firing back. She emptied the weapon into his body with a vengeance. Only when the gun clicked, the slide locking back because the gun was empty did she lower it, breathing heavily. She saw the bloody mess that had been Robbins. She stared at it for a moment, thinking of what he had done to her, what he'd done to Joe and Randy, and what he had done to Rick … Rick!

She turned to him, sliding to her knees next to him. She pulled out her cellular phone and dialed for an ambulance, telling them to come code three, an officer was down …

****

Later in the hospital, Midnight sat watching the monitors and machines that were hooked up to Rick. Her face was a mask of sorrow.

He hadn't regained consciousness yet. The doctors had done everything they could. The bullet had barely missed his heart, but had managed to do some serious damage to his body. Midnight knew that he could easily die, much like Joe could have when he had been shot. But Joe hadn't died, and Rick wouldn't either, she just had to hold onto that. She sat in the darkened room and as she held his hand she cried silently. He couldn't die, he just couldn't.

In another room in the hospital, the doctor was looking Joe over, coincidentally the same doctor who had treated him previously. The knife wound in his chest wasn't as bad as it appeared. Fortunately, she had missed his heart altogether. His breastbone had kept the knife from going very far into his chest. There was some minor muscle damage, and he had lost a lot of blood. His shoulder wound was more severe. Fortunately for Joe, the bullet had gone all the way through, so it was not in his shoulder. The doctor explained that having to do surgery to remove a bullet of that caliber, a forty-five, would have probably caused more muscle damage to his shoulder than the bullet had done. There was some minor repair work necessary to make the shoulder usable again, but that could be done under a local anesthetic, avoiding the general anesthetic that had taken Joe almost three weeks to get over previously.

Randy was hovering nearby, a worried look on her face. He smiled at her, wincing as the doctor touched his shoulder again.

"Now that we've stabilized your blood pressure, Sergeant, I'd like to get to work on that shoulder," the doctor said.

Joe nodded and the doctor said he would go and get the nurse to prepare the local. Randy walked over to Joe and touched his face gently, worry written all over hers.

"I'm okay, babe, I swear," he said, smiling down at her.

"Yeah," she said, grimacing. "So okay they have to do surgery on you again …" She thought he was downplaying things.

"Randy, it's not like last time, I'll be fine," he said, trying to reassure her. He was astounded at how calm and clearheaded she was. He was sure it hadn't hit her yet that she had actually killed Tasha. He dreaded the questioning she was going to get from the department; he knew it would be rough on her. But he'd be there with her and he'd defend her all the way. He was sure the department would dismiss any charges against her; she was only defending him after all. He smiled at her remembering again that she had saved his life. He wondered if that had occurred to her yet either. He didn't think she had come to grips with any of what had happened yet, and he knew he'd better be there when she did.

The doctor came back then with the nurse and told Randy she had to leave. It was an hour later when the doctor came out and told her she could go in and see Joe. She walked in the room; he was sitting on the edge of the side of the bed, his feet planted firmly on the floor. He wasn't wearing a shirt, and he was still wearing his blood-stained jeans and his boots. He hadn't heard her come in and was staring down at the floor, going over the events of the last twenty-four hours in his mind. She stood at the door looking at him. She could see the still red scar from where he had been shot. She walked over to him, still not making a sound, and leaned down to kiss his good shoulder. He jumped a little in response, then turned his head and he smiled at her.

"C'mere you," he said softly.

She walked around to face him. She was taller than him, since he was sitting on the bed, but not by much. He reached out with his good arm and pulled her to him to hug her close. Her hands went around him, one hand burying itself in his hair, the other grasping his good shoulder.

They were still hugging when Darrell Curtis walked into the room, with Donovan trailing not far behind him. Darrell stood watching them for a few minutes. He had been told that Randy and Joe had been kidnapped and held by a gang. He had also heard that Joe had been shot, again, and that Randy had shot someone. He hadn't been too happy to hear that his sister had shot and killed another person, but he wanted to hear the whole story from her before he made a judgment. He was doubly unhappy to walk in and find his sister hugging the guy that had gotten her into all this mess in the first place.

Randy looked up and saw Darrell. She stared her brother down for a long moment, not making any move to leave Joe's embrace. Joe felt Randy tense though, and looked up at her. He saw she was staring challengingly in the direction of the door. Joe turned his head and saw Darrell. He started to stand, but Randy's hand on his shoulder stopped him. He turned, bringing one leg up onto the bed so that he could look at Darrell without twisting his neck around. Randy's hand remained on his shoulder, and Joe's arm remained around her waist. Joe and Randy stared Darrell down not saying anything. Darrell did the same. It was Donovan who broke the silence.

"Hey," he said, as he walked around his brother and over to the bed. "So you got shot again, huh?" he asked, his youth overriding any notice of the tension in the room.

Joe smiled at the young man. "Yeah, that seems to keep happening."

"Yeah," Darrell said derisively, "and my sister seems to keep getting involved."

Joe looked at Darrell with narrowed eyes. "I didn't mean for Randy to get involved, Darrell, it just happened that way ..." He was feeling a bit guilty, knowing the consequences could have been much different.

"You see, Randy, even Mr. Wonderful can't protect you all the time," Darrell said, his eyes narrowing at Joe.

Randy looked down at Joe. Her hand touched him under the chin, lifting his eyes to hers. Without a word, she leaned down and kissed him softly on the lips. Then straightening, she looked at her brother.

"That's where you're wrong again, Darrell. Joe did protect me. If it wasn't for him, that bastard Robbins would have raped me, but Joe distracted him," she said indignantly. "He kept them all from hurting me. So I wouldn't say he can't protect me, he did, and he protected the others too, that's how he ended up shot. So don't you dare presume to tell me how *Mr. Wonderful*, which he is by the way, can't protect me, because he can and he has!" There were tears of anger in her eyes by the time she'd finished speaking.

Darrell stared at her for a long minute, surprised once again by his sister's newfound boldness. "So who did you shoot?" he asked then, his voice accusing.

Randy was taken back by the tone of his voice. She didn't speak, she just stared at him. Certainly, he couldn't think badly of her for what she had done.

"*She* was protecting me, Darrell," Joe said. "She saved my life." He looked up at Randy who stared down at him, her eyes reflecting surprise at his words.

She started to shake her head, but Joe stood, taking her face in his hand. "Yes, Randy …" he said, his voice stern, "that's what you did. Tasha was bent on killing me and if you hadn't shot her, she would have."

He hoped that he was getting through to her, even as she stared up at him, her eyes wide. Then she slowly closed her eyes, and after a few moments nodded acceptance of what he was saying. She brought her head up again, resolve clear on her face.

"I saw her turn on you, and then I saw the knife. I yelled at her to stop, but she didn't … she'd already stabbed you once, so I fired, I had to stop her, Joe … I couldn't let her … she would have killed you …"

Her voice pleaded with him to agree. It was now becoming real to her. She had killed someone, and she could go to prison for it.

Joe pulled her into his embrace again, his good arm holding her tightly.

His lips were in her hair. "Yes, baby, she would have. You were defending me … It'll be okay," he said, his voice soothing as he stroked her hair. "I love you, Randy," he whispered to her, "and I'm gonna be there with you through this. It'll be okay."

She nodded. She trusted him completely and it was that faith and devotion that had gotten him through the night before.

Darrell watched as they hugged. He heard what Joe told her and he saw the look in his sister's eyes. The love and devotion she felt for Sinclair was very clear, and though Darrell didn't think much of what

Sinclair represented, he had to grudgingly admit that Randy obviously loved him. He only hoped that Sinclair really felt the same.

"You'd better be there for her, Sinclair," Darrell said, eyeing Joe, who still held Randy against him.

Joe looked up at Darrell, a sardonic grin on his face. "Oh I'll be there for her alright, for a very long time, in fact."

Randy turned then, staying within the circle of Joe's arms. Joe continued to watch Darrell over Randy's head.

Darrell stared at the two them standing there united like a strong front. He knew he wasn't likely to have any effect on their commitment to each other now. Until that moment, he'd still held out hope that things wouldn't work out. The thought died as he stared at the two of them.

"What?" Donovan asked, looking between Darrell, Randy, and Joe.

Randy smiled at her younger brother, realizing that Darrell obviously hadn't told Donovan about their engagement. She knew it was because Darrell was hoping it would change.

"Joe and I are getting married," Randy told Donovan.

"Wow, serious?" Donovan asked, his teal-blue eyes shining brightly.

"Yep," Randy said, smiling as she nodded.

"So cool!" Donovan said, smiling from ear to ear as he stepped over to Joe and held his hand out to the older man.

Joe took Donovan's and shook it smiling.. At least one of the Curtis men was happy for them. His eyes trailed over to Darrell whose lips were twisted in derision. Joe quirked his lips in a sardonic grin.

****

Rick remained unconscious and Midnight refused to leave his side. Eventually, Joe and Randy came in to see Rick. Midnight was relieved to see them and Joe hugged her tight. "Joe, he's gotta be okay, he's gotta be ..." Midnight said, her face against his chest, her fresh tears wetting his shirt.

"He'll be okay, Night," Joe said soothingly. "He's strong. He'll come out of it."

Midnight nodded, her eyes on Rick. She looked at Randy then. "You okay?" she asked the younger girl.

Randy nodded. "I'm fine ... Joe took the brunt of the punishment," she said, her voice expressing her anguish over that fact.

"That's his job," Midnight said, looking up at her partner, glad that he was okay.

"How did you find us anyway?" Joe asked. He hadn't had a chance to ask until now.

"Well, you know that's an interesting story," Midnight said, leaning back against the wall behind her. Her eyes kept straying over to Rick as she talked.

"I got a call from the watch Captain that one of my people had been hurt, it was Dibbins. He had been hit in the back of the head and left for dead down in Chula Vista. He's okay, just got a nasty concussion, and a big lump on that hard head of his. So I got on the phone to you, even though you told me not to call ..." she said then, grinning at him. He was very glad she had not listened to him.

"Anyway, I found that you weren't home, and I thought that was a little weird, but I figured you and Randy had stopped off and had dinner or something, even though it was eight o'clock by then. So I tried your cell phone, with no answer, so as a last ditch effort I texted you. I even put 911 on the end of the message ...Nothing. I decided I better check your house out then. Rick and I went over there and realized you'd never made it home. Of course, we checked for traffic accidents and all that, but something told me that this was no coincidence. So Rick and I went back to the office and started looking through everything we had seen recently on the Scorpions. We put an APB out on your car, and we checked to see if you had gotten any call outs over the radio, which you hadn't ..."

"Yeah someone called me on my phone, at around five thirty. They said Dibbins needed an okay on a search," Joe put in. Midnight nodded, adding that piece to the puzzle.

"Okay, so that's how they got a hold of you ... we never did figure that out. Well anyway, we were getting mighty desperate by this time. Nothing had turned up on any of our leads, and no one had seen you or Randy since you left the office. But then we got a break, one of the guys was looking through some of the surveillance photos that we got from BNE and he thought he recognized something about one of the cars that was parked in front of one of the houses. It was Tasha's, that white Beemer she drove wasn't exactly low profile. It clicked then, I remembered what you'd said about Tasha's strange behavior when you two broke up and that you thought she might be on drugs. I took a chance. We started running everything we could on Tasha then. We put an APB out on her car. We decided that since Dibbins had been hit in Chula Vista, and the Scorpions were working with the Riveras, Mexican Nationals, that they'd be between Chula and the border.

Then I got the idea to give a call to David Bollings, on the off chance that he could remember something about any properties being used by the Scorpions within the perimeter we were checking. At first he was drawing a blank, but then he remembered going to a house in San Ysidro to pick up some dope … He couldn't remember where exactly it was though, so that took a lot more time. But eventually we thought we had the house. We did some quick surveillance, again with the assistance of BNE, and decided to go in. Rick, Tiny, Spider, and me went in behind a BNE entry team … those guys are good, you know. Well we didn't expect you to be in the basement, so we sent BNE to secure the rest of the house, Rick, Tiny, Spider and me made our way through the kitchen, and we ran into more of them. Tiny and Spider were taking care of them, when Rick spotted door to the basement ajar. We went over to it and started down the stairs. I heard and recognized Robbins' voice right away. I knew we had found you then." She smiled once again grateful for luck to have been on their side.

"Good police work there, partner," Joe said, grinning at her, his eyes showing the respect he felt for Midnight.

"Yeah, thank Rick. If he hadn't seen noticed Tasha's car … we could have been chasing our tails for a while." She looked over at Rick's motionless form then, her eyes filling with tears again.

Joe and Randy stayed with Midnight. Three hours later Rick's doctor came in and saw the group in their varied states of waiting. Joe was sitting in a chair, leaning his head against the wall his eyes on Midnight. Randy sat on the floor in front of him, between his legs, her head rested on his knee, her arm wrapped around his leg with Joe stroking her hair. Midnight was sitting in a chair next to Randy, closer to the bed, her right hand holding Rick's as she stared down at him. Her left hand by her side was clenched in Randy's other hand.

Human support chain, was the thought that came to the doctor's mind. He knew that his colleague had done some minor surgery on Sinclair, and that he should be resting. The doctor had been ready to tell Joe that he should leave, but when he saw the four of them, he couldn't do it. No matter what his twelve years of medical training said, he felt that a cocoon of love and support around his patient may be the only thing to bring him out of the coma his body had slipped into.

The story of what had happened had spread through the hospital like wildfire and the doctor felt very sorry for these four people, who were, after all, the good guys. The doctor found himself praying, which he hadn't done much of over his forty-two years, for the recovery of this patient. The doctor quietly checked Rick's chart, disappointed to see no change in his condition. His blood pressure was still dangerously low, and he had yet to regain consciousness. The doctor left as quietly as he had entered, saddened that he couldn't give them any encouraging news.

CHAPTER 5

Rick remained unconscious for four days. Midnight was almost frantic with worry. She hadn't eaten or slept the entire time she had been at the hospital. Joe and Randy had stayed with her, alternating between going to get coffee or food. Joe hadn't wanted to eat either, but Randy knew that he needed to for his own recovery, so she had forced him to. She knew he should be resting too, but she understood that Rick was his best friend and Joe needed to be there for both Rick and for Midnight. Randy felt that she needed to be there too. Rick had come for them, he wasn't a police officer, yet he had put his life on the line to help rescue them, and he'd been shot doing it.

It was twilight outside on their fourth day at the hospital. The light in the room was dimming. Randy was sitting in a chair and Joe was sitting on the floor in front of her. Her hands were massaging his neck and uninjured shoulder. She could feel the tension in them and she knew it wasn't good for him. Joe's elbow rested on her knee, the back of his index finger rubbed back and forth across his lips as he stared off into space. His injured arm was held gingerly in front of him, slightly bent. Midnight had just stood to stretch when she thought she saw some movement from Rick. She watched him closely, and saw that his mouth was moving. He was grimacing, as if trying to come out of the coma was too much of an effort.

"Joe!" she said, then motioning to him.

Then she leaned over, her lips only inches from Rick's ear.

"Rick? Come on, babe, you can do this … come back to me." Her eyes watched his face, he was definitely hearing her voice.

She watched as he opened his eyes. He stared up at the ceiling for a moment, then his eyes moved to look at her.

She touched his cheek. "Hi there," she said softly, her eyes gazing down into his.

He didn't say anything at first then a slow smile spread over his face.

"Hi …" he said quietly.

"Hey man," Joe said, coming to stand behind Midnight.

Rick looked at Joe and grinned weakly.

"How ya feelin'?" Joe asked.

Rick looked at Joe for a long moment, then he looked at Midnight, then down, as if trying to assess how he felt before answering.

"Chest … hurts," he said finally.

Midnight smiled at him. "That's because you tried to stop a forty five slug with it, babe."

"Oh," Rick replied simply, grinning at her again.

He closed his eyes, swallowed, then opened them again. "Did … we … win?" he asked his words halting.

"Of course we won!" Joe said, with mock indignation.

Randy had run to get the doctor and came in with him then. The doctor looked Rick over, checking his blood pressure, checking his reflexes, then nodded approvingly.

"He's out of the woods, it's all downhill from here." He smiled at them then, as they collectively sighed with relief.

Then he looked down at his patient. "Now that you're awake," he said seriously but with a grin, "do you think you can make your friend, his girlfriend, and your girlfriend get some sleep and eat something? Or else I'm going to have three more patients soon."

Rick's eyes went to his friends, as if seeing them for the first time. He now saw how tired they all looked, even though they were all smiling at him. Midnight looked the worst; he could tell she hadn't been eating or sleeping.

"Babe ..." he said, touching Midnight's hand.

"Don't start on me, Debenshire," she said. "I'll rest now that I know you're okay, but I'm not leaving this hospital till you do."

When he turned to Joe and Randy for support, Joe held his hands up in a surrendering gesture.

"Yeah, yeah," Joe said, laughing, "we'll go." Then he smiled somberly at Rick. "Glad you're okay, man."

"Me too," Rick said then, returning Joe's smile.

"Randy ... take this guy home ... and make him rest," Rick told her.

Randy nodded. "I will."

She leaned down, kissing Rick on the cheek. "Glad to have you back," she said, then smiling down at him.

"Glad to be here," Rick replied smiling back at her.

Joe and Randy left and Midnight sat down in the chair again, taking his hand in hers. They were silent, each lost in their own thoughts. After a while, he fell asleep, and Midnight curled up under her FORS jacket and went to sleep too.

Midnight spent the next week at the hospital with Rick. She slept off and on, the hospital staff had finally brought a cot in for her, so she could actually lie down when she did sleep. Rick continued to get better. The doctor released him a week and four days after he had been shot. The hospital was astounded at his recovery, but the doctor felt that it was the love and support of his friends that had done it. All of the members of FORS had been to see him at least once, and in the case of Spider, Tammy, Dibbins, Tiny, and Kana, they had been to see him every day. Joe and Randy had also been at the hospital a lot. Randy had made Joe stay home for the first couple of days, so he could regain some of his strength. After that, he and Randy had alternated between the office and the hospital.

Joe found out that Tasha hooked up with Robbins a few months after they'd broken up. An associate of Robbins had been supplying her with the drugs she had been taking when she and Joe had argued. When she had needed another fix she had tracked her source down, and when she had told him about what an asshole Joe Sinclair was and how she'd like to see him dead, the source had put her in touch with Robbins. Robbins had seen the potential for her kind, and had hooked up with her. Tasha had supplied the Scorpions with all of the information she had on Joe and Midnight.

She'd given him Midnight's address. He'd failed to get it previously when he'd followed her home one night. That's when he'd had the encounter with Mike Harlow. Luck had been on Midnight's side that night, but nothing could divert the discontent of ex-lover. Fortunately, Tasha did not have the addresses for the rest of FORS, since none of them were law enforcement personnel officially. Midnight had not filed the listing of their confidential addresses with the DMV. Tasha had no access to that information. Although she had mentioned to Midnight that having that information on file might prove useful in an emergency situation, Midnight had declined. That one decision had kept both Midnight and Joe alive in situations that would have meant their instant death normally. Robbins had become obsessed with killing all of the members of FORS, to exterminate them, as he had said. He'd wanted the information, and refusing to supply it had kept Midnight and Joe alive long enough to be rescued. Ultimately, Tasha's obsession with making Joe pay for not loving her back had gotten her killed, as had Robbins' obsession with killing FORS.

It bothered Joe that Tasha had become so crazed about loving him. It scared him. He had never considered himself attractive or a good catch. But Tasha had been obsessed. When her apartment had been searched, the police had found a diary, and since Tasha was dead and no charges had been filed against Randy for her death, the police gave it to Joe. He was the main subject of it. The chief of police himself had exonerated Randy of any wrongdoing. He felt the same as every other police officer in the department that she had been defending a police officer, Joe.

The night before Rick was to be released from the hospital, Joe and Randy were at home in bed. Joe was holding her close. After she had fallen asleep, Joe had gotten up, and gone into living room. When she stirred two hours later, Randy realized that Joe wasn't in bed. She got up, and padded down the hallway, noting the light on in the living room. She found him sitting on the couch, a bottle of tequila next to him on the end table, reading Tasha's diary. He didn't notice her come in. She watched him; his face was drawn and unhappy, as he read Tasha's words. He took another swig from the bottle next and saw Randy standing there. He smiled at her grimly.

Holding up Tasha's diary he said, "What a great guy I am." His voice was self-depreciating, and depressed.

Randy kneeled in front of him, her eyes on his. "You are a great guy, Joe. I don't know what Tasha wrote, but she wasn't all there, and you shouldn't take anything she said in there to heart." Her voice was strong and sure, she knew she was right about this.

"She says," Joe said, reading from one of the pages, "I love him, why can't he see that? I don't know what else to give him. I thought my heart and soul was enough, what else could he want? He yelled at me again today, but I know he's just frustrated, that Midnight keeps him wound pretty tight, always needing him, always calling him. I wish she'd just get shot or something and die, then he'd be mine like he should be. I took more of those pills today, but I needed them. I can't leave Joe alone that way, the pills keep me calm, they keep me serene. I think Joe needs someone serene in his life with all the craziness he deals with at work. He needs me. I just have to be right for him, that's all … these pills make me right … most of the time." He looked up at Randy then, the look in his eyes miserable. "She was taking the pills to be 'right' for me …" he said quietly.

"Joe," Randy said, touching his cheek, "you can't think that you should have known why she was doing that, you can't blame yourself. What Tasha did was her decision. She was crazy, there's no way around that. You were just the object of her obsession, that doesn't mean you're to blame …" She waited to see if he'd listen to what she was saying.

After a few long moments, Joe nodded. "I know, you're right, it's just weird you know?"

"Yeah, it is," Randy answered, taking the book from his hands. She crawled up into his lap. They wrapped their arms around each other. "I love you, Joseph Michael Sinclair."

He kissed her. "And I love you Randissi Curtis."

Randy pursed her lips, her eyes sparkling excitedly. "Randissi Sinclair … hmmm …" Then she smiled. "I like it."

"You better," he said, smiling down at her.

They kissed again and Joe eventually, gathered her in his arms and carried her back to bed, leaving Tasha's diary sitting on the coffee table. They made love for the first time since the incident with Robbins. The next morning Randy took Tasha's diary and threw it away, not wanting Joe to read anymore. She knew that Tasha had been partially insane and she didn't want Joe feeling guilty over her lunatic rantings. Joe didn't say anything about its disappearance He was glad it was gone … he didn't want to read anymore.

****

When Rick was released from the hospital, Midnight took him to her house. The doctor had cautioned her that he was not to overexert himself. Midnight had given Rick a pointed look and he knew she intended to enforce that edict. She set him up in her bed and sat down next to him.

"Well, Mr. Debenshire, you managed to scare the hell out of me," she said, her voice sounding accusing, but she was still smiling.

"Sorry, love," he said sincerely.

"Rick …" she said looking down at the bedspread and industriously picking at invisible lint on it.

"Yeah?" he replied, not sure what to make of her change in mood.

"Do you still … you know …" She didn't look up at him, she just shrugged.

"Do I still what?"

"You know … love me?" She said the words as if they were taboo.

He reached out then, touching her under the chin, and bringing her eyes up to meet his. "Yes, I still love you … why?" he asked, with a lopsided grin starting on his face.

"I just wondered, because you haven't really said it … lately, I mean …" Her voice trailed off as she shrugged helplessly again, avoiding his gaze.

He stroked her cheek. "Baby, I haven't said it, because I knew it bothered you, but that doesn't mean I didn't feel it. I love you, Midnight, that's not going to change …" He was worried, he wondered if she was trying to get around to telling him she didn't want to see him anymore.

But that would be in complete contrast to her actions of the last week and a half. A small light of hope started in his heart then.

"Babe, what is it?" he asked, seeing her struggling with her emotions.

Still not looking at him, she started rubbing the palm of her hand with the thumb of her opposite hand. She often did it when she was agitated.

"I just … well, when you were in the hospital, when you didn't wake up … I guess … I did a lot of thinking. I was so afraid you wouldn't wake up, and then I couldn't tell you, I couldn't say …" Tears started in her eyes.

Rick was about to say something but when she looked at him, he caught his breath at the look in her eyes, and he knew even before she said the words.

"I was afraid I wouldn't get to tell you that I love you, Rick."

Rick almost couldn't believe what he'd just heard. It took him a few long seconds to let the words sink in. Suddenly, he was happier than he'd ever been in his life, but he was damned if he could think of anything to say. He pulled her to him and hugged her close.

"Night, I didn't even want to dream it …" he said, his voice wondrously happy.

Midnight smiled against his chest then.

"More like a nightmare …" she said laughing, and he laughed with her.

"Not hardly."

He held her, feeling like the whole world was right. He couldn't believe that she loved him. He thought about what it had taken, and he decided he'd get shot all over again, if that's what it took.

Midnight was relieved that her attitude about his feelings hadn't put him off and that he'd changed his mind. She always thought that there was one person for everyone, but she'd also assumed that when she met her soulmate, she'd know it right off the bat. She and Rick had spent so much time pushing and pulling away that she'd decided he couldn't be 'Mr. Right.'

While she'd been sitting in the hospital praying that he'd be okay, she'd looked back at all that they'd been through. Rick had been the one man she couldn't ignore, or dismiss from her thoughts. Her heart had been his from the moment she'd met him, she was just sure that her head had been the one fighting it. That and her independent spirit that wasn't ready to be tamed. But Rick didn't want to tame her, he loved her for who she was. That's what was amazing about him.

"Thank you," she said as she lay against him, her face against his chest.

"For what?"

"For loving all of me," she said, curling her lips in self-disgust, "even the stupid, stubborn parts."

"Well, I do love that about you too," Rick said, a smile playing at his lips. He touched his finger to her lips. "No conditions, babe," he told her softly. "I just love you."

Midnight drew in a deep breath, tears misting her eyes as she nodded. "No conditions," she repeated.

****

Two weeks later, Joe and Randy left for England. They planned to get married there in three weeks' time. Rick and Midnight took them to the airport.

When their flight was called, Midnight gave Randy's shoulder a nudge. "Now don't do all the shopping before I get there, we have to go out together and spend some of Joe's money," she said, grinning at the younger girl. Randy laughed, holding her arms out to Midnight and they hugged. Joe and Rick shook hands, and then Joe and Midnight turned to each other.

She looked up at him, grinning, her eyes already shining with tears.

"Don't do that, dammit!" Joe said, smiling at her. "I'll see you in two weeks."

"I know, I know," Midnight said, wiping at her eyes with the back of her hand.

Joe gave Rick a stern look. "Keep an eye on her, huh?"

Rick put his arm around Midnight, pulling her close to him and kissing the top of her head, "I will, and we'll see you in England in two weeks." Joe nodded. Midnight moved out of Rick's arms and into Joe's. Joe hugged her close then his head bowed down to hers.

"Thank you," he whispered.

"For what?" she replied, whispering too.

"For letting me go so I could find Randy …" He hugged her tighter then, as he heard her sob softly. "Night … you have Rick now …"

"I know, I just hate all this goodbye shit … it scares me …"

"Two weeks …two weeks … then you're in my town." He grinned down at her and she laughed.

"Oh shit, then I'm really in trouble, huh?"

Joe nodded, nodding to Rick, as he released Midnight, as if handing her back to Rick. "You take care of her, okay?"

"I promise," Rick said, grinning at Joe. He pulled Midnight back against him, crossing his arms in front of her, his hands holding her shoulders. He kissed the side of her head, as Joe and Randy went to board the plane.

"You okay?" he asked, his lips still in her hair.

"Yeah," she said, watching as Randy and Joe disappeared around the gangway. She turned to him then, looking up at him, her eyes searching his.

"What?" he said, not sure what she was looking for.

After a long moment, she shrugged and said, "Nothing." She had been searching for any sign of anger or jealousy over her and Joe's goodbye, but she didn't see any. What she didn't know was that Rick was very good at hiding what he was feeling.

****

Once on the plane, Randy knew she was going to go crazy. She was on her way to another country, with the man she loved, and was going there to get married. Things in her life were changing so fast, she could barely keep track of them. But she loved it all. Most of all she loved Joe. They were flying first class, so the stewardesses were especially nice to them, but Randy knew that they were being very attentive of Joe because he was so good looking, never mind the little blond girl sitting with him. That was Randy's first taste of the jealousy she would endure being engaged to Joseph Michael Sinclair.

The flight was very long, almost ten hours, and Randy couldn't sleep since they had taken off at nine o'clock in the morning. Joe did sleep, however. He was still on mild painkillers because of his shoulder. There had been a couple of further complications, requiring two more minor surgeries. Randy watched him sleep, thinking how lucky she was. He was handsome, kind, fun to be with, incredibly sexy, and just all around wonderful. She still couldn't believe that he loved her, it was just too unreal … but he did, and they were on their way to his homeland to make it official.

When they arrived at Heathrow Airport, it was raining and cold.

"It's always like this," Joe said, smiling despite himself.

He looked out the windows as the plane rolled into the gate, feeling a little strange being back. When they deplaned, Joe put his arm around Randy as they walked up the gangway. Randy stopped by one of the windows in the passenger area, taking her first long look at England. Joe stood next to her, looking out too.

"Master Sinclair?" a clipped English voice inquired behind them.

Joe turned around, looking down at the small man dressed in black with a white starched shirt, and a black cap.

"Yes?" Joe answered. Randy was staring up at him, eyes wide, mouth agape at the title he had attached to him name.

"The car is this way, sir," the man replied, bowing just slightly.

"Thank you," Joe said as the man led the way to, "the car."

"What?" he asked, smiling down at her having seen the odd look on her face.

"*Master* Sinclair?" she said, her eyes still wide.

Joe laughed. "Oh yeah, I forgot to tell you about that, it's … I don't know, an old time English thing."

"I see," Randy said, once again impressed with a new aspect of her fiancé's life.

They reached the car, a limousine. The driver stood holding the door open for them. Randy looked around her eyes taking everything in. "Wow … I've never been in a real limousine before … well, okay once, but it was this rental one, and it was awful … this one's …"

"Not a rental," Joe finished, and her eyes grew wider.

"Oh my …" Randy said then, sitting back against the soft leather seats.

She noticed that Joe was looking at her with an odd smile on his face.

"What?" she said, having picked up from him the habit of asking that whenever someone stared at her.

Joe shook his head, his smile growing wider. "It's just nice to see your reaction to things like this … I've always taken them for granted. It's interesting to see it through your eyes."

She smiled up at him then, and pulled his face down to hers and kissed him. They were still kissing when the driver returned from getting their luggage. Randy blushed furiously when he got in the car and waited patiently for Joe's orders. Joe instructed the driver to take them to his parents' home. The driver nodded, and put the car in gear.

Joe sat back, his arm still around Randy. The drive to Joe's home took forty-five minutes. As they got closer Joe got quieter, and his face took on a closed look. Randy held his hand, stroking it with her other hand. She took in the beautiful countryside as it slid past, but she couldn't enjoy it, knowing what Joe was going through. Her heart ached for him.

It had been nearly eight years since Joe had left England. Being back was bringing everything back and making him feel the weight of guilt and anguish pressing in on him again.

When they turned into the long driveway that would take them to the Sinclair home, Randy sat up, looking out the window. She felt her heart almost stop at her first glimpse of Joe's childhood home. It was absolutely incredible. It was a Tudor-style mansion, white with brown trim. She had seen homes like this in magazines and books, but she never even dreamed that she'd be staying in one like it.

She didn't realize she was squeezing Joe's hand convulsively until he laughed. She bit her lip, realizing she was being a bit overexcited. Joe couldn't help but be warmed by her reaction to his parents' home. He thought for a moment he was going to have to resuscitate her.

His eyes went to the front door, he dreaded walking through it. All the way home he had relived his parents last days … and there were moments when he wanted to tell the driver to turn around. He wanted to go back to America, where he could be far from all these memories. But he had swallowed down on those impulses, knowing that he needed to do this.

Now looking at the house again, he found his courage failing. Randy turned to him, seeing the almost scared look in his eyes. "Are you sure you want to do this?" she asked then, her voice concerned. The driver opened the door, and she glanced over her shoulder at the open door, then back at Joe. "Maybe it's too soon …"

"No …" Joe said, taking a deep breath. "I'm okay." He looked at Randy seeing the skepticism on her face. He grinned at her lopsidedly. "So maybe *okay* isn't a good word for how I am but I can do this, as long as you're by my side."

Randy stared up at him for a long moment, then she kissed him softly and turned to get out of the car.

A man in a butler's uniform opened the front door for them. Randy was assailed with the scents of wood, flowers, and lemon. She looked around the entryway of the house in complete awe. The floors were hardwood. The sweeping staircase in front of her was built completely out of mahogany. She looked up and saw the cathedral ceiling of the entryway, detailed in intricate gold scrollwork. She couldn't believe her eyes.

"Randy ..." Joe said, smiling down at her again.

She looked at him, and suddenly realized that there was a small line of people standing in front of them. They all wore uniforms of some sort. As the butler began introducing the others to her, she realized they were servants. *Oh my God,* was all she could think.

"Miss Curtis, this is Annie, she is the downstairs maid, and this is Joy, she is the upstairs maid. This is Frederick, the cook, and Sandra Bender, the overseer of the Sinclair home. I am Mason, at your service." The older gentleman bowed, and Randy was sure she was going to faint.

"Nice to meet all of you," she managed to say, her eyes going to each of them.

Annie was a small woman with brown hair, and glasses. To Randy she looked like she was in her early thirties. Joy was taller, with lighter hair, and brown eyes. She looked about thirty. Frederick was heavyset with long gray hair pulled back in a ponytail, and looked about fifty. Sandra Bender was blond haired with blue eyes. Randy thought she was perhaps in her late forties and found out later she was actually fifty-five. Mason was the epitome of the classic butler. He had hawk like features, very sharp. He had brown hair that was graying at the temples and thinning at the crown. He looked about sixty.

Joe started to show her around the house, but it was obvious to Randy that he was not handling being home very well. She gently suggested that they save the tour for later, and that they rest up a little. They were both exhausted from the last few weeks at work. They had been frantic wrapping up everything that could be wrapped up before Joe left. Neither of them had slept enough, plus Joe's extra surgeries had set him back a little. Joe nodded to Randy's suggestion of resting, and led her upstairs to what was apparently his room, before he left.

Randy didn't realize until later that he had not been in this room since the night his parents had been killed. The servants that tended the house had kept it dusted, and straightened up, but they had not presumed to move or remove anything. Randy tried not to look around too much, knowing her curiosity would get the better of her. She knew that Joe needed to rest now, and she would wait until she had gotten him to sleep before she took the time to properly look around. Her first impression of his bedroom was that it was imposing, not just in the surprisingly large size of the room itself, but also due to the large, heavy antique furniture. The colors of the room were dark, navy blue and greens, and there was a definite masculine look to everything, and to Randy it very much felt like a rebellion of sorts. While the furniture seemed expensive, the room itself had a different feel from the rest of the house. It wasn't elegant or aristocratic, rather it seemed an antonym to the rest of the house. It gave Randy a little bit of insight into the younger, more rebellious Joe.

Joe, like Randy, didn't look around, but because he didn't want to remember at that point. He lay down on the bed on his stomach, breathing in the familiar scent of his room, and feeling sick to his stomach.

Randy sat down next to him on the bed, stroking his hair. "This is really rough on you, isn't it?"

Joe nodded, his face buried in a pillow.

"What can I do, Joe?" she asked, concern filling her voice.

Joe turned over looking devastated. "Just be here, babe ... be here with me ..."

Joe sat up and Randy reached out, taking him into her arms. He leaned against her for a long time, drawing strength from her warmth. After a while, Randy moved to lean against the headboard, pulling Joe with her. Joe eventually fell asleep, his head resting against Randy's stomach. Randy stroked his hair, watching him sleep.

When she was sure he was asleep, she let her eyes wander around the room. First, she noticed the pictures on the bureau; there was a picture of what was obviously Joe and Rick. They both looked very young, and both wore leather jackets and jeans. Randy noticed that even then Joe was very handsome. In the picture, his face seemed set in stone and his eyes were very cold. Rick looked like his usual self, only younger.

The next picture was obviously Joe and his parents. Randy saw how beautiful Joe's mother had been. She glanced down at him, seeing the resemblance immediately, but he looked like his father too. He was definitely the best of both parents. She saw a picture with Rick in it, and four girls. At first, she thought it was his harem of girls that Joe had told her he always had in England, but then she started to see the resemblance between them, and realized she was looking at Rick's sisters. There was also a picture of a dark-haired woman who Randy didn't recognize, nor could she figure it out. Shrugging, she looked at the next picture.

She got up off the bed carefully so as not to disturb Joe. She moved closer to the picture. It was a group photo. She could see now, that almost everyone in the picture wore a leather jacket. They were standing on what looked like the edge of a cliff, overlooking a dark stormy sea. Joe stood in front of the group, his head tilted down, but his eyes looking up at the camera, menacingly. Rick stood just to his right and slightly behind Joe. He was looking at the camera, but he had the sardonic grin on his face that Randy had come to know. The rest of the group ranged out behind them. As Randy looked at the different faces, she heard Joe's voice behind her.

"That's the Knights …" His voice sounded a little strange, and Randy turned her head to look at him. His eyes looked very haunted.

"Big gang …" she said, turning back at the picture.

"Fair sized, yeah," Joe responded, his voice sounding a little more normal.

"And you were their leader …" Randy said, sitting back next to him on the bed.

"Yeah," he replied simply. Then his eyes moved past her, and fell on the chair next to his bed.

Randy followed his gaze and saw the leather jacket lying on the chair. She looked at him again, his gaze was fixed on the jacket. Randy stood and picked up the jacket. It had what was obviously the Black Knights logo of crossed black and silver swords and the words Black Knights written in silver in calligraphy script on the back. Randy could smell the mixture of the cologne Joe still wore, and leather. It smelled like Joe. "Try it on," he said then, surprising her.

Randy shrugged into the jacket. The sleeves hung well past her fingertips, and the bottom of the jacket came down to her mid-thigh.

She laughed, knowing how silly she must look, and surprisingly Joe laughed too. Randy put her hands in the pockets, and to her surprise found things in the pockets. Out of one pocket, she pulled out a pack of cigarettes, a silver lighter, and what Randy assumed to be money.

"How much would this be in American dollars?" she asked curiously.

"Well that's about a hundred and fifty pounds …" he said, looking up at the ceiling calculating the exchange. "Today it'd be worth about one hundred and ninety-five … back then it was more like a three hundred and forty."

"Two hundred to three hundred *dollars*?" Randy repeated, totally shocked.

Joe chuckled. "That was nothin' … I'd drop that at the pub in one night."

"You were bad, weren't you?" Randy said then, smiling down at him.

She reached into the other pocket and her hand touched something hard and cold. She pulled it out of the pocket and stared down at an ivory handled switchblade. She looked at Joe then, not sure why she was surprised.

"Never left home without it," Joe said, his voice low, his eyes on the knife. "You look surprised."

"I am. I guess … I mean I know that you were different back then but …"

"I didn't use it much," Joe said, taking if from her hand.

He depressed the switch and the blade snapped out.

"I like to fight with my hands. But one never knew …" He shrugged then, closing the blade as his eyes looked up at her. He could see she was taken back by this revelation. "There's a lot about me you don't know …"

"That's true," she said sitting down next to him, still wearing his old gang jacket. Her hand reached up to touch his cheek, her eyes looking directly into his. "But there's nothing you can tell me about yourself that can change the way I feel about you."

Joe looked at her for a long moment, then he slowly pulled her to him and kissed her, feeling the need to be close to her. As they kissed, he removed his jacket from her. She entwined a hand in his hair while the other unbuttoned his shirt, and touched his bare skin. Joe groaned softly, against her lips. His hands were at the small of her back, holding her close to him. He moved one to the base of her neck, caressing her.

They had just got themselves settled on the bed when they heard a voice say, "Master Sinclair?" It was Mason.

Randy was instantly red from embarrassment. Mason had not actually entered the room. He stood on the threshold. The door was still open, but his eyes were averted from them politely.

"Yes?" Joe answered, grinning at Randy.

"Taylor is here to see you, sir."

"Already? Damn!" Joe said, then he sat up. "Okay, Mason, escort her to the sitting room, we'll be down in a few minutes."

"Yes, sir," Mason answered, and then turned and left.

"Is he always going to do that?" Randy asked still embarrassed at having been caught making out, even if it was with her own fiancé.

"If we forget to tell him not to disturb us, he will … Very proper household here … I forgot to warn you." Joe was grinning at her, and she swatted at his arm.

"You, cad!" she said. She looked at Joe, worry starting in her eyes. "Taylor, huh?"

"Yeah … you ready for this?" Joe said, eyeing her.

"No!" she said. Then she sighed. "But will I ever be?"

"Probably not," he said, touching her under the chin then, and looking her straight in the eye, "just remember that I love you."

She smiled at him. They both went into his bathroom and straightened up. Joe watched Randy, a slight smile playing at his lips.

"What?"

"Nothin'" he said, still looking at her.

A few minutes later they sat on an antique couch with Taylor sat across from the in a Louis the IX chair. After a couple of minutes, Annie came in bearing a tray with silver tea service on it. Joe nodded to her, and she left the room without a word. Taylor made show of preparing tea for herself, asking Joe if he was having any.

"No … I'm kind of on coffee now," Joe replied.

Taylor made a face. "Can't abide by the substance myself. Too bitter." Then she looked at Randy, who was sitting right next to Joe, her hand in his. "What about you, Randy … or are you a coffee person too?" She made the question sound more like a jab, and Randy felt Joe squeeze her hand slightly, indicating he had heard it too.

"I don't really drink coffee either …" Randy said quietly, her eyes staring down at the Persian rug. The rug was very beautiful, and she was dying to concentrate on something other than Taylor's cold blue eyes. She leaned back, and Joe moved to give her a little more room. She heard him suck in his breath, and she knew he had moved wrong and hurt his shoulder again. He hadn't taken a painkiller again since they had boarded the plane in California. She looked up at him her eyes showing her concern, but he shook his head at her.

"What's wrong, Joseph?" Taylor asked. His wince hadn't escaped her.

"I … well I got shot a few weeks back and—"

"Honestly, Joseph, why do you continue with this ridiculous course of action?" Taylor huffed.

"I know you don't understand, Taylor, but deal with it," Joe said, his tone short.

Taylor shook her head, but thought better of arguing with him again. She'd already had to apologize to him for her comments previously and assure him that she did not believe that he'd killed is parents for their money. She didn't want to push him again. Unfortunately, in searching for a new topic, she backed into another disastrous direction.

"Are you going to see Roslynn while you're here?" she asked.

"Why would I see her?" Joe asked, his look pointed.

"Well, you two were betrothed, Joseph. I don't see how it would be harmful for you to simply see her," Taylor said plaintively.

'I'm not going to have time," Joe said.

"I thought you were home for three weeks," Taylor pointed out. "Surely there's enough time …"

"I'll be busy," Joe said. The pointed look on his face should have warned her.

"What will have you so very busy?" Taylor asked, her tone exasperated.

"We'll be making wedding arrangements," Joe said simply, grinning down at Randy.

"You'll be what!" Taylor practically shrieked.

Joe chuckled, squeezing Randy's hand. "Randy and I are getting married, Taylor."

"You wouldn't dare ..." Taylor breathed.

"Wouldn't I?" Joe queried.

Taylor stared back at him openmouthed. Joe's light blue eyes widened and he thoroughly enjoyed his aunt's reaction to his news. Without a word, Taylor stood up and hastened out of the room.

"Did she just leave?" Randy asked Joe in a hushed voice.

Joe canted his head, listening for the front door to slam. He heard it a moment later and grinned widely. "Yep," he said, sounding pleased by the thought.

"Wow," Randy said simply. Joe just laughed at the shock on Randy's face.

****

The next morning, Randy woke up before Joe, since he'd had a few drinks with dinner, and had taken a painkiller before they'd gone to sleep. Randy put on her jeans and a sweater, and wandered around the huge mansion. Eventually she made her way into the kitchen, having gotten totally turned around, and more or less, lost. She walked into the huge kitchen and saw Sandra Bender sitting at the kitchen table, drinking tea. Sandra Bender looked up at Randy then, smiling kindly at her.

"Good morning, miss," the older woman said.

"Good morning," Randy replied, as she sat at the kitchen table. "Would you like some breakfast, miss, cook is just …" Sandra started to say, but Randy shook her head.

"No I'm fine, thanks."

"How about some tea then?" Sandra said, her voice coaxing.

"Okay," Randy said, shrugging.

"Would you like it in the formal dining room?"

"No!" Randy said. Then she smiled sheepishly at her outburst. "I mean … I think I just wandered through that room … it's so big!"

Sandra smiled warmly. "Indeed it is," she said. She stood and got Randy a cup and saucer. She poured some tea from the china pot that sat on the table. "How do you like your tea, miss?" she asked, her hand hovering over the sugar.

"I um, I'm not sure …." Randy said. She wasn't used to anyone serving her.

"Have you ever had milk in your tea?" Sandra asked.

"I can't say that I have," Randy said, shaking her head.

"Let's give it a go, shall we?" Sandra asked, smiling.

"Okay," Randy replied, liking the other woman immediately.

When Sandra handed her the cup, Randy took a tentative sip and then smiled brightly. "Oh this is so good …" she said.

"That's the English way," Sandra said, winking at the younger woman.

"I didn't realize there was an English way," Randy said, smiling.

Sandra raised an eyebrow at Randy. "Then Joseph hasn't been teaching you properly." she said, her tone light.

"Joe does that too," Randy said, smiling up at the older woman.

Sandra sat down. "Does what?"

"Raises his eyebrow at things …" Randy said. She looked up at Sandra then. "Did you know Joe … before …" Her voice trailed off again, not wanting to bring up a sore subject.

"I've known Joseph all his life," Sandra said, smiling fondly at the memory.

"You have?" Randy asked, surprised.

"I was his nanny when he was young."

"You were?" Randy replied. Then she looked up at Sandra, a little abashed. "What was he like when he was little?"

"Oh, that one!" Sandra said, laughing. "He was the most mischievous little boy I have ever had the pleasure of governing."

"Mischievous?" Randy said, testing out the word. "Yes, I can believe that."

"Oh believe it, miss, he was the worst. But you know," she said, leaning toward Randy, in a confidential way, "those baby blue eyes of his, always got him out of whatever kettle of fish he'd gotten himself into."

Randy nodded then, laughing. "And I can believe that too!"

"But he did change …" Sandra said then, her eyes taking on a shadowed look.

"Change?" Randy said then, surprised by the woman's change in mood.

"Yes, as he got older, I saw him grow more handsome every day. He never realized how handsome he was, but he knew what effect he had on people, and he used that effect to put people off. He grew angry and cold. I suppose that it had a lot to do with the pressure his parents were putting on him …" Her voice trailed off, as she remembered those days.

"What kind of pressure?" Randy asked curiously. She had always wondered what would make a man as handsome and well off as Joe turn to a gang.

"Well, Joseph was their only son. They wanted him to follow in Joseph Senior's footsteps, and that required grooming. They wanted Joseph to attend the right parties, know the right people, date the right girls …" She shook her head.

"That is what his aunt still wants," Randy said, her eyes sad.

"Well never you mind about that, miss. Joseph knows his own mind … never liked the arrangements that were made for him anyway."

"Arrangements? Oh, the girl they wanted Joe to marry?"

"Joseph told you?" Sandra asked.

"Yes," Randy said, her voice somber.

"Well, it was definitely not something Joseph wanted, in fact when they told him he went absolutely mad. He yelled, he cursed, which he did not normally do in front of his mother. Finally, he stormed out of the house. He didn't come back for a week. By this time, his parents were absolutely beside themselves with worry. When Joseph finally came back, he told them then that he would do as they wished. He changed totally then; he was silent, cold. He was a stranger, but he was doing as his parents wished. He came home later and later, and always with a new cut, or bruise. His father tried to talk to him, but Joseph wouldn't listen, he smiled and nodded, but it was obvious he wasn't listening ... then the accident happened. Joseph was so badly injured ... he never came back to this house after the night of the accident, except for a few moments before he left for America, until now ..."

"Did he talk to Rosylnn about the engagement?" Randy asked after a few moments of silence.

"No ... she visited him once in the hospital. He wasn't even conscious at the time. Joseph didn't want to see her, and she didn't come back. I wouldn't be surprised if they have never spoken again ... but there's no doubt in my mind that she still wants him ..."

"Really? Joe said he'd heard she was married, but Taylor said that the marriage was not working out ..."

"I'll just bet that had to do with Joseph returning to England, but she didn't bargain for you, I'll wager," Sandra said, giving Randy an approving look. "I think that you are very good for Joseph and he'll be doing right to marry you."

"Thank you," Randy said, embarrassed at the compliment, but happy at the same time.

"Sandra ..." she said then, looking shyly up at the older woman.

"Yes, miss?"

"Taylor said something about Joe's responsibility to his family name, and that his parents wouldn't approve of me …" Her voice trailed off, not sure how to ask the question she wanted to.

"Never you mind about all that rubbish, miss. They would have loved you, because you love their son and he obviously loves you. Taylor can't know what they would have thought. She just has her bonnet set for Joseph marrying the Ellington girl, that's all."

"You don't think he'll be disgracing his family name … by marrying me?" Randy asked softly then.

"Oh good Lord," Sandra said, rolling her eyes dramatically. "Taylor has always carried on about that nonsense. I don't know why, it's not even her name!"

Randy looked at Sandra for a moment, then she started to smile. That's right, Joe had said that Taylor was his mother's sister.

Sandra put her hand on Randy's, looking directly into Randy's eyes. "You are the woman that Joseph should marry, or else you wouldn't be here. I assure you, it took a great deal for Joseph to return here, and you must be worth it to him."

Randy felt better knowing someone who knew Joe so well approved of her.

She felt even better that evening when Joe took her to meet Rick's parents. Annabelle Debenshire was totally enchanted by Randy. She told Joe over and over what a lovely girl she was, and that he had better be doing the honorable thing by her. Joe had smiled warmly, and Randy was reminded of what Sandra had said about how he had changed. She couldn't imagine him any other way than the way he was now.

At one point during the evening, Joe said something about Midnight.

"That's the girl that Richard has gotten himself involved with isn't it?" Annabelle said, her voice not sounding pleased. Randy felt Joe tense next to her. They were sitting in the Debenshire's living room.

"*That's* my partner," Joe said, his voice cool.

"Now Joseph, you know Richard, probably better than any of us, if you take my meaning ..." Annabelle said, her eyes looking into Joe's.

"Yes, I do," Joe responded, his face set in a stony look, "and he knows that if he hurts her, I'll kill him." It was obvious from his tone of voice that Joe was deadly serious.

Annabelle was obviously taken back by Joe's tone as well as his words. "She means that much to you, Joseph?" she asked.

"Yes, Belle, she does," Joe responded, his voice strong and sure.

Robert Debenshire looked very uncomfortable, and leaning forward he said, "So have you seen Taylor yet?"

Joe gave the older man a sardonic grin. "Unfortunately."

"Now Joseph, why would you say that, you are her favorite nephew after all," Anabelle said, when Robert was too surprised to respond.

"Well that doesn't seem to be the case anymore," Joe said, his grin widening.

"What does that mean?" Anabelle asked.

"Never mind."

After a few moments of silence, Randy spoke up. "She doesn't approve of me, I'm afraid."

"Good Lord, why not?"

"She doesn't have the right *breeding*," Joe sneered.

Anabelle looked sharply over at her husband. They'd had a discussion about the very same thing, when it came to Midnight. Although he hadn't said he was marrying the girl or any such thing.

"Well," Anabelle said, her smile warm, "leave it to Taylor to be blunt and rude. Joseph you need to do what's right for you."

"That's about what I told Taylor. She reminded me of my 'duty' to my family name …"

"Joseph, marrying a beautiful girl like Randy won't sully your good name. Pay Taylor no mind."

Later that night, when they were back at Joe's house, Randy was still thinking about their earlier conversations. They were in his room, in bed. Joe's arms were around her.

"Joe," she said cautiously.

He looked down at her, recognizing the hesitation in her voice. "Yeah?" he asked softly.

"Were you ever in love with Roslynn?" she asked after a long moment of indecision.

Joe didn't answer for a few long moments, then he shook his head. "No … I tried … but she was just too much like all the women I was trying to avoid."

"Avoid?"

"Yeah, I mean, being in a gang, that keeps you pretty far away from the social scene, you know." He laughed, a sardonic grin on his face. "The few times I did get an invitation to some ball, or something, I went in a leather jacket and jeans, and made a general nuisance of myself. That earned me the rep I needed to keep as far away from all that crap as I could get."

"So that's why you started the gang?" Randy said, still looking at him.

"More or less," Joe said shrugging, "and it worked too. Until my parents decided they were going to head me off at the pass, as it were. They *arranged* for me to marry Roslynn, and *told* me I was doing it. I just about went off the deep end. I spent the next week drinking and sleeping with any girl I could get my hands on, but nothing would change the fact that this was what my parents wanted. By the time I went back home, I had resolved that I would do what they wanted, but I had no intention of settling down, even if I did marry Roslynn."

"And your father changing his will to cut you out of it was his way of making sure that happened, right?"

"Yep," Joe said, his look slightly haunted then.

"That's why people think you killed them," she said quietly.

Joe nodded, closing his eyes for a long moment.

"Did you even know about the appointment?" Randy asked.

"No ... I didn't find out about it till after Scotland Yard did. Then Rick's dad decided he better tell me before they did."

"My God, that must have been awful, having them investigate you, and treat you like a criminal, when you were still grieving your parents ..." Randy said, her eyes misting with tears.

Joe looked down at her, seeing the love and trust in her eyes, and he knew she had no doubts about him. He was once again amazed at her devotion to him, how could someone who barely knew him be so trusting of him, and believe him no matter what? It was crazy when he thought about it, especially when his own aunt, who had known him all his life, didn't even believe him.

"Randy, how can you believe in me so much?"

Randy hesitated, thinking about her answer.

"I don't really know …" she said, her face composed in thought. "I just know that I would and have trusted you with my life, and you've been there for me …" She shrugged. "I guess it might have something to do with my parents. They weren't there for me and because of that I've had a hard time trusting anyone to be there for me. But you have been, and you love me. You've given me what I've needed for a long time, you've given me someone to lean on, and depend on. You've given me yourself. I guess in return I've given myself to you, and all the trust and love that goes with me." Her eyes stared up at him, she reached up and touched his cheek. "I love you, is that so hard for you to believe?"

Joe looked down at her. "I guess in a way it is. I mean, you don't hold anything back, there's no reserve there, you don't hide anything. I guess I'm used to love coming with conditions, and you don't give me any. You love me no matter what."

"Well, believe it," Randy said, reaching up to kiss him. Her lips moved to his cheek, then right next to his ear. "I love you, Joseph Michael Sinclair, and nothing is ever going to change that."

He hugged her close to him bringing her lips back to his with his hand. When their lips parted, his hand held her face, gently, his eyes searching hers. "And I love you, I don't care what Taylor or anyone thinks, we belong together, and nothing is going to tear us apart."

"I won't let it," Randy said, her eyes shining in the semi darkness of the room.

She moved her lips to Joe's chest, and felt his hand tighten on her waist in response. She moved her lips to explore the muscles on his chest. She looked up at him, and saw that his eyes were watching her. She could see the desire clearly in his light blue eyes and it sent a thrill of excitement through her. Randy moved so that she leaned over him, her hair brushing his chest. She kissed him. Joe's hand entwined itself in her hair, while his other hand pulled her body down against his. It was clear from the intensity of his kiss that he wanted her.

Randy moved away, removing her nightshirt. She had been nervous about not wearing anything, in case Mason walked in on them again. Joe watched as she removed the shirt, admiring her body. His hands reached out to touch her and he sat up, bringing himself within inches of her. He touched her shoulders, then slid his hands down to her waist, his eyes never leaving hers. He leaned down, his lips taking possession of hers once again. His hands at her waist pulled her slight frame to him, crushing her against his bare chest. The fire between them ignited, and his hands caressed her back. His lips left hers, and traveled down to her throat. Randy's hands grasped at his shoulders, and she felt him jump when she touched his still healing gunshot wound.

"I'm sorry," she said, her voice husky with passion, but her eyes showed genuine concern.

She gently kissed the now healing scar. He held the base of her neck with one hand and kept the other around her waist. Randy kissed his neck and heard his low moan in response. She continued to kiss his neck, as she slid her hands to his chest, her nails trailed lightly over his skin, and she heard his sharp intake of breath, as his hands tightened on her body.

"Randy ..." he said, his voice a deep groan.

She moved to his lips, kissing him with all the passion she was feeling. He returned that passion with all of his own. For the first time in their relationship, Randy made love to him. She delighted in her ability to make him respond to her, and it made her feel powerful and confident.

Afterwards they lay entwined in each other's arms. Joe looked down at her, with a wide grin on his face.

"My … what a little power will do to a woman," he said, his voice still husky from their lovemaking.

"No," Randy said, looking up at him, "it's what you do to me."

"Hell, tell me what I did, I'll do it again, gladly!" he said, and she laughed.

They fell asleep a half hour later. Joe woke the next morning to the sound of someone knocking lightly on the door. He had been half-awake anyway or he wouldn't have heard the light tapping.

Assuming it was Mason, he made sure that both he and Randy were covered, then he said, "Come."

It wasn't Mason, it was Roslynn.

"Well, well now," Roslynn said quietly, looking down at Joe, taking in his bare chest and the girl sleeping next to him.

"What do you want, Roslynn?" Joe whispered harshly. He was hoping to keep Randy from waking, but she was already stirring.

"I'd say a little of what she obviously had," Roslynn said, her voice still low, her eyes staring down into his.

Joe was shocked by her brashness. Randy's eyes, to his dismay, were now open and she was staring up in amazement at the nerve of the intruder.

"Sorry, dear, didn't mean to wake you," Roslynn said with a conciliatory tone.

"Roslynn," Joe said, keeping his voice calm and cool, "get out of here."

"Why Joseph, you haven't gotten shy on me have you?" Roslynn said, her eyes widening at him.

She sat on the chair across from the bed.

"Roslynn ..." Joe started to say, his voice issuing a warning.

"Oh Joseph don't be a prude," Roslynn said, waving her hand at Joe. Then she looked at Randy, who was staring at her almost dumbfounded by her boldness. "You see dear, Joseph and I ... well we're no strangers. Well my parents they thought that I was a sweet innocent virgin, but Joseph he changed all that, and—"

"Roslynn!" Joe yelled then, cutting her off with a swift gesture of his hand. "Get the fuck out of here, before I have you thrown out."

"Oh, now you wouldn't do that Joseph. I know you remember the good times we had, and we can have those again, if you'll just come to your senses ..." She looked at him, her eyes those of a vixen.

Joe just shook his head, not believing that this was the same blushing girl his parents had wanted him to marry. To his utter shock, Randy sat up, her eyes staring defiantly at Roslynn. The marks of their passionate lovemaking were evident on Randy's neck and Roslynn's eyes narrowed at the sight of them.

"I believe Joe asked you to leave," Randy said, keeping her voice cool.

"Well ..." Roslynn said, measuring up her adversary. "Don't think that you won't be next, dear."

"She's not going anywhere," Joe put in, as he sat up and pulled Randy back against him.

"But you are," Randy said, settling herself against Joe, still facing Roslynn, her eyes never leaving the other woman's face.

"Is that so?" Roslynn said becoming very haughty.

"That's so," Randy replied.

"You think you can handle a man like Joseph *little girl*?" Roslynn said, her voice full of derision.

"I think I have," Randy said, her voice full of meaning, her smile provocative.

"He'll get bored with you in no time," Roslynn said, her eyes narrowing.

"Like he got bored with you?" Randy asked, her voice mockingly sympathetic.

"You dirty little bint!" Roslynn said, her eyes flaring with anger. Randy knew she'd hit her mark.

Joe chuckled, still astounded at Randy's fire.

"Takes one to know one, doesn't it Roslynn?" Randy fired back.

"Well, you won't keep him," Roslynn said, trying to regain her composure. "No one ever does."

"No one else has ever married him and that's just what I'm going to do," Randy replied, placing her hands on top of Joe's where Roslynn could see them clearly.

Roslynn noticed that Randy wore Joe's signet ring on her left ring finger. Randy caught Roslynn's eyes on the ring, and noted the subsequent widening of her eyes. She smiled evilly at the other woman then.

"I think you'd be wise to leave now, Roslynn," Joe said, his voice derisive, "while you're ahead." Then he snapped his fingers. "Oh, that's right you're not even ahead now … better yet you better leave before Randy here actually beats you into the ground."

He grinned, moving his head down to nuzzle Randy's neck. Her hand came up to touch his face. Joe looked up at Roslynn from the tendrils of Randy's tousled blond curls, his light blue eyes reflecting victory. Roslynn inhaled sharply at the look in his eyes, then she looked at Randy. Randy had her head tilted down, so that Joe's lips could touch the hollow of her neck, but her eyes stared at Roslynn. Joe was her man, and nobody, not even a ghost from the past could have him. Roslynn got the message loud and clear. She stood without a word and walked out of the room.

Roslynn walked outside the room, closing the door, and leaning against it. She had expected Joe to be ready to jump into her bed. She had grown up a great deal since he'd seen her last, and she thought that she would make him drool. She hadn't expected this "Randy" to be the blond-haired vixen she had turned out to be. Taylor had said that Randy was very meek, but obviously Taylor had underestimated the girl. As she leaned against the door, she could hear what was going on in the room. She reluctantly listened to Joe and Randy for a moment, then strode away down the hall, tears gathered in her eyes.

"Jesus!" Joe said, after Roslynn left and closed the door. "Where did you come from?"

"I've always been here, I guess it just took someone like her to bring out that side of me," Randy said, leaning back against him, enjoying the feel of his skin against hers.

"Well, stay, please …" Joe said seductively.

Randy looked up at him, smiling. "Oh I intend to," she said, her voice low and sexy.

"Good …" Joe said. He leaned down to kiss her lips and his hands caressed her breasts.

She gasped as she felt his hands on her, and the intensity of their kiss increased. After a few minutes, Joe turned her around to face him, his eyes burning with desire.

"God," he said, his voice husky, "You're gonna be the end of me yet."

"Not the end, Joseph," Randy said, her eyes staring seductively up at him, her voice like silk, "just the beginning …"

She ran her hand through his hair and brought his head down to hers. Joe found himself reacting strongly to her sudden change of character. He very much liked this side of Randy too. He had enjoyed being the teacher, guiding her through lovemaking, but now that she had discovered her power over him, she was using it, and he liked it, a great deal.

As they kissed, her nails skimmed the sides of his head as her hands moved through his hair. Joe found himself responding wildly to the sensation. His hands gripped her and he dragged her body over to him, and pressing it against his, which only served to excite him more. Her tongue slid seductively along his lips, and once again he responded with an intensity that surprised him.

"Baby …baby …" Joe murmured over and over, as he felt himself losing all control.

She pushed him back on the bed and slid her body along the length of his, her own pulse racing at having excited him so much. As she slid down and his body entered hers, they both groaned loudly. They made slow passionate love, both of them holding back, wanting to extend the sensations they were feeling. When they finally reached the height of their passion, they both exclaimed loudly, their hands clasped tightly.

Afterwards, Joe stared up at Randy, knowing the student had now surpassed the teacher, and glad of it. She grinned down at him, feeling absolute power, and reveling in it. Just let Roslynn try to take this man away from her now!

****

Over the next week, Joe showed Randy around London and, at her gentle insistence, around the estate. They rode horses over the hundred acres of the land that was the Sinclair estate. Randy was surprised to find out that her husband to be was also a generally accomplished horseman too. She wondered if there would ever be an end to the things that she didn't know about this man.

Randy herself was slightly afraid of horses, but Joe talked her through the saddling of the horse and helped her onto the back of the Arabian mare he had chosen for her to ride. Once she was on the horse, he gave her gentle instructions to keep the horse in line. A few times he gave the black Friesian stallion he rode a quick kick and galloped off ahead. Randy watched as he rode; he was even more attractive astride a horse. It reminded her of the movie they had watched "Ladyhawke." It had starred Rutger Hauer, who played the

Captain of the Guard. In the movie he had ridden a Friesian stallion, known for their grace and beauty as well as their exceptionally long manes and tails. Joe looked as handsome to Randy as Rutger Hauer had in the movie. Even more so because she loved him.

They stopped for a while and sat under a huge oak tree on the estate. Joe was a little quiet, and she noticed a far off look in his eyes. It had been a week and three days since they had left America.

"Hey," Randy said, laying down next to him in the grass, and looking up at him.

He was sitting with his knees up to his chest, his ankles crossed, and his arms resting on his knees. He looked down at her smiling.

"What?" he asked.

"What are you thinking about?" she asked, her voice in no way suspicious or prying.

"Home," he answered simply.

"I thought you were home?" she replied, smiling up at him.

"No, I mean America."

"You consider that home now?"

Joe thought for a moment, realizing what that would mean to him. And after a few long moments he nodded. "Yeah, I guess I do, I mean, all this"—he gestured to the wooded area around them—"it's not mine, it's theirs. It's like I'm just keeping it for them ... you know?"

"Is that how you feel? Like this isn't really yours anymore?" Randy asked, sitting up, and her eyes searching his.

"It never was mine, Randy. It was always their house. I didn't buy it, I didn't earn it. It's their money, their house, and their land."

"But they left it to you. Don't you think they'd want you to have it?" Randy said.

"I guess so, but it's hard, you know, taking what they left. It seems so wrong somehow."

Randy reached out, touching his cheek. "You loved them, and they loved you, and they left you all of this so that you could live your life the way you wanted to, and that's what you're doing. Does this have to do with that stuff with Roslynn?"

He looked at her, eyes not giving anything away. They hadn't talked about Rosylnn since the morning she had barged in on them.

"I guess in a way it does. Knowing that my father was going to change his will, and knowing that he didn't want me to have all of this if I didn't marry her. I guess it has a lot to do with that, now that I think about it," he said, coming to the realization as he spoke.

He looked apologetically. He didn't want to hurt her, but she had asked him and he didn't want to lie to her.

Randy was silent for a few minutes, looking out over the land-scape. They were sitting in a clearing, surrounded by big beautiful trees, the sky was clear, but there was a definite chill in the air. Then she finally brought her gaze back to him.

"Joe, I think that your father was going to change his will, because he wanted to make sure that you did something that he felt would, in the end, save you from yourself," Randy said, her tone reasoning. "Okay, so you didn't marry Roslynn, but you did save yourself from yourself didn't you? You went to the States and straightened yourself out. You became a police officer, you've done so much …" she said, her voice trailing off as she canted her head. "Don't you think that you've done so much more than they could have hoped for? Don't you think they'd be proud of you now?"

"Marriage isn't the only thing that can straighten someone out, or settle them down," she continued when he didn't answer. "It's very unfortunate that it took the loss of your parents to make you realize what a foolish path you were headed down, but you did realize it, and it made you stronger for it. So now, you're marrying me. You're doing one better than your parents wanted, you've straightened yourself out, you've settled down and now you're marrying for love. What could possibly be wrong with that?"

Her voice was very calm during her speech, and he could see that she honestly believed every word that she was saying. Joe once again found himself astounded by her way of seeing things.

It was obvious from her words that she had been thinking about this. Joe found himself loving her even more, for the fact that she worried about him enough to try and 'save him from himself' as she had put it. He pulled her into his arms, hugging her close and kissing her.

"What if someone rides by or something?" Randy said, suddenly realizing they were totally out in the open and feeling like an errant teenager necking in the woods.

"Randy, this is my land … no one rides on it but me … and you." He smiled at her then.

She had caught the fact that he had said 'my' land. She hoped that meant that she had gotten through to him. She had wondered what he was thinking about the situation with Roslynn, but she hadn't wanted to bring up a sore spot.

Later that night he suggested that they take a trip.

"A trip?" Randy echoed.

"Yeah, somewhere like Paris …" Joe said, his eyes twinkling at her surprise.

"Paris?" Randy repeated, her eyes widening.

"Love, it's only a hop, skip, and a jump from here."

"It is?"

"Yeah, it's a two hour drive to Dover, and then a three hour drive from Calais. Not too bad a trip if you want to go."

"Yes, of course I want to I'm just not used to the idea that we can do things like that … I mean … Paris."

After a little more discussion they decided to leave the next day and stay in Paris for three days, which would put them back in England the day after Rick and Midnight were due to arrive. They figured they should have leave Rick and Midnight to have a day to themselves to get over the jet lag. The next day they left the Sinclair estate with Joe driving one of the Mercedes that were kept on hand. He thought to be chauffeured was too pretentious. Once on the ferry Joe pointed out the fabled white cliffs of Dover to Randy and hugged her closer at her childlike joy. He enjoyed showing her new things. He knew she would appreciate all the things that people like Roslynn, and even himself, took for granted. But this was all new to Randy and he loved that he was the one that was showing it all to her. He loved her.

CHAPTER 6

When Rick and Midnight's flight touched down at Heathrow Airport, Midnight was asleep. She'd slept most of the way over. Rick chalked it up to the hectic two weeks that they'd had since Randy and Joe had left. There had been loose ends to tie up, and all kinds of last minute things to work out. FORS was not equipped to have both its leaders out of the office at the same time. Spider was taking over, with the assistance of Tiny. They had both been set to start the police academy the day before, but Midnight needed them at FORS for the time being so special arrangements had been made for them to split the time between the academy and FORS.

"Night," Rick said, rousing her gently, loathe to wake her.

"Hmmm?" she responded, rubbing at her eyes like a little girl. Rick smiled down at her.

"We're here babe."

"Wow," she said, opening her eyes and looking out the window. "I thought it was supposed to be a really long flight?"

"It was, you slept through most of it," he responded.

She looked at him. "I'm sorry … guess I'm not much of a travelling companion am I?"

"Not the best, no." He leaned down and kissed her on the forehead. "but I love you anyway."

"Oh good, so I don't lose points for that one?"

"Don't push it," he said, smiling.

He stood and stretched. Midnight noticed there were other admiring glances at him, besides her own. *Let 'em look,* she thought to herself, *he's mine.* She reached up touching his waist, when he looked down at her, she just smiled up at him. He responded by leaning down and kissing her on the lips, his hand touching her face gently. *Let 'em look now!*

Later on the drive to his parents' house, Midnight had a chance to look around the countryside.

"It's really green here," she said, her voice surprised.

"It does nothing but rain, what'd you expect?" he replied, humor in his voice. He was driving a rented jaguar, and of course to Midnight's way of thinking on the wrong side of the car and the wrong side of the road.

Midnight was silent for a while, taking in the scenery and trying to orient herself with her new surroundings.

"So, how does it feel to be back?" she asked after a long while.

"I've only been gone for a year."

"Yeah, but I thought you Englishmen were supposed to get homesick real easy."

Rick laughed. "Well I wouldn't say real easy. I did miss it if that's what you mean and it is good being back, especially with you here to share it with. My family will be thrilled that I've brought you home with me." He glanced in her direction, his blue eyes shining.

He noticed she looked uneasy for a minute, but then she smiled and he figured he had imagined it.

When they reached the Debenshire home, Midnight was surprised at the size of it. By her standards, it was a mansion, but Rick said it was nothing compared to Joe's and that was obviously what he judged a mansion to be. Rick's home was, however, a very charming looking three-story Victorian-style home, painted an elegant pearlized cream and accented with hunter green and sea foam green. The house was set back from the street, with a low elegant white rod iron fence around the beautifully landscaped front yard. Midnight stood looking up at the house, her eyes on the second story balcony.

"Hey," Rick said, coming to stand right behind her, his arms going around her waist.

She leaned back against him, her eyes still on the house.

"This is absolutely beautiful," Midnight said her voice awestruck.

She felt Rick shrug behind her.

"It's home," he said in her ear.

"You should see my 'home' sometime. You won't be so nonchalant about yours anymore." There was no anger in her voice, but he knew what she was talking about.

One late night she had told him about where she and Thomas had grown up. She said it was basically a shack with three bedrooms. The walls were paper thin, so she and Thomas could always hear when Jack and Carrie were going at it, whether it be sex or fights. Half the time there was no electricity because Jack wouldn't have worked enough that month to pay the bill. Food was scarce, but she made a point of getting some for her and Thomas, she never was sure how Jack and Carrie ate.

It had made Rick ill to think of all the rough times she'd been through when he had everything in the world he could want, and took it all for granted. Now standing in front of his family home, he was determined that his family was going to accept Midnight and make her feel welcome and loved. He had heard the skeptical tone in his mother's voice when he had told her that he was bringing Midnight home with him, and that he was in love with her.

Of course, he couldn't really blame his mum. He had been "in love" so many times before, but it had never felt like this. Most of the time he had been just said it so he could put his mother's worry to rest. Annabelle Debenshire despaired that her only son would never settle down and start a family.

Once inside the house, Rick found the note that his mother had left. It said, "Small emergency at Deborah's, be home soon as possible, not to worry. Love, Mum."

"Guess we're on our own for a while," Rick said, looking at Midnight. She was looking around the kitchen, wide-eyed.

The interior of the house was very elegant, but cozy, with lots of wood furniture and throws over chairs and couches. The kitchen was decorated in antique blue and cream, and Midnight found it hard to believe that anyone actually cooked in this kitchen.

"Does your mom cook?" Midnight asked, looking over at Rick who was leaning against the refrigerator watching her.

"My mum?" Rick said, rolling his eyes. "Lord yes! And you're in a whole lot of trouble when she sees you."

"Why?"

"'Cause she's gonna feed you like you've never been fed before. I can just hear her now complaining over how thin you are. My poor sisters had to fight her off constantly."

"What happened to you then?" Midnight said, walking over to him, and sticking her finger into his ribs. Rick laughed.

"I was too fast for her, besides I've been out from under her roof for a year …"

"No you were thin when you got to America, I know …"

"You do, 'ey?" Rick asked, holding her against him.

"Oh yeah, I checked you out that first night."

"You did, huh?" he said, smiling down at her.

"Oh yeah …" she said, her voice trailing off seductively.

"Then why didn't you do anything about it?" he teased.

"You were Joe's best friend, what was I supposed to do?"

"Jump me on sight."

"Oh that would have gone over well." She laughed.

"That's what I wanted to do to you," he said, his voice low.

"Is it now?" she said, pulling back to look up at him. "And why is that?"

"Because," he said, leaning down to kiss her, "you are the most incredible woman I have ever met, and I wanted you the minute I laid eyes on you."

"I see …" she said, laughing.

They kissed for a few minutes leaning against the refrigerator. Then Rick showed her around the house. Midnight's first impression of the house as being cozy and warm was only further justified upon closer inspection. Rick's mother seemed to like the Victorian colors of deep greens, rich mauves, deep burgundies, and pale peaches.

The house was very warm and cozy, yet at the same time, Midnight could tell that Rick's parents definitely had money. There were numbers of antiques, and expensive-looking crystal and china in the formal dining room. Confirming that Rick, too, came from money, only made Midnight more apprehensive about meeting his family.

After showing Midnight around the house, they settled on the couch in the family room. Rick sat with his back to the corner of the couch, with one foot on the floor and the other up on the couch. Midnight sat between his legs, leaning against him, her head resting on his chest. It had been two hours since they had arrived and Midnight was starting to feel a headache coming on, and her head was getting congested. She sniffled, and Rick looked down at her immediately concerned.

"You okay?" he asked.

"Yeah," Midnight replied, reaching up to rub her temples, "I think I might be getting a cold though." She sniffled again.

"Oh boy," Rick said, touching her forehead, "you do feel a little warm. Let me see what my mum has here for a cold."

Moving carefully, Rick got up and Midnight rested her head on the arm of the couch, looking around the room again. It was very homey. It was what she would have liked her home to have been like. There were all kinds of pictures on the walls, pictures of Rick when he was younger, pictures of his four sisters, family pictures, pictures of Rick playing soccer, pictures of his sisters dressed in their Sunday best.

It was nice; it was family. Something that Midnight knew very little about. It scared her in a way. They were a family, and here she was some homeless waif trying to gain their acceptance. She was just sure they wouldn't like her, but she loved Rick, and for him she would try this. But she knew they held all the cards, and she held none, save Rick's love for her. Rick came back a few minutes later, and gave her some pills to take. She took them obediently, and they settled back on the couch.

"Baby, maybe you should go lay down," Rick said, worried about her. She wasn't one to get sick easily.

"No, I'm okay … I'll just lay here, okay?" she said softly.

"But, Night …"

"Rick, I don't want to lie in some strange bed alone and I don't think your mom would like it too much if she came home and we're in bed together, okay?"

He could hear genuine concern in her voice, as well as a touch of anger. Rick knew she was not happy to be placed in the position of having to gain acceptance from anyone. He knew how hard this was going to be for her, he only hoped his family would make it easier.

"Okay, baby, okay … just lay here."

Midnight rested in his arms, the pills eventually taking effect and making her sleepy again. She fell asleep, with Rick's arms around her, one hand stroking her hair. Rick was sitting back against the corner of the couch again. She was turned toward him, her head resting against his shoulder, one small hand curled around a handful of his shirt. Rick's head was bent so that his lips rested against her forehead.

Anabelle Debenshire's first impression of her son and Midnight was the obvious tenderness between them. When she entered the family room, she saw her son with his head resting against a young woman's copper-blond head. Careful not to make a sound lest she disturb the tender moment, Anabelle stepped closer. She could see that the young woman was asleep, and Rick was holding her close soothingly stroking her hair. Anabelle couldn't help but see the affection he held for her. Loathe to disturb them, but knowing that watching them too long without their knowledge would constitute an invasion of privacy, Anabelle stepped closer, and whispered, "Richard."

Rick looked around and smiled up at his mother.

"Mum, hi," Rick whispered.

He looked down at Midnight then, smiling. "She wasn't feeling well ..."

"No?" Anabelle said, concerned. She moved around to look at the young woman. "My, she is lovely, isn't she?" Anabelle said, taking in the small features, free from makeup or anything artificial.

"Yes," Rick said, looking down at Midnight again tenderly, "she is."

As if she knew she was being discussed, Midnight stirred. Before even opening her eyes, she reached up, almost childlike in her gestures, and rubbed at her eyes. Then opening them, she stared up at Anabelle Debenshire, her golden-green eyes wide with surprise.

"Hi," she managed, her voice sounding small and timid.

"Hello there," Anabelle countered with a warm smile. "Richard tells me you're not feeling well."

As if to prove it Midnight sniffed, sounding even more congested after her sleep. She nodded in response.

"Well, we'll have to do something about that," Anabelle said. She looked at her son then. "Richard, why don't you take ...?"

"Midnight," Rick supplied.

"Ah, yes, Midnight, intriguing name that. Anyway, take Miss Midnight down to that second bedroom and I'll make up some tea and bring her something to take for that cold. Go on with you then," she said, shooing her son down the hall.

Rick stood, and picked Midnight up in his arms.

"I can still walk you know," Midnight said, looking at him with an arched eyebrow.

"I know, but this is faster," Rick said, laughing at the face she made.

A little while later, after Anabelle had fussed over her and made her take the medicine she brought for her, Midnight fell asleep again. Rick and his mother sat in the kitchen talking.

"So how are you, young man?" Anabelle asked, looking at her son with a critical eye.

"Fine, good as new," Rick responded, knowing that his mother had been almost sick with worry when he'd been shot.

"I see. Is that what you say, or is that what the doctors say?"

"The doctors released me, Mum, I'm fine, really."

"This new career of yours may be the end of me," Anabelle said, clutching at her chest dramatically. Rick laughed.

"Where's dad?" Rick asked then.

"Oh he's with Deborah, one of the girls got hurt. Little Susan. She hurt her arm, broke it I think. Poor child."

"So how is Deborah, and … Wilson … is it?" Rick asked trying to remember his sister's husband's name.

"Richard Debenshire, you know very well it is, and don't you start going on about that rubbish again, you know that your sister's perfectly happy with him."

"No, way, Mum, he's too stuffy, even for Deborah."

"Well, you must see your sister dear, she has changed a great deal since you left, she's quite the lady of the house now."

"Yeah, I'll bet," Rick said, distain coloring his voice, "but is she happy?"

"Richard ..." Anabelle's voice warned.

Rick had been against Deborah's marriage to Wilson Endicott from the beginning. Wilson was the kind of man that Rick despised, an over-groomed, over-stuffed pompous ass with 'breeding' to the eyeteeth, but not a warm bone in his body. But Deborah had set her cap for him, and had eventually won his hand in marriage, much to Rick's dismay. He never knew what his sister saw in the man, but if she was indeed happy, then he couldn't fault her.

"Now what about you, Richard?" Anabelle asked, narrowing her eyes at her son.

"Me?" Rick asked blankly, trying to postpone the talk he knew was about to occur.

"Yes, you," Anabelle said, knowing her son's tactics. "How serious are you about this young lady?" she asked, gesturing the direction of the room in which Midnight slept.

"Very," Rick answered simply.

He saw the look of skepticism on his mother's face instantly.

"Mum, I love her ..." he said, trying to come up with the words to explain.

"Richard ... " His mother's voice was patient and gentle. "You've been in love before, or so you've said ... What makes this any different. Is it?"

"Oh, God, Mum, yes," Rick said, his eyes shining in the soft light of the kitchen. "Midnight is not like any other woman I've ever met. She's as tough as nails, but then gives people everything. She gives everything of herself, and she doesn't ask for anything back. You've got to see it to believe it, Mum. This woman, this tiny woman leads some of the fiercest looking people I've ever met, and she does it without taking anything away from them. And believe me those people will follow her anywhere. They'll give up their lives for her, it's absolutely incredible." He shook his head as if he couldn't even believe what he was saying.

"People like that have very high highs, but they also have very dismal lows, Richard," Anabelle cautioned.

"Oh, don't I know, when she lost a member of her unit, I thought it would kill her. But it didn't, she went on. In fact, she helped a lot of other people through it. She has so much strength in her spirit, being near her makes you feel like you can take on the whole world. But when she was vulnerable ... the only thing I could think of was protecting her. I've never felt that way about any woman."

Anabelle looked at her son for a long moment, surprised at his words as well as the look of utter love and devotion on his face as he spoke about Midnight. She wondered what kind of spell this woman had put on her son. She was about to comment on that when a scream pierced the silence of the house. Rick was out of his chair, and running toward the bedroom in an instant. Anabelle followed closely behind. When she got to the open doorway, she saw Rick holding Midnight against him. The girl was obviously very upset, she was shaking, her hands were clenching at Rick's shirt.

"Oh, God ... oh God," Midnight was saying over and over.

"Babe, it's okay, I'm here …" Rick said, soothingly, stroking her hair. "It's okay." He was rocking her back and forth. Anabelle watched, mesmerized. She had never seen this side of her son before.

"Oh God, Rick, it was him …" Midnight was saying her voice full of anguish and fear. "Robbins!"

Rick hugged her closer, kissing her hair, his hand running rhythmically along her back trying to soothe her. "Baby … he can't hurt you anymore … he's dead … he's dead, okay?"

"No, he was there … I saw him … Rick!" Her voice rose hysterically as the dream came back to her again.

"Come on baby, calm down!" Rick said, his voice a raised whisper. He took her face in his hands and tilted her face up to his. "No one's ever going to hurt you again, not while I'm alive. I'm here, baby, you're okay, I'm here …" He kissed her forehead, then her cheeks. "It's okay, I love you, baby, and no one is ever going to hurt you again … you trust me?"

Midnight was clearly still rattled by the nightmare. It was obvious she was trying to regain her bearings as she nodded slowly.

"Okay," he said, smiling down at her. "Now I want you to lay back down here, and relax. It was only a dream, and I'm here now, okay?"

Midnight nodded again as Rick moved to gently lay her back on the bed, still holding her. Her arm went around his waist, her head snuggled against his shoulder. Rick lay, half sitting up against the headboard. Midnight lay next to him. He looked up at his mother, realizing for the first time that she was standing in the doorway. The look in his eyes told her everything that a mother needed to know. Anabelle leaned against the doorjamb watching her son. She thoroughly enjoyed seeing this side of her sometimes taciturn son. After a little while, when he thought she was asleep, Rick tried to move. Midnight's grip on his waist tightened,

"Please ..." she pleaded quietly. "Don't leave ... stay here with me."

Rick looked up at his mother, knowing her view of men and women "sleeping together" unmarried, especially under her roof. Anabelle looked at Rick for a long moment, then down at the young woman snuggled against him. A small smile crossed her face and she nodded to her son.

"Okay, baby, I'll stay," Rick said, kissing her gently on the forehead.

The next day Rick showed Midnight around London. They drove around the countryside, and took in some of the tourist attractions, such as the Tower of London and the Crown Jewels. Midnight was still battling the cold, so they didn't stay out too long. Just before the evening meal, Rick's parents got an opportunity to see Midnight in her role as the Lieutenant of FORS. Just as they were sitting down to dinner, the phone rang. Anabelle answered and after a few moments held the phone out to Midnight. "It's a Spider ..." she said, her voice perplexed over such a strange name for a young man.

Rick and Midnight looked at each other. Rick grinned and shook his head. Midnight looked almost embarrassed as she took the phone from Rick's mother.

"Yes?" she answered, glancing shyly at Rick's parents, who were trying to pretend not to listen to the conversation. She listened for a few moments and slowly but surely Rick could see Lieutenant Chevalier coming out of the shy girl who had stood holding the phone a moment before. "No … No! Spider, aw geeze! No, don't do that, no!" She rolled her eyes dramatically. "You can't do that … no I mean, *you can't do that.*" She shook her head emphatically. "Spider, listen to me … are you listening?" She was now using her 'lieutenant voice.' Robert and Anabelle were taken back by it, but impressed too. "Now … you can't arrest him on vehicular … if you arrest him on vehicular, then we can't get him for murder one … why? Because Spider, there's this little thing called jeopardy … and it can only attach downward … Yes that's a legal term Spider … well I know that. That's why I have the degree in law and you don't." Anabelle looked at her husband, since he was a barrister, or the American equivalent of a lawyer.

Robert Debenshire was nodding his head. This young lady knew her stuff, and he was pleasantly surprised to hear she had a degree in law.

" … Now … if you will just hold on … " Midnight continued, as if talking to a child. "We'll get the DNA evidence and we'll have him for murder one … so just chill out, Spider, okay?"

She listened again for a few moments. She stood with her free hand on her hip, and her teeth worrying her lower lip. She focused on a spot on the floor as she listened. "He's not gonna bolt, Spider … he's on parole, BNE's got him tagged. We've got him tagged, he's got nowhere to go … so just sit back and relax okay?"

She rolled her eyes again, sighing. "We've only been gone a day and a half, do you think you can hold it together for another twelve days?" Her voice was skeptical.

Then she grinned at Rick, he was leaning against the opposite wall, shaking his head and smiling.

"Okay, good … geeze, you guys are going to make me old before my time! Okay … fine … I'll call you sometime next week, okay? Tell Tammy hi for me, and the rest of the gang too. Okay … bye."

Midnight hung up the phone and looked apologetically at the Debenshires who were now watching this little woman with a new respect. "Sorry about that … they're not used to me being gone …"

"Nothing to be sorry about, dear. You're obviously very important, and they need your advice, not to worry. Robert gets calls at all hours too," Anabelle said, looking at her husband on the last.

The rest of the meal proceeded quietly. Rick knew that Midnight had just earned a lot of respect from his father. Robert Debenshire hated nothing more than a beautiful woman without a brain in her head. After dinner, Midnight went to bed, to try to get more rest and hopefully beat her cold.

Later that night, once again Rick and his mother ended up in the kitchen. Rick told his mother about how Midnight came to be in the type of business she was in. He told her about how Midnight's little brother had wanted to join her gang, and how she had decided it was the lesser of two evils to let him into hers. He also told her how Thomas had been killed and how Midnight's parents had disowned her from that point on.

"I can't believe that …" his mother started to say, but he shook his head.

"I didn't either at first," he said, feeling the knot in his throat tighten, "but her father called her a while back, and before the conversation got very far, he was right back to accusing her of murdering their son. It's like they think she's still in the gang and they're ashamed of her."

Anabelle was aghast; she could understand Midnight's parents being upset about losing their son, but for her parents to treat her so badly, after all she had accomplished was just ludicrous. She couldn't imagine cutting one of her children out of her life. She felt all the more sorry for the girl.

"And how did you two get together? Through Joseph I imagine," she said smiling at him. She looked on Joe as one of her own children.

Rick nodded. "Midnight is Joe's boss, if you can believe that!"

Anabelle shook her head, laughing. "Not really!"

"Yeah, he works for her, and I ended up working with Joe. I think I loved her the first time I met her though …" He looked at his mother, trying to see if she'd think him crazy, but all he saw was love and acceptance. He had rarely ever seen anything else in her eyes when she looked at him.

"Love at first sight?" she asked, her smile still in her eyes.

"I guess," he said smiling at the thought. "I thought she was gorgeous—"

"And you were right," she injected.

He smiled at her, happy that she thought so too.

"But man she was tough. She didn't want to have anything to do with me. Although we had a brief go around, but when Joe was shot … and she was …"

He couldn't finish the sentence. He didn't like to talk about that time, it had been so awful. His mother knew about Joe getting shot. Of course he had called and told her that, and she had been extremely worried about him having been cut up so much and Joe being injured so gravely. He hadn't told her about Midnight at the time, because it would have taken more energy to explain than he had, and then the time had never seemed appropriate. Now the time did seem right. He told her everything, about Midnight being kidnapped and raped, and how he had found her and gotten her out of there. Then he told her about how a woman who was involved with Joe at one point had been involved in the plot to kill Joe, Randy, himself, and Midnight and shut down FORS.

"And now Joseph is getting married, and what about you? What are you thinking to do with Midnight?"

Rick thought for a minute. "You know, Mum, I honestly don't know, we've never talked about it. God I haven't even been crazy enough to think of marriage with her. It's a lot to ask for from someone like her." Then he grinned, shaking his head. "Getting her to slow down long enough might be the hard part."

"Well lad, you just have to keep trying …" She too was grinning.

They were both startled to hear Midnight's voice from the kitchen doorway. "And what's this? A plot?" but she was smiling, she knew they had been talking about her. She walked over to Rick taking his outstretched hand and he pulled her down onto his lap.

Even with no makeup and her hair tousled from sleeping, she looked so beautiful to him, he couldn't resist reaching up to kiss her. Her hand came up to touch his cheek tenderly as they kissed. When their lips parted they looked into each other's eyes, smiling. Anabelle cleared her throat, looking the other direction, although it did her heart good to see her son so obviously in love.

"So," Midnight said, picking up his cup and taking a sip. She had learned to like tea since the days after Tim's death. She had come to think of it synonymously with Rick's soothing voice and sweet manner. She looked at Rick over the rim of the cup. "What are you two planning?"

"Oh nothing," Rick said, his deep blue eyes wide and innocent.

Midnight looked at Anabelle, smiling. "Something tells me you saw that look a lot when he was growing up."

"Aw indeed I did, dear, he was a little devil that one."

Midnight laughed, her eyes shining. She was happy here, and glad that Rick's parents seemed to like her. They spent an hour or so going over what a mischievous little boy Rick had been. When they finally stood to go to bed, Rick walked her to her room. She leaned up against the doorjamb looking up at him. He stood with is arm over her head. "So what *were* you two planning when I came in?" she asked. Her finger traced a pattern down the front of his shirt. She looked up at him through the veil of her hair.

"Are you getting paranoid?"

"Probably," she said, laughing, "who wouldn't be after all the shit we've been through." Grimacing, she looked around hoping Rick's mom wasn't within hearing distance to hear her cuss.

"Hey!" he said softly, touching her under the chin, lifting her eyes to meet his, "don't worry, she likes you, *a lot.*"

"Does she?" she asked hesitantly. He realized then how much she wanted his mom to like her. For someone who hadn't cared about what people thought of her for a long time, that was a huge step.

"Yes, love, she does." His voice was sincere.

"Well that's a relief. One down, only five to go ..." she said, her hand trailing a little bit lower.

Rick sucked in his breath, eyeing her. "You're mean."

"Who me?" she said, her hand moved further down.

"Midnight!" he said in a harsh whisper.

But she laughed as she moved her hand back up to his face, touching his cheek and then his lips. He kissed her fingers, then bent down to kiss her on the lips. In moments, they were both breathless.

"Oh God!" he groaned, holding her close to him. Her head rested against his bare chest, as she'd already unbuttoned his shirt.

One of his hands was entwined in her hair, the other stroked her back.

"Why do you do this me?" he said, his voice still ragged from the passion she'd ignited.

She smiled against his chest. "Oh, I'm so sorry" she said, her tone full of mock concern.

"No you're not, you evil wench." But he laughed, knowing she was getting him back for talking about her behind her back. Then he became serious. "Are you okay with all of this? My family and all, I mean I know it's a lot for you ..." He wanted to know, he really wanted his family to like her, because they meant a great deal to him, but so did she.

"Yeah, it's okay. It's weird, but it's okay," she said, sighing.

He let his breath out in a rush, and smiled back at her, taking her in his arms and hugging her fiercely.

"I love you, babe," he said into her hair.

"I love you too," was her response.

Then it was her turn to groan.

"What?" he said looking down at her.

She gave him a mournful look. "Tomorrow," was all she said.

He laughed. "It won't be that bad, love, they won't eat you."

"The hell you say!" she said, smiling at him.

She was meeting his four sisters the next day. She was terrified, she knew they wouldn't like her, the one she was most worried about was Katherine. Rick had told her about Katherine, and she knew that this one was going to be trouble. Rick had told Katherine, his oldest sister, about Midnight's checkered past on the phone before they'd even left America, meaning to win Katherine over with the sad tale. Unbeknownst to Rick, Katherine had decided that Midnight was a gold digger from America.

Katherine was the oldest and therefore the one with seemingly the most power in the circle of the siblings. Even Anabelle admitted that Katherine could control the other girls and usually Rick too, so Midnight was worried.

CHAPTER 7

The next day Midnight was supposed to meet the sisters at Harrods. But since she was still feeling tired and nothing seemed to help for long, Anabelle suggested that they make a trip to the urgent care doctor first just to make sure everything was alright. Rick had agreed, and they had been gone a long time. By the time they got back, Rick was rushing her off, because he wanted a chance to take her to lunch before she met his sisters.

He took her to lunch at the Hard Rock Cafe London, at her insistence. "I have to have something normal in my stomach before I meet them," she had said.

"Normal?" he asked.

"Yeah, you know, burgers, fries, all that stuff"

"I see." He was smiling at her; if Katherine thought she was a gold digger, she had another thing coming.

She never wanted to go to expensive restaurants or buy expensive clothes, he practically had to force her to try on clothes when they went shopping, and then he had to talk her into letting him buy them for her. She'd say it's too expensive, that she didn't need it, or already had one. But he wanted to buy her things and give her everything that she ever wanted. He sincerely hoped that Katherine would like Midnight, but even if she didn't, Rick didn't care. He loved Midnight and that's what mattered, he didn't care what anyone else thought.

After a nice lunch at the Hard Rock, Rick drove down to Harrods. Once in front, Midnight turned to Rick in almost a panic and grabbed his arm. "Come with me!" she said, her voice shaky. He had never seen her like this, she was actually nervous, and he didn't think that happened too often.

"Night, it'll be okay," he said holding her hand. He had to pry the other one off his arm so he could hold it too.

"No it won't be, she's going to hate me, they all are." She breathed a heavy sigh, throwing herself back in the seat of the car.

Then she looked at him, eyeing him in mock anger. "I hate feeling like this, ya know."

He couldn't help but smile at her petulant look.

"Midnight come on, you've faced gang members and drug dealers, you've dealt with police chiefs and you even had a show down with the Attorney General himself once, *you can handle this.*"

He had to laugh, because she was scowling at him, as if all those things were nothing compared to this meeting.

She sighed, laughing at herself. "I guess you're right, I just hate relatives." She grinned sardonically. "Hell, I think half the reason Joe and I got along so well is because I never had to *meet* anyone!"

"Sorry," he said, his face schooled in a look of mock sorrow.

"Oh bullshit!" she said, laughing. Her face brightened up a little and. she swatted at his arm. He grabbed her hand and pulled her over to him to kiss her.

They were still kissing when someone tapped on the window. They looked up together, and Midnight knew she was looking at Rick's sisters. They all looked a lot like Rick; they all had brown hair and blue eyes in varying shades. And they all looked very excited to see their brother. Midnight moved back to the passenger side of the car, trying to straighten herself up, thinking what a great impression she had just made. She was pawing their brother in front of a historic English department store. *Great!* she thought to herself.

Rick got out of the car and was pulled into a group embrace by all four of his sisters. Midnight could hear the squeals of delight. She was happy for the opportunity to reapply lipstick and run her fingers through her hair. Then Rick was there opening her door. He took her hand to help her out of the car and held it as he was introducing her to his sisters.

"Night, this is Allison, Mandy, Deborah, and this is Katherine."

They were all looking at her and she hated it. She had never felt self-conscious about her appearance, but now she was and it wasn't a good feeling.

"Hi!" Allison said, smiling brightly. She was small like Midnight and her eyes were almost the same shade as Rick's. Her hair was cut in an attractive bob and she wore a beautifully cut light blue silk suit.

Midnight tried to remember what Rick had said about each one of them as she shook hands. Allison was still single, although she was engaged to a young man from their father's firm. Rick said that Allison being the youngest at twenty-five years old was the most bubbly of the four. She was two years Midnight's junior, which made Midnight feel a little better, less overwhelmed.

"Hello," Mandy said.

Midnight remembered that Rick had called her his willowy sister. She could see why; Mandy stood almost as tall as Rick and she seemed like she weighed almost nothing. Her hair, like her sister's, was cut in a bob, but longer and tapered in the front that made her angular face even more fascinating. She had the same high cheekbones as Rick, but her cheeks were almost hollow. She wore a black sleeveless pantsuit and looked very chic. Then Midnight remembered that she was a model. Mandy was very reserved, but Midnight wasn't sure whether or not it was actually that she didn't like her or if it was just how she was. Rick had said that she was very quiet.

"Hello," Deborah said.

Deborah she was more sophisticated than the rest of them. Her hair was up in a French twist, and she wore a cream wool suit with elegant gold jewelry. Her makeup was absolutely perfect, her hands perfectly manicured. She was married, Rick had said to a banker, a man Rick didn't like at all. Deborah had two children that Rick said were just great, but Midnight couldn't imagine this woman having "great" kids. She figured they'd be as manicured and coiffed as their mother.

Katherine remained silent, and as she was shaking hands with each of the sisters, Midnight saw, out of the corner of her eye, Katherine shake her head at Rick, as if to say that his choice was not suitable and that she couldn't believe he was subjecting them to her. Midnight looked at Rick immediately and saw the anger in his eyes. Even though he tried to smile at her, she could tell he was angry at Katherine. She knew it should make her happy that he would stand against his own family for her, but in some remote way, it made her sad. She turned then to Katherine, determined to try for Rick's sake.

"Katherine," she said extending her hand to the other woman.

Katherine just looked at her, raising an eyebrow at her extended hand. Midnight heard Rick take an angry breath, to say something but she spoke first.

"I've heard a lot about all of you," Midnight said, moving her hand subconsciously to the small of her back where she usually carried her gun.

Rick didn't miss it and, knowing Midnight the way he did, he realized that her subconscious was warring with her good intentions. He laughed then taking the hand that Midnight had moved behind her. She turned her head, smiling at him.

"Well, let's move along then, shall we?" Deborah said.

When Rick didn't make any move to leave, Katherine looked at Midnight as if she was holding him there forcibly, but she spoke to Rick. "Are you staying, Rick?"

"I think I'll meet you back here in a while. I have to go down the street to meet Joe for tux fittings, but I'll hang around after that."

Midnight squeezed his hand gratefully, but because of the look on Katherine's face, Rick found it necessary to say, "That is if you ladies don't mind …"

Allison, Mandy, and Deborah assured him that they didn't mind at all. Katherine just shook her head all the while looking at Midnight, as if trying to figure out what kind of spell she had put on their brother.

As far as Katherine was concerned, Midnight was a gold digger and she was in no way suitable for Rick. Midnight could see her opinion in her eyes. *I always thought the English were supposed to be good at being discreet about how they really felt* she thought to herself. She looked at the woman who at thirty-nine years old was twelve years her senior. She knew from Rick that Katherine had always been the serious one. She also knew that Katherine only had one soft spot and that soft spot was Rick, which made her extremely protective of him.

Katherine stood looking at the girl who thought she was in love with her brother. Katherine was older than Rick by ten years, and she had always kept an eye on him. When he was little, she had been his constant vigilant mentor. As he grew older and more handsome, she had become his protector from the vultures. She knew that because their family had money and because he drew women like flies to honey with his deep blue eyes and his long hair, that he would be a prime target. She had kept a close watch on his relationships over the years and had managed to keep him from making any number of mistakes. Although she had to admit she had lost a great deal of her power when he had moved to the states.

It was therefore her opinion that the only reason Rick actually thought himself serious about this one, was because he hadn't had her there to talk him out of it. But there had been no wedding plans yet, so she still had plenty of time. She was already convinced that the whole relationship was purely sexual. Midnight was a very sultry looking young woman and she probably used that to every advantage on Rick. She was happy that their mother had put them in separate rooms at the house. Maybe this way Rick would cool off and realize that the relationship he thought was love was really only sex. It wouldn't be the first time for him to have thought that way.

Rick seemed loathe to let go of Midnight's hand and she really didn't want him to. Deborah noticed and suggested that they meet Midnight inside. Midnight smiled a silent thank you to Deborah. The four women went inside, and once inside Deborah turned on Katherine.

"Just what are you doing?" she asked accusingly, narrowing her eyes at her sister.

"Whatever do you mean?" Katherine said. She kept her eyes on the couple outside. Midnight was leaning against the car facing Rick as they talked.

"You know what I mean, why are you giving that girl a difficult time?"

"She's not right for him," Katherine pronounced as if that was the final judgment.

"I see, and you know this from meeting her once?" Deborah sounded disgusted, and she was, Katherine tried to run everyone's life, especially Rick's.

Deborah was happy for Rick, and she thought that he seemed very happy, but she knew Katherine always discounted people's appearance and how they *thought* they felt. Katherine only nodded in response to her question. She was still watching them.

Outside Midnight moved back toward the car, she was wearing white jeans with a white camisole top, and the emerald-green Italian leather jacket Rick had bought her on one of their few shopping trips. She'd argued with him about even that, saying that he didn't need to, but he had said he loved the way it looked on her, so he bought it. Now standing in front of her, he was fingering the tassels on the jacket, not sure what he could say to her to make her feel better.

Midnight was watching him. "You don't have to change your plans for me," she told him, already feeling foolish for not being able to handle something as simple as meeting Rick's sisters. This was all just too new to her.

"I want to, okay?" His voice was soft. Then he quirked a wry grin. "I guess I should be happy you're not carrying today, eh?"

She laughed, knowing he had known what she had wanted to do earlier. "Yeah, I guess you should be. Look I know you and Joe were going to go around to some of your old stomping grounds. I don't want to screw up your plans, I'll be okay ..." She took his hands in hers then, laughing ruefully. "This is unbelievable you know."

"What?" he asked.

"To think that just two weeks ago we were knee-deep in murder attempts, deceptions, drug deals, everything and now ... I'm worried about surviving a day of *shopping with your sisters*!"

She made a face and he had to laugh, thinking about how ridiculous it sounded.

"You're right love, it is unbelievable. All the same, I want to be here with you. The difference between then and now is that you had backup then, okay?"

"Is that what you are?" she said, smiling. "Backup?"

He brought his face down close to her ear then said, "I'll always be your backup."

His voice was so serious and sincere Midnight felt her eyes well up with tears. He kissed her, a slow passionate kiss, that made her feel like she could face anyone with him standing by her side. When their lips parted, her hands were up around his neck and she didn't want to let go of him. She just wanted to run away with him and not have to deal with families or expectations. But she knew he couldn't do that. His family meant too much to him, and for that reason she knew she had to try harder with his sisters, even Katherine.

"I better get in there," she said.

"I'll be back in about an hour," he said and his voice brooked no argument.

"Okay" she said, smiling at him again, "thanks." Then she turned and walked to the double doors of the store.

Before she walked in, she turned and saw that he was watching her. She winked at him and went inside.

After she went inside, Rick leaned against the car thinking about her. Poor girl wasn't used to all these entanglements. He knew another difference between then and now was that she was way out of her element now, and she was struggling to adjust. He felt terrible for putting her in that situation, that's why he was changing his plans. He loved her and he didn't want her to have to go too far away from who she was to adjust to his family. Rick knew that who Midnight was, although the best thing in the world for him, would get her eaten alive by Katherine. The last thing he wanted was for Midnight to be exposed to his overbearing, disapproving sister for very long. As it was, he was considering skipping the fitting, but he knew Joe would already be there. He also knew that Midnight was the type of person to take challenges head on, and she would probably resent his trying to protect her too much. It would be too suffocating for her. He turned and got in the car, glancing again at the door she had gone through. He shook his head ruefully, she was tough enough to deal with Katherine. So off he went, but promising himself he would hurry.

Once inside the store Midnight joined the other women.

"I need to find a dress for tomorrow night," Deborah was saying as she joined them. "Midnight, would you help me?" Midnight looked at her for a moment. She wasn't sure why this sophisticated woman would want her advice on a dress for a dinner party. Then she saw that Deborah was looking at her as if to say *just say yes.*

"Sure," Midnight said, feeling relieved that someone seemed to be on her side.

"I need to pick up some things upstairs," Katherine said. "Mandy you come with, we'll meet you three down here in a little while." With that she turned and walked away with Mandy in tow.

Allison turned to Deborah and she was smiling, obviously pleased to have been left behind. Midnight was further relieved when Deborah entwined her arm with hers and said, "So let's go look at those dresses, come along Allison." Allison fell into step beside Midnight.

Once they were in one of the private dressing rooms, Allison and Deborah each tried on a new dress. Midnight sat in one of the chairs.

"Aren't you going to try anything on?" Allison asked, her eyes watched her in the mirror.

Midnight shook her head. "No, I don't need anything else, your brother was on a shopping spree for me yesterday." Her voice reflected her chagrin at the idea.

"Rick likes to spend money," Deborah said, she too was watching Midnight.

"Yeah," Allison said laughing and looking at her sister, "remember the time he bought Teddy Anne that diamond necklace, and Dad almost killed him!" She laughed, but then she looked embarrassed. "I'm sorry," she said turning to Midnight. Midnight looked at her for a minute perplexed, what had she said that she should apologize for?

"For what?" Midnight asked.

"Well for mentioning another woman of course," Allison said walking over to sit down next to Midnight. "It was unthinking of me, and I'm sorry"

Midnight waved her hand to dismiss what Allison was saying. "Allison, I know Rick has been with other women." She shrugged. "It doesn't bother me. I had a life before him, if anyone's has grounds for jealousy it'd be him."

"But …" Allison started to say.

"What my little sister is trying to say," Deborah broke in, "is that she shouldn't bring up the past, it's not important. Rick was always a bit of a tramp, but he's changed now, and that's what's important." She looked at Midnight, a little smile on her face, her eyes shining mischievously. "But what would Rick have to be jealous of in your past?" She grimaced then, knowing she was as bad as Allison. "I'm sorry, ignore that question"

Midnight laughed. "It's okay, I don't have anything to hide here. I just meant that Rick has more of a reason to be jealous or worried about someone in my past, because he knows him"

"Knows him?" Allison said perplexed. "But you're from America, and the only person he knows there is … " Her voice trailed off as she put two and two together. "Joe?" She looked at Midnight with what looked like admiration. Midnight didn't understand that, but then she remembered that they all knew each other.

"Oh yeah," she said, almost sorry she'd said something now. "I forgot you guys grew up together."

"Yes we did," Deborah said. Then she smiled. "And I had the biggest crush on Joe Sinclair when we were teenagers!"

"Really?" Midnight said, again thanking her lucky stars to be here with them, rather than Katherine.

"Oh he's gorgeous!" Allison said, her eyes shining.

"Oh yes," Deborah said, "and from what I've heard that's not all ..." Her voice trailed off suggestively.

"Deborah!" Allison said her voice aghast, but she laughed evilly.

"Well," Deborah said, shrugging at her sister. Then she turned to Midnight her face intense, but her eyes reflected humor. "So, how was he?"

Midnight just laughed, shaking her head. She could not believe her good fortune. Not only had she not totally screwed up by saying something about Joe, she believed that she had actually just earned their respect. "He was ..." She looked at them slyly lingering on her answer. Deborah grabbed one of her hands and Allison the other.

"Midnight!" they both said.

"Okay, okay ... yes what you heard was very true ... but ..." Her voice trailed off and her face took on a kind of secret look.

"But?" Deborah said, wanting to know what that look meant.

Midnight shrugged. "But, Rick is better."

"Ugh!" Allison said, grabbing her stomach and flinging herself back in her chair, laughing. Deborah too was laughing, shaking her head. Midnight laughed too realizing that they wouldn't appreciate the difference since they were Rick's sisters. They all three laughed, until they were almost in tears when they heard Katherine's voice.

"And what's going on in here?" All three women stopped laughing.

"Oh, Midnight was telling us … some things." Wisely, Allison didn't explain the nature of the conversation.

"I see … well we could hear you, four aisles away." It was obvious from Katherine's tone of voice that she did not approve of their public display of gaiety.

"Lighten up, Katherine," Deborah said, standing up.

"Well what is it that was so funny?" Katherine asked, her eyes on Midnight.

"She was telling us about Joe," Allison blurted out, trying to help Midnight, but not succeeding.

"Joe?" Katherine said, surprised at hearing his name. "What about him?" Her eyes narrowed as she saw the abashed look on Allison's face. Allison never could hide her thoughts well and she could never lie to Katherine. She always felt that somehow she'd know. "Well, they were together in the States …" She shrugged, looking at Midnight apologetically. Midnight only smiled at the girl.

"So you were with Joe *first*?" Katherine said, making the whole thing sound sordid. Midnight's look didn't waiver, she only nodded, her eyes never leaving Katherine's face. She knew that looking away would make her look scared. She was worried about what this would do to the already poor relationship with Katherine, but she knew that her relationship with Joe was not what Katherine thought it was.

"So you couldn't catch that fish, so you caught our brother instead." Katherine's words fell like stones in the room.

Instead of answering her, Midnight just stood and walked out of the room. Tears stung her eyes as she walked away. For some reason it had really hurt her to have her relationship with Joe treated so off handedly. She hadn't seen Joe in two weeks, and she missed him. Now here she was in this awful place with nasty people like Katherine. Suddenly the weight of all the pressure was too much on her. She stood outside the dressing room, facing the wall, her head leaning on the wall, and the tears started to flow. She heard the dressing room door open and heard them come out. She didn't even look up until she heard Allison say, "Joe!"

Joe had just found them having finished at the tailors before Rick. Rick had asked him to go and "save" Midnight. He hadn't realized how true that would be. Midnight turned to see Joe standing not ten feet away. He was dressed all in black, every bit the dark knight. Without stopping to think Midnight ran to him. He grabbed her up in a hug, squeezing her so tight she almost couldn't breathe, but she didn't care. He was here and he was going to keep Katherine away from her. Her tears flowed freely now.

"Night, what's wrong?" Joe asked, but she shook her head. He looked up at Katherine accusingly. "What did you say to her!" His voice was deadly cold.

Katherine just stood looking at him, her face cold. "I guess the truth might hurt sometimes."

Joe took one menacing step toward her, but Deborah stepped in front of Katherine. "Joe! Katherine was being mean. Midnight told us about you two and Katherine accused her of going after Rick since she couldn't *catch* you." Joe's eyes shifted from Deborah to Katherine, shaking his head.

"As usual Katherine is shooting her mouth off about something she doesn't understand." His voice cut like ice. He shifted his attention back to comforting Midnight. "Night? Come on, love. It's okay. Just ignore that stupid fool, she doesn't understand anything." His hand stroked her hair as he talked to her. The four sisters stood watching. Joe, was so tall, Midnight's small frame was dwarfed by his as he held her protectively. And watching him hold her all four women, even Katherine, felt a pang of envy for the depth of caring they saw on Joe's face.

Rick turned up and looked around at the scene. The smile on his face disappeared when he saw Midnight in Joe's arms. Katherine was sure that he was just realizing what kind of woman Midnight was, that he was shocked at seeing his best friend holding his girlfriend and she assumed he would be appalled. When he strode over to them, Katherine was so sure that he would have harsh words to say to Midnight. She was totally shocked when Rick took Midnight's hand from Joe's shoulder and held it in his, and turned his accusing eyes on her.

"Katherine what the hell have you done now?!" His voice was harsh, but he certainly wasn't addressing Midnight.

"Me?" Katherine said stunned he was turning on her.

"Yes you, Katherine Don't try to play that game with me, what the fuck did you say to her? What is your problem!" His eyes flashed angrily.

Katherine's mouth gaped. "Your girlfriend stands there in another man's arms and you have the nerve to cuss at me Richard Debenshire?"

"Another man's ..." Rick started to say then he realized what she meant. He knew now what was happening. The smile he gave Katherine was ice cold. "You are so wrong Katherine, you've never been more wrong in your life." He gestured to Joe with his head. Joe released Midnight and without another word, the two men led her away.

The four sisters just stood staring at their departing figures. Deborah shook her head. "Wow," she said quietly. "I wish someone was that protective of me."

"Me too," Allison said in complete awe.

"She must be something special to have the two of them as her knights in shining armor," Mandy said, pressing her lips together as she widened her eyes dramatically.

The other three turned to look at her in shock; she rarely spoke out. Katherine made a noise in the back of her throat, thoroughly chastised and feeling a little foolish. She turned on her heel and walked down the nearest isle. The other three followed her, but suddenly she didn't seem to be their leader anymore. Rick had never spoken to Katherine the way he just had. He usually went along with her on things.

"He must be really in love with her to stand up to Katherine," Allison whispered to Deborah. Deborah only nodded, her eyes on Katherine's back. She knew that Katherine was not happy about that confrontation, but she wasn't sure if Katherine was going to give up now or not. She hoped so, she genuinely liked Midnight.

****

Joe and Rick walked Midnight outside. Rick turned to her. "Baby, what happened? What did she say?" Midnight just shook her head, wiping at her eyes, feeling a little foolish. She knew she had just caused not only a major scene but also a major rift between Rick and his sister.

"Katherine," Joe said angrily, "said that since Midnight couldn't catch me, that she went for you instead …" His voice trailed off ominously, indicating what he thought of the accusation.

"Ah, Jesus!" Rick said, looking up at the sky, wanting to take Midnight away from all this crap. He felt like he was being pulled in a million directions. "Midnight, I'm sorry, I didn't tell them about Joe … and—"

"No," she said, straightening up. "I did." Her voice was strident, she didn't like having to defend or hide her relationship with Joe. "I told them." She eyed Rick angrily.

He held up his hands in a defensive gesture. "Hey! I didn't say you shouldn't. I just meant that Katherine's the type to figure that I didn't know about the whole thing and take it the wrong way."

"She still didn't have the right to say that to her," Joe said, putting his arm around Midnight's shoulders.

"I know, I know," Rick said, looking tired. "Shit!" He turned away from them, staring down the street, trying to sort out all his emotions. When he had approached them in the store, he had known that Katherine had been behind it all. He couldn't believe his sister's attitude, but he couldn't fault her for trying to protect him. His loyalties were being pulled in a dozen directions and it was making him nuts.

"Rick," Midnight said, moving to stand beside him, "I'm sorry, I shouldn't have snapped at you." She sighed, putting her head on his shoulder. "This has not been a good day." Her voice sounded tired too.

"C'mere," he said, pulling her around to face him. He took her face in his hands and smiled warmly as he said, "I think you and I need some time alone," he said, kissing her lightly on the lips. "Let's go to dinner tonight."

"Just you and me?"

He smiled at her. "Yeah, just you and me." He hugged her. He turned to Joe, still holding her, and he reached out his hand. The two men shook hands. "Thanks man."

Joe nodded. "Anytime," he said and they smiled at each other. They both knew that Joe would still do anything for Midnight, and the thought nagged at Rick, even as he smiled at his best friend.

That night Rick and Midnight went to dinner. They reveled in being alone together. They drank wine and talked about inconsequential things, including Joe and Randy's wedding. They talked about the engagement party that his parents were throwing for them the next evening. Since Joe's parents weren't around, Anabelle had decided that it would be her responsibility to give them a party to celebrate their engagement. Midnight was almost dreading it now, with what had happened with Katherine.

"I'm so glad Randy and Joe will be there tomorrow night," Midnight said with relief.

"Me too," Rick said, thinking of that afternoon.

"Thinking that Joe will have to rescue me again?" she asked, her eyes watching him.

"Sort of …" he said hesitantly. He really didn't want to get in to all that now. Midnight detected a change in his mood.

"What's wrong?" she asked quietly. She'd been waiting for this since they had gotten together. She had always suspected that he felt threatened by Joe's place in her life more than he'd ever say. Rick shook his head, his eyes averted from hers.

"Nothing," he said, standing to leave.

They had finished their dinner almost an hour before, but they had lingered over drinks and now he wanted to get out of there before she could corner him on what he was thinking. It had been a cold fear in the smallest darkest place in his mind for the past few weeks, that he would tell her how he felt about the situation with Joe and that she would turn away from him and never return. He didn't want that, not for anything in the world and if it meant keeping his mouth shut he would. It wasn't a real problem, it just had nagged at him more since that afternoon. He felt like a jerk not telling her how he felt about his feelings so deep down that he barely acknowledged them normally. His nerves were raw and Midnight could sense it.

When they walked outside she grabbed his hand and turned him around to face her. Her eyes were shadowed with fear. Rick had never shut her out before, he had always been honest with her and now he wasn't. It scared the hell out of her.

"Tell me what's going on," she said angrily.

He started to shake his head again. "Rick!" she all but screamed, as tears of anger and fear sprung to her eyes.

She turned away from him and started walking down the street, unshed tears in her eyes. Her mind was churning. She was afraid that now Rick had brought her home to meet his family, he'd decided that she wasn't right for him. After the confrontation with Kathrine that day, she was sure he was just ready to throw in the towel and didn't know how to break it to her.

She'd finally given her heart to this man, and now she was terrified that he wanted to give it back. The independent part of her screamed, *Good, I don't need anyone!* but the part of her that loved him, and wanted to be vulnerable and yielding to him cried, *What will I do if he leaves me?*

When Midnight walked away from him, Rick got scared. He strode after her, catching up to her easily.

"Midnight," he began, reaching out to touch her shoulder, but she wrenched it away and kept walking. "Damn it!" he said, angry at her stubbornness. He hadn't wanted to get into any of this. They'd had a nice evening, and smoothed everything over and now it was all going to hell.

This time he had to run to catch up to her. He got in front of her and stopped her by grabbing her by the shoulders. She tried to evade his grasp but he tightened his grip and his fingers bit painfully into her shoulders. She gasped, but refused to cry out. Rick could see the accusation in her eyes and it almost physically hurt to see it. When he didn't speak for a moment, she managed to wrench away again, this time turning and walking across the street.

When he caught up with her this time, he spun her around to face him and backed her up against a wall. It was late and there were no people around. His hands pinned her to the wall, but she struggled to get away anyway. Again, he tightened his grip.

"Goddam it, Midnight! Just stop!" His voice was so harsh and angry. She felt like someone had thrown cold water in her face and she stopped struggling.

She leaned her head back against the wall, refusing to look at him. A couple of tears slid down her cheeks, glistening in the light from the street lamps.

"Will you just relax," he said, his voice calmer now.

She turned her look to him. "Not if you're not going to be straight with me."

Rick exhaled, shaking his head. "Midnight, you don't understand."

Her eyes flashed anger again. "Then make me understand, damn it!" When he hesitated again, she pinned him with a deadly glare. "Don't fuck this up, Rick. It's too damned important to me." The tears welled in her eyes again, but she wouldn't look at him. Her head leaned against the wall again, her face turned to the side.

"Shit!" Rick said. He was screwed. If he didn't tell her, he was going to lose her, but maybe if he did he would too. He felt tears of anger and frustration sting the backs of his eyelids. If he lost her now, after all they'd been through together …

"Midnight, I'm sorry." His voice was shaking.

The defeated tone made her look at him again. She saw the tears in his eyes and she could see that he was shaking.

"Please, just tell me what's going on in your head," she pleaded trying to stop their downward spiral.

She touched his cheek. His eyes closed in response to her touch. Part of him had been terrified that she would never touch him again. It was that part of him that made him let out a small cry of relief as he took her in his arms.

"Midnight, Midnight," he murmured in her ear, his voice low and almost tearful. "Baby, I don't want to hurt you ..."

"Not talking to me is hurting me," she said, keeping her face buried in his jacket.

Sighing, Rick looked around them. The building they were standing in front of was the Royal Hilton. Making a quick decision he said, "Come on." He took her hand and led her into the hotel. He left her standing in the lobby as he strode to the front desk. She watched him as he requested a room. When the desk clerk had registered them and gave him the key, Rick walked back over to her, took her hand, and led her to the elevators.

Once in the room he took her in his arms again, holding her tight, trying to delay the talk he knew they needed to have. She wasn't fooled. She disengaged herself from his embrace and walked over to the windows. She stared unseeing out at the lights of London. It was foggy that night and it seemed to be symbolic of their situation. Rick stood on the other side of the room watching her. He felt like they had grown miles apart in a matter of minutes. His heart ached thinking the gap could widen further when they talked. Midnight surprised him by turning around. It was obvious she was upset and doing everything she could to deal with it.

"This is about your family, right?" she said, her voice clear and business like for all her appearance begged to differ.

"What? No," Rick said, shaking his head.

"Then it's about Joe and me, right?" Midnight asked, that having been her second thought as to the source of his sudden reluctance to talk.

For a moment Rick didn't make a move, he just stood watching her. When he saw her eyes narrow angrily he nodded miserably.

"Tell me, Rick," she said quietly. He could see she just wanted him to say whatever he needed to.

"I just ... Oh God ..." He looked away his teeth worrying his bottom lip. He was afraid to say something that he'd never be able to take back.

Midnight waited stoically, letting the silence stretch. He didn't know how to start, what to say. He felt like he wanted to hit something, scream, something, anything to get over this tense sick feeling. He clenched his fists against the feelings that wanted to overwhelm him.

"Damn it, Rick!" Midnight said, striding over to stand right in front of him. She grabbed him by two fistfuls of his jacket. "You've always been so goddamned straightforward with me, why can't you be now when it's important!" The anger and intensity in her voice snapped him out of his reverie.

"Alright!" he yelled back. "It is Joe, it's the whole fucking idea that I was second choice and that you'd rather have him!"

Midnight was so shocked by his outburst that she let go of his jacket and backed away from him. Her eyes were wide, she couldn't believe what he had just said.

"Is that what you think?" she asked incredulously. "Or is that what your fucking sister has convinced you of?" she asked then, her tone suspicious.

He was in turn surprised by her reaction. He had expected her to be angry, but he had expected her to defend her relationship with Joe, and she wasn't doing that.

"Katherine has nothing to do with this!" he said his anger flaring at the insinuation.

"Then what is it, Rick?" she asked, her voice quieter now, the whole thing starting to weigh heavy on her.

"I guess I've always felt kind of ... jealous," he said miserably, his tone indicating that the word 'jealous' was distasteful to him. "But I never really acknowledged it. It was in my head though, back in the deep dark part of my mind. Then when that shit happened today, I thought that maybe that's what it was, that I was second choice and I knew I'd never be what Joe is to you."

She shook her head. She had expected something like this, but she knew he was so wrong too. It amazed her to think back on the day's events and realize that he had defended her staunchly even though he wasn't totally sure of her himself.

"But what about today? You told Katherine she was wrong. Or was that just bullshit too?"

He was taken aback by her attitude and her responses. She hadn't said a word in defense of Joe or their relationship. She was busy trying to figure out why he had defended her if he didn't believe her.

"Midnight, nothing was bullshit." He sighed again feeling very tired and hurt. "I told Katherine she was wrong because I know you're not after money, and because I know you really care about me ... " His voice trailed off as he saw her anger flare.

"*Care* about you?" she repeated incredulously. "Oh Jesus Christ, *what is wrong with you*?" She was shaking her head as if to clear it of all the things he'd said. "I *love* you, you stupid son of a bitch, or haven't you believed that all along either?"

Rick didn't answer. He moved wearily to the bed and sat down, not knowing for sure anymore what he thought. He knew he had just screwed up badly with her. Yes, he'd always believed that she loved him, but the he'd still had the nagging thought that he was second choice and the happenings of the day had brought that thought into the forefront in his mind. In some insane irony, he knew that his doubting her love could cause the rift to separate them forever. If indeed she did love him.

"Midnight, I don't know what's happening. All I know is that I love you and the last thing I wanted was to hurt you. I know that Joe means a lot to you, but I guess what I need to know is. does he mean more to you than me?" The last was said in the merest whisper as if by saying it quietly he could keep the answer from being something he didn't want to hear.

Midnight stared at him, shocked. Her first reaction was to be mad, but she had never seen Rick unsure of himself and right now he seemed like a lost little boy. Her love for him made her want to reach out to him, but she knew that wasn't the answer he was waiting for. Her eyes never left his as she answered him.

"No he doesn't," she said, and in those three words Rick felt his soul restored.

He believed her. There was never a question of whether or not she had lied, but only whether or not she had "settled" for him. He wanted to take her in his arms and hug her until she was breathless, but he knew that doing that right now was impossible. There was still a distance between them. He closed his eyes against the pain that he felt for that distance. He had been wrong and he had let that mistake cause the relationship possibly irreparable damage.

"Rick," Midnight began, her tone even. It made him hope that she might be able to forgive him.

She walked over to him, sitting down on the chair across from where he sat on the bed. "Joe is someone that filled a hole in my heart a long time ago. When I was starting out setting up FORS, I was alone. Nobody believed in me, everyone figured I was just some dumb broad making noise. Hell, I think the chief was only humoring me because I was female. But when Joe got there ... he believed in me, he backed me up on everything, he was my friend. We spent hours and hours together sweating over FORS, trying to make it work. And by the time we finally got it going, we were best friends. He looked out for me and I looked out for him. I finally had someone in the world who cared about me, what happened to me, whether or not I got home safe at night, all that. Sure, guys took me out all the time, and they wanted to make me into what they thought I should be, but not Joe. He was like a rock that I could hold onto in a storm, and believe me there were plenty of those. But not once did he say he didn't think I could do something, not once did he let me down. And I loved him for that.

"When we got together it seemed so natural and it was comfortable. We were like two old shoes that fit so well. But we were too much alike. He was very protective of me anyway, but when we got together he was impossible. I felt like I was suffocating. He wouldn't let me be the cop I was, and I let him change me a little. I was so busy all the time, worried about getting hurt, that I got too careful, and when that happened I did get hurt. Some gang member knifed me in the back, because she'd figured out I was a cop. Joe and I decided then that being together like that wasn't a good idea, that it was causing too much friction between us."

She reached out and took his hands in hers, hoping he was hearing everything she was saying.

"When we looked back later, we realized that we just didn't totally fit. Sure, we made great friends, but being lovers takes a lot more than either of us was willing to give. We are both very guarded people, we don't love or trust easily and we're not real good at sharing of ourselves. It took the right people to make us want to give up our independence and to share our lives with someone. For me that right person was you." Rick had been listening intently and when she said the last he felt even worse for all he had just put her through.

He groaned, throwing himself back on the bed, the heels of his hands pressing into his eyes. "And I'm so goddamned dumb, I went and fucked that all up, didn't I?"

His self-deprecation, in spite of being heartfelt, made Midnight smile. She decided then that even if she wanted to, she couldn't be angry at him. It had been unfair of her not to have talked to him about this before. She had just skated past the thought a number of times, selfishly expecting him to just understand and not ask questions. She got on the bed and straddled his waist. She removed his hands from his eyes and held them down on the bed on either side of his head. Then she leaned forward to look him straight in the eye.

"You, my beautiful man, did not fuck anything up." She grimaced apologetically. "I wasn't very fair to you, I'm afraid."

"Oh babe ..." he said the relief on his face almost painful to her.

She leaned down and kissed him, and they melted into a passionate embrace. The lovemaking that followed was intense and poignant as if they were both trying to recapture something they both were afraid they had lost. Midnight knew that she loved him more now than ever. She had seen how much he loved her by the way he had reacted to the thought that she might not really want him. He hadn't been angry, he had been sad. She had never had any doubts about how much he loved her, but if she had, the argument they had just had would have dissolved any of those doubts in an instant.

Later as they lay together, their bodies still close together, Midnight smiled. "So I take it we're okay again …" she said lightly.

He leaned over to kiss her again. "More than okay, love," he said, his voice still husky.

Midnight looked over at the clock on the bedside table then. "Oh shit," she said, seeing that it was after one o'clock in the morning.

"What?" he said.

"It's late, Rick, your mother's going to freak!" she said, laughing at the fact that they were adults having to worry about what his mother thought.

"I'll call her," Rick said, standing and putting on his jeans. Midnight got up and went into the bathroom. Rick watched her go with a fond smile on his lips. He picked up the phone and dialed his home number. His mother answered on the fourth ring, sounding tired.

"Sorry to wake you, Mum," Rick said sounding chagrined, every bit the chastised young man.

"Richard …" his mother said sounding worried. "Is everything okay?"

"Yes, Mum, everything's fine. Midnight and I just needed some time to sort some things out." He hesitated, making a quick decision. "We're going to stay at a hotel tonight, Mum. We really need some time alone."

"You take all the time you need, we'll be here when you come home." Her voice was soft, and supportive, and Rick smiled warmly, thanking the God above once again that she was his mother.

"Thanks, Mum."

Midnight came out of the bathroom as he hung up. He smiled at her. She looked disheveled, but incredible.

"C'mere," he said, beckoning her.

She walked over to the bed, and stood, with her hands on her hips.

"Everything okay on the home front?" she asked.

"Yep," he replied. "By the way, what did the doctor say this morning?" He asked as he reached for his jacket, his eyes on her. She sat down on the bed shrugging.

"Nothin' much, just a cold." She watched him as he pulled something out of his jacket pocket. "What's that?" she asked, pointing to the box he held.

"This?" he asked. "Oh, I wanted to show it to you …" He shrugged nonchalantly as he opened the box.

Nestled inside was a ring of emeralds and diamonds. It was a marquee cut emerald, with diamond and emerald baguettes inset into the gold band. It was the most beautiful ring Midnight had ever seen.

"Wow!" she said, staring at it. "It's beautiful! It looks antique, is it?" she asked, her eyes shining.

Rick grinned at her. "It is, as a matter of fact. It was my grandmother's and she left it for me, when she passed away."

"Wow, that's cool. I'd just like to have grandparents," she said, rolling her eyes.

"Well my grandmother, she left it for me, and said that I was to give it to the woman I married." He looked at her pointedly then. "I want you to have it," he said, his voice was very soft.

Midnight looked up at him, not sure she had heard him correctly. "But Rick, she said the woman …" She stopped as a slow smile spread across Rick's face, and he nodded when understanding dawned on her face. "You want me to … but you …"

Rick laughed. He took the ring out of its box, took her left hand in his, and placed the ring on her finger, looking directly into her eyes. "I'm asking you to marry me, Midnight. I want you to be my wife."

Midnight stared up at him for a full minute. "I … you …this …"

"Yes, this. I want you to marry me," Rick said smiling at her apparent fluster. "Will you?"

Midnight blinked a couple of times. He could see her mind working through what was happening, and he sensed something else. But then when she smiled and nodded to him and said a simple, "Yes," and he promptly forgot everything else, and hugged her to him.

They began kissing and nothing else existed. His hands touched the body he had grown to love so much. He felt her respond to his touch, as his own body responded to her. Their lovemaking was slower this time, more gentle, although as was common with them, it grew in intensity as they reached their climax together. And as they laid in each other arms, Midnight smiled up at Rick.

"Well, I guess, there is one little thing I should share with you … now …" she said, her tone holding hint of mystery.

"What?" he asked suspiciously.

"Well, the doctor told me that I have a cold, and something else … something that won't go away as easily …"

"And what is that?" Rick asked, worry starting to cloud his eyes.

Midnight touched his cheek, grinning at him. "Well, it'll go away, eventually, in about eight months."

It was Rick's turn to stare at her dumbfounded. Then as understanding started to dawn on him, Midnight started to laugh.

"Midnight, are you telling me that you're pregnant?" he said, his voice indicating that he wasn't even daring to hope.

"You got it," she said, grinning at him.

"A month?" he asked then, trying to keep the worry out of his voice.

"Oh believe me, that was the first thing I made him verify, no more than a month, Sorry, love, it's yours." For a moment he'd worried about Daniel Robbins, and the possibility that it had happened then. Midnight knew and understood that.

"Sorry, my ass!" Rick said, smiling at her as he pulled her into a fierce hug. Then he pulled back and gave her a suspicious look. "Why didn't you tell me earlier?"

"I … well I wasn't really planning on telling you tonight … but since we just got engaged and all … I thought you should know …" she said, sounding a little evasive.

"When were you planning to tell me?" he asked seriously.

She looked up at him, hoping she hadn't just screwed up. "Well, maybe when we got back to the states. I don't know, I was waiting for the right time, I just didn't want …"

"Didn't want what?" he asked, almost sharply.

"I didn't want … " she started again, sighing. "I didn't want you to ask me to marry you, because of this." She gestured to her stomach, still flat as ever. She prayed he'd understand what she meant. "I wanted your love, not your sense of *duty.*"

Rick looked down at her for a long moment, then a slow smile crossed his face. "So I beat you to the punch, did I?"

"I guess so."

"Babe, I love you, I would have married you either way."

"Well, I guess I know that now, since your mother doesn't even know."

"You didn't tell her either?" he asked, surprised his mother hadn't pumped her for the information after leaving the doctor's. His mother was slipping.

"Nope, she was very nice about the whole thing. I think she might suspect though, because doctors don't usually run blood tests for common colds." Midnight grinned. "I think you're in trouble, Mr. Debenshire."

"That's okay, as long as I get to have you in the end, I don't mind." He looked down at her. "What's say you and I get married when Joe and Randy do," he said, watching her for her reaction.

She looked up at him, suspicion clear in her eyes. "You little shit, you had this planned all along, didn't you?"

"Well sort of. I hoped and I wanted to ask you at dinner, but the timing was wrong, with all the shit this afternoon and all, but then tonight, it just worked out."

"Okay … so have you talked to Joe about impeding on his wedding, what about Randy?"

"Yes, I talked to Joe, and Randy's okay with it too."

"Great so everyone's in on it but me, huh?" Midnight replied, smiling ruefully.

"Just us three."

"Okay, I think I can live with that."

They lay together silently for a while. Midnight was thinking of a song that Rick had been playing in the car on the way to the restaurant that evening.

"Rick," she said softly.

"Hmmm?" he answered. His eyes were closed, he opened one eye, just barely.

"That tape you were playing on the way to the restaurant, who was that?"

"Def Leppard, why?" He closed the eye he had opened.

"Well that song, that talks about not being able to stop the feeling of love … What's it called?"

"It's called 'Hysteria,' " Rick said.

"I like it."

"Yeah, I like it too, makes me think of us. How we both seemed to fight these feelings."

"'Cause we were both chicken shits," Midnight said, chuckling as she did.

Rick laughed softly too. "That's pretty accurate, yeah."

"Do you think it would be a cool song to play at the wedding for our first dance?"

He was happy to hear her talking about the wedding already. He opened his eyes looking at her "A rock song? At a wedding? Is that traditional?"

"Well," she said, laughing, "I'm not exactly the traditional type bride, and I don't think you," she said pulling at one of his long brown curls, "qualify for traditional groom of the year either."

He laughed. "Yeah I guess that's true enough."

CHAPTER 8

The next day Anabelle and Robert Debenshire were very happy to add their son's engagement to the celebrations taking place that evening. Anabelle hugged Midnight warmly. Robert hugged her too, to everyone's surprise. Robert Debenshire was a loving man, but he wasn't given to emotional gestures. He was just so happy with his son's choice. Katherine was still fuming over the scene at Harrods, but the other three sisters congratulated Midnight and Rick warmly.

That night at the engagement party, Katherine found solace with Teddy Anne, who was Rick's ex-fiancée. Teddy Anne was a tall dark-haired blue-eyed model type. While very pretty when made up, she paled in comparison to Midnight who looked absolutely breathtaking in a black gown that accentuated her delicate features perfectly. Her copper-blond hair was pinned up, with ringlets dropping in silken tendrils around her face and down her back. She had used more makeup than she usually did, accenting her gold-green eyes with just the slightest touch of emerald-green shadow, and hunter-green eyeliner.

A thin chain of gold suspending a deep emerald heart sparkled at her throat, and emeralds sparkled at her ears. Rick had given them to her earlier in the evening, calling them an engagement gift. The Debenshire family had been waiting in the front room when Midnight had entered. Rick had stood staring at her speechless, he had always considered her beautiful, but on this night she was absolutely gorgeous. Midnight had laughed at his reaction, as the rest of the family told her how beautiful she looked, except for Katherine of course, who had stood back and said nothing. Rick had taken her aside, touching her gently as if she were made of glass, and told her over and over how incredible she looked, how much he loved her, and then he had handed her the box that contained the emerald heart and earrings. He had made a point of not making them too extravagant, knowing Midnight would refuse to accept them if he did.

Now in the grand ballroom of the Royal Windsor Hotel, Rick stared at his bride-to-be from across the room. Midnight was standing with Joe and Randy, laughing at something Joe had just whispered to her. Joe had been overwhelmingly happy to hear about Midnight's acceptance of Rick's proposal. Joe had told Rick he really didn't know if she would accept, he had said that it wasn't that he didn't believe Midnight loved Rick, but he had said, "She's just not into that commitment stuff, ya know?" But Joe had been very glad to find out he was wrong.

Rick watched Joe and Midnight interact, and he thought again of their conversation the night before. He was now very happy they had gotten their feelings out into the open, it had taken a huge weight off his heart. Rick had hated feeling like he did about their relationship, he felt like he was betraying his best friend by thinking the way he had, and he had felt horrible hiding his feelings from Midnight. Now everything was cleared up and he felt like everything was going to go right for them now.

Rick was about to join Midnight, Joe, and Randy when his mother approached him.

"Richard, could I have a quick word with you, dear?"

"Sure, Mum, what's up?" Rick answered smiling at his mother.

"Well, I didn't know if you and Midnight had talked about the wedding. I mean other than actually deciding to get married and all ..." Anabelle hesitated looking at her son.

"Well, no we didn't really, I guess. We'll have to here soon, why?"

"I was just wondering, do you think Midnight would take it the wrong way if I offered to help out? I have been through this with Deborah, so I know what all is involved ..." It was obvious she didn't want to interfere, or put her two cents in where they weren't wanted.

"No, Mum," Rick began, his eyes going to Midnight again, "I think that would be great. Maybe Deb, Mandy, and Allie could help too. I know Night likes them."

"That's a good idea. You don't think she'll mind?"

"Well, as long as you let her make all the decisions. She's used to that you know. I don't think she'd mind at all. In fact she'd probably welcome it. Planning weddings isn't really her forte." His eyes trailed over to Midnight again. Joe and Randy had moved to talk to someone else and he saw Katherine, with Teddy Anne in tow heading toward Midnight. He wanted to get over there, but he didn't want to be rude to his mother.

"It's settled then," Anabelle said, smiling as she put her hand on her son's arm. "I'll try to talk to her tonight about it." She tightened her grip on Rick's arm, looking directly into his eyes. "I think you made a very wise choice there, Richard. She is a very special girl, and very beautiful too. You make a handsome couple."

"Thanks, Mum," Rick said, glad that his mother obviously liked Midnight a great deal. He saw Midnight looking up at Katherine, a blank look on her face. Then he saw a familiar look cross her face. It was look she gave people who made the mistake of taking her for a fool. She was obviously doing fine with Katherine this time.

Midnight wasn't altogether surprised when Katherine approached her with a dark-haired woman in tow. Midnight was almost sure that this woman was the fabled Teddy Anne. Rick had told her about Teddy Anne the night before. They had talked about a lot of things last night. Rick told her that he and Teddy Anne had been engaged before he left England. His parents had wanted him to get married, and since he couldn't stand most of the society types he had dated, he had opted for Teddy Anne.

Teddy Anne was the closest thing he had been able to find to a rebel in London society. She did things that made her stand out in a crowd. She was a little on the wild side. They had been a good pair, Rick told her. They got into all kinds of mischief together. He had decided that if he had to marry someone, she would at least be a little more fun than one of the stoic, impeccably groomed dolls of English society. He had eventually decided that marrying her would be a mistake too, he didn't love her. He liked her, but there was no great love there. So he had broken it off with her right before he had gone to America. He had described her to Midnight, and now Midnight was sure that the woman standing beside Katherine was her.

Midnight looked at Katherine, and smiled, a cool smile.

"Midnight," Katherine said, managing to make her name sound inferior. "I'd like you to meet Theodora Emerson." It was obvious she was watching for some kind of reaction from Midnight.

Midnight looked at Teddy Anne and inclined her head slightly, her eyes not leaving the other woman's. "Nice to meet you," she said, keeping her tone level.

"Katherine has told me a great deal about you," Teddy Anne said. She accent made her sound very sophisticated, but her eyes sparkled with sarcasm.

Midnight's gaze didn't even flicker. "Really? That's strange, she knows absolutely nothing about me." Her smile remained on her face, and she was happy to note that Katherine's waivered. Teddy Anne looked surprised at Midnight's words.

"Well she told me that you and Richard are engaged," Teddy Anne said, having recovered quickly.

"I see," Midnight responded, leaving no room for further comment.

There were a few moments of silence as Teddy Anne and Midnight looked at each other, neither one willing to be the first to lower her eyes.

"Teddy Anne was engaged to Richard, before he left for America," Katherine said conversationally, but it was obvious from the way she watched Midnight that she was expecting it to be a surprise to the younger woman.

Midnight didn't say anything for a long moment. She kept her face composed in a look of superiority. Her catlike eyes shifted from Katherine to Teddy Anne, then she smiled a lopsided sardonic smile. "You should have held on to him when you had the chance."

Teddy Anne's mouth all but dropped open at Midnight's statement. She made a startled sound, as her blue eyes widened slightly at Midnight. But again, she recovered quickly and her face took on a knowing, haughty look. She shook her head, as if about to address a dull-witted child.

"Don't be too confident, dear," she said, her eyes staring down at Midnight. "I can take him back, all too easily."

Midnight looked calmly at Teddy Anne, her lips curling in derision. "Go ahead and try," she said challengingly.

Teddy Anne looked at the younger woman in open surprise, as did Katherine. After a few moments, a triumphant smile crossed Teddy Anne's face. Midnight only stared at her calmly, the picture of serenity and confidence.

Teddy Anne looked around the room, seeing Rick heading toward them. She moved to intercept him and put her arm through his.

"Richard Debenshire, you haven't danced with me once this evening," she chided, her voice sweet and affectionate.

"Can't have that, can we?" Rick said smoothly. They made their way to the dance floor, and Rick caught a fleeting glimpse of Midnight watching him, a confident smile on her face. He knew something had just transpired between his bride-to-be and the woman he now held in his arms.

After a few moments, Teddy Anne moved her hand up to the base of his neck possessively, as she always had when they were dating. Her eyes gazed up at him. "I've missed you terribly," she said, her voice petulant. "And you never even called me. I thought we were closer than that." Her voice turned seductive on the last part.

"Things got a little complicated in America," Rick said apologetically. "But I'm here now," he finished, his smile warm.

"Yes," she said, her fingers stroking the back of his neck, "with a fiancée no less." She said the word "fiancée" as if it didn't mean anything to her, just another word for girlfriend.

"Well," he said, moving his lips closer to her ear, "I was under the impression from our last parting words that you never wanted to see me again. What was it?" His voice took on her sophisticated tone. "*A cold day in hell* before I'd see your bed again?" His tone was playful.

"Well, you can't blame me for being angry with you, the way you broke things off, without much of an explanation …"

"I know," he said. "I was a bit of a shit, wasn't I?"

"Yes, Richard you were … but I'm willing to forget about it …"

"You would be?" he said surprised. She shuddered as his lips brushed her ear. She could feel his warm breath on her cheek.

"Yes," she breathed, feeling the old familiar warmth start in her body.

"But your parents don't think I'm fit for you," Rick said remorsefully.

"My mother commented just a few minutes ago how you seem to have settled down a great deal over the last year," Teddy said, smiling winningly up at him.

"Really?" Rick said, smiling like a kid at Christmas.

"Of course," Teddy said, frowning prettily, "there would be the matter of your current engagement." She gazed up at him through the veil of her long lashes.

"That's true," Rick said, nodding, pursing his lips in thought. "It could pose a problem."

"She's from limited means, isn't she?" Teddy said then.

"Well, yes …" Rick said, his face brightening slightly.

"I'm sure that between our two families and our own trust funds we could come up with a decent … settlement for her." Teddy's voice sounded triumphant. And that little bitch dared to challenge her hold on Rick … ha! She'd grabbed him back right out from under the girl's nose, without even having to try very hard, a few looks, a caress and he was hers once again.

"Well …" Rick began, looking down at Teddy Anne. "There are still three little problems," he said mournfully.

"And what would those be, love?" Teddy said, gazing happily up at him. There was nothing that money couldn't solve, she'd always known that.

"Well, first of all, I gave her my grandmother's ring."

Teddy Anne shrugged. "So make that part of the settlement, you get the ring back."

"Well, the other thing is a little more complicated."

"What is it?" she asked, smiling at him.

"Well … she's pregnant." His voice was very repentant.

"Oh, my … that is a little more complicated, but nothing a little more money won't handle, I'm sure. How far along, do you know?" she asked then, thinking an abortion might be a quick answer.

"Only a month, I think," he answered, looking down at her like a child begging to be forgiven.

"Don't worry about a thing, darling. We can deal with that easily." She gave him an indulgent smile. She had always known Rick was kind of a slut, he just got into trouble this time. "Now what's the third problem, dear heart?" she asked, feeling very generous with her forgiveness. She may even let him make love to her later tonight.

"Well, the third problem," he said, his voice pained, his eyes apologetic. He hesitated, then averted his eyes from hers furtively.

"Richard, whatever it is, it can't be that bad ..." She touched his cheek. They had stopped dancing now and stood on the edge of the dance floor. To Teddy's happy surprise, ironically, they stood very close to where Midnight stood watching them, and definitely within earshot. "What is it Richard?" she asked, her voice soft and sweet.

Rick looked her straight in the eye then, his face a calm mask. "I happen to be in love with her, think you can solve that?" His voice took on a mocking tone on the last, as his lips curled in a sardonic smile.

Teddy stood stock still, staring up at him openmouthed. She could hear Midnight laughing behind her, but she continued to stare up at Rick, sure that he was going to tell her he was only joking. He didn't. He took a step back from her, and bowed mockingly, his eyes never leaving hers, the twisted grin still on his lips. He turned, and as she watched, he walked over to Midnight and took her in his arms, kissing her passionately. Midnight's arms went around his neck, and her hands entwined themselves in his hair. Teddy was sure she was about to die from embarrassment. Blindly she turned and walked out of the room.

"Whatever did you say to her, Mr. Debenshire?" Midnight asked, laughing.

Rick grinned down at her. "I knew what she was up to, I didn't think she'd take it that far ... but ..." He shrugged, smiling. His face became serious for a moment as he looked down at Midnight. "I love you," he said softly.

"I love you, too," she said, pulling his head down to hers to kiss him again.

A few minutes later, Joe and Randy wandered over to Midnight and Rick.

"What was that about?" Joe said, nodding toward the dance floor.

"Oh," Rick said, his arm around Midnight. "Teddy thought she'd just make her last play, that's all."

"I see," Joe said, grinning at his friend. "Didn't get too far, did she?" Joe said, his tone matter of fact.

"She was coming on to you?" Randy said then, her voice incredulous.

Rick laughed, but Midnight answered. "She told me she could get him back if she wanted to, I told her to go ahead and try it," she said, shrugging.

Randy shook her head, at the nerve of Teddy. She excused herself then, deciding to try to find the ladies' room.

She walked through the ballroom, receiving appreciative glances from many of the men, but she didn't notice. She was wearing a white gown, with just a dusting of iridescent crystals that made her seem to glow. She was wearing the diamond and sapphire necklace Joe had bought for her in Paris, and there were small, but exquisite sapphire and diamond earrings at her ears. Her golden-blond hair flowed down her back, making her look like a fairy princess.

On her left hand sparkled the diamond ring, that Joe had had custom made for her at a jewelers in London. He had taken her into the store and the owner had personally helped her pick out the perfect setting and just the right size diamond. She didn't want anything too big or gaudy. She had settled on a marquee cut diamond set at an angle on the band, and Joe had suggested putting blue topaz baguettes along the band. The color of the blue topazes was called London Blue, and Joe said that they just about matched her eyes. The ring was absolutely magnificent, and the only one of its kind. The owner of the shop had christened the ring The Randissi.

The ring and other jewels sparkled on her as she walked under the lights of the ballroom. When she reached the doorway, she heard someone call her name softly. She turned and saw Roslynn, who beckoned her. Roslynn was wearing a sky-blue dress and plenty of jewels. "Hello," Roslynn said, when Randy was in front of her. Randy inclined her head to other woman. They were about the same height so they stood eye to eye.

"Hello," Randy said, keeping her voice even and polite.

"I wanted a chance to speak to you privately, can we go outside?" Roslynn said, moving toward the veranda. Randy nodded and followed her. Once outside, Roslynn turned to her. "I don't think you realize what your marrying Joseph will do …" Her voice trailed off, as if to indicate such dire consequences.

"Roslynn …" Randy sighed, leaning against the stone railing of the balcony. She had half hoped that Roslynn had wanted to apologize for her behavior of a couple of weeks ago.

"Now, just hear me out," Roslynn said, holding up a perfectly manicured hand. "Joseph, is the last of his father's line … he needs to marry a woman who can produce an heir to the Sinclair fortune …"

"As far as I know," Randy said, canting her head to the side, "I am capable of bearing children." Her voice was calm.

"Yes, but you aren't … well, frankly you aren't, how can I say this? You're not from the right background." She looked at Randy again, and rushed on when she saw a slow irritated smile start on Randy's face. "Joseph needs to marry a woman from a good family. He needs to come back to society, before his family name is removed from the societal rolls. You don't understand the importance of one's status here. And Joseph marrying you will put his family name in an abysmal pit, and I feel a responsibility to try and keep that from happening. I am a close friend of the family, and I feel that out of duty to the Sinclair's I must beseech you to consider your actions, and the repercussions they could have on Joseph in the future." Roslynn was clutching her hands together dramatically.

Randy found herself staring down at Roslynn's hands. She noticed that Roslynn no longer wore the diamond wedding ring she had on at their last meeting. She didn't say anything. She couldn't think of anything to say. Roslynn's speech hadn't left much room for response. Randy could see that there was more the woman wanted to say, and she hoped that by keeping silent Roslynn would just get on with it so she could get back inside and back to the man she loved.

"I know," Roslynn said, her voice taking on a companionably tone, "that you think you're in love with Joseph, and who could blame you? But you couldn't possibly understand everything he's gone through, everything he went through when his parents were killed. I know that he's just shut out his parents' memory to keep the pain away, but that doesn't mean that he shouldn't do what's right. Maybe, if you … left … if you told him you'd changed your mind … maybe …"

"Maybe," came Joe's voice from just behind Roslynn. He stepped out of the shadows, his eyes narrowed at her. "If you and Taylor would stay the hell out of my life, I could finally get some peace." His voice was cold and hard. He walked over to Randy, and put his arm around her. She leaned against him gratefully. "I think we've heard just about enough of this crap," Joe said, looking down at Randy.

Randy shook her head slowly, her eyes locked with Roslynn's. "Why don't you work on your own marriage, Roslynn, and I'll take care of Joe," Randy said, glancing up at Joe. She caught his proud smile. Without another word, they walked back into the ballroom, arm and arm.

****

A week and a half later, Randy and Midnight stood in the dressing room to the Christ Church in Turnham Green, London. Joe had been right, the church was absolutely beautiful, and not too overwhelming. Both women wore white gowns. They laughed together nervously over the fact that neither one of them was entitled to wear white.

"At least your closer to it than me," Midnight said, with a mock grimace.

"It's all in the mind, you know …" Randy said, laughing.

"Being a virgin?" Midnight said, raising an eyebrow at the younger girl. "I think you have that confused with mental health."

"Probably," Randy said, smiling. "I'm so nervous right now I don't even think I can remember my own name."

"It's Randissi Curtis," came a familiar voice from the doorway. Randy turned, and cried out. Darrell and Donovan stood in the doorway. Randy all but hurled herself into Darrell's arms, she was so surprised at seeing them. She knew Joe had something to do with this, somehow.

Actually, he had everything to do with Darrell and Donovan's appearance at the wedding. Joe had written Darrell a simple letter, telling him that Randy's happiness should be more important than Darrell's pride. He also wrote that since Randy's father was who knew where, the honor of giving her away would fall to Darrell, and Joe knew he'd regret having missed the opportunity. Joe's final words in the letter were, "You won't be doing this for me, you'll be doing this for your baby sister." Joe had included two open-ended round trip airline tickets to England in the package, and sent it off. Joe had been surprised to receive a note in return telling him that they would be there. He had kept it a secret, wanting to give Randy one last happy surprise on their big day.

She was happy and so surprised. Darrell admired his little sister, and couldn't believe how beautiful and happy she looked. Randy was wearing a traditional wedding gown, although the beauty of the gown was anything but average. It had a high collar and a sweetheart neckline. The bodice was covered with thousands of tiny iridescent seed pearls and was form fitting and cut in at the waist, making Randy's already small waist seem even smaller. The skirt flared from the waist, and was draped with antique hand-stitched lace, that also made up the twenty-foot train. Her veil was a halo of seed pearls and tulle. Her long hair was pulled back in a braid that had baby's breath braided into it. At her throat, she wore the intricately designed filigree gold and diamond necklace that Joe had given her as a wedding present. She had been speechless when she had opened the box the night before. He had bought her matching diamond earrings too. Randy had chided Joe about being so extravagant, but he had only shrugged and said that she was worth every penny. Now standing in the dressing room gazing up at her brother, she was an absolute vision of purity and innocence.

"When did you get here?" Randy asked Darrell happily.

"Last night … but Joe wanted it to be a surprise …" Darrell said, for once not referring to Joe by his surname. Randy took note of it, but didn't comment.

"I'm so glad you came …" Randy said, smiling, "and you both look so nice in those tuxedos, especially you Donovan." She gave her little brother a sideways glance and hugged him a moment later as he started to blush.

There was a knock on the door, and Anabelle slipped inside. "It's time ladies," she said, smiling. She nodded to Darrell and Donovan; she'd already met them a few minutes before, when Joe had introduced them, before asking Anabelle to show them to the dressing room.

Randy and Midnight looked at each other.

"Oh shit," Midnight said, grinning and placing her hand on her stomach. "I don't know if it's the baby, or the nerves, but I'm in one big knot here …" She laughed nervously. Anabelle walked over to her daughter-in-law to be.

"Now Midnight, you look beautiful." She looked at Midnight pretending to be serious. "You're going to go out there and marry my only son, so if anyone has a right to be nervous around here it's me …" Midnight laughed at that.

"I guess you're right," Midnight said then, still smiling.

Anabelle and Midnight had spent the evening before talking. Midnight had finally gotten up the nerve to tell Anabelle about the baby. She and Rick had omitted that part when they had announced their engagement. Rick hadn't been sure how his parents would take the news, so he wanted to wait. But Midnight had felt guilty about hiding it from Anabelle. She had been so helpful and nice about everything, and Midnight felt that she deserved the truth. Anabelle had been silent for a moment, nodding her head understandingly when Midnight had explained that that wasn't the reason she and Rick were getting married. She explained that he hadn't known she was pregnant when he had asked her to marry him. Midnight had held her breath wondering what Rick's mother would say. After a long moment, Anabelle had surprised Midnight by taking her in her arms and giving her a warm hug.

"You love my son, and he very obviously loves you. That's a good enough explanation for me, Midnight. I'm very happy for you. I hope a baby is what you want right now, though." She had looked concerned, remembering what Rick had said about her being very work oriented.

Midnight had looked reflective for a moment, then looked directly at her mother-in-law to be. "You know, when the doctor told me, I wasn't really happy about it. My job ... well it's not really one that I can easily work around being pregnant. But then I thought of Rick, and how much he means to me and I figured what better way to show him how much I love him, than by having his child. Sounds kinda corny doesn't it?" She had said the last shaking her head.

"Not in the least. In fact, it's music to a mother's ears, to hear a woman speak so lovingly of her son. The fact that you are willing to give up some of your own hard-won freedom for him is what every mother dreams of for her son." Anabelle's eyes had grown misty with tears, thinking of her son and Midnight together over the last couple of weeks

Now standing looking down at Midnight, Anabelle felt a need to comfort the girl.

"Come now, Rick tells me you've fought the biggest and baddest gang members in the western hemisphere," Anabelle said. "What have you got to fear from a little priest …" Her voice trailed off challengingly.

Midnight grinned at her, she knew what she was doing, but she appreciated it. She took a deep breath, closing her eyes and centering herself, much like she did before a confrontation. Then opening them, she nodded. Randy walked out first with Darrell and Donovan trailing after her. Anabelle walked out, and Midnight followed. Randy was to be escorted down the aisle first. Midnight had jokingly said that if anyone was going to trip, she wanted Randy to be first. As Midnight stood at the back of the church waiting nervously, she was surprised by a familiar voice.

"Fancy meeting you here."

Midnight turned and looked into the eyes of Tom Ryan, looking very dapper in a tuxedo. "Tom!" she whispered fiercely, as she hugged him. "Oh my God! How did you … When …" she stammered, trying to ask a million questions at once.

"Your fiancé," Tom answered simply. Midnight smiled, remembering that she and Rick had discussed the "giving away" part. She had said that there was no way in hell she was even considering her own father. Finally, she had shrugged and said, "So I give myself away, I've done everything else for myself over the years, why not this too."

It had occurred to Rick then that Tom Ryan would be a likely stand-in for Midnight's real father. He had put in a call to Tom and Tom had been more than happy to oblige. He had even refused Rick's offer to pay for the plane ticket. Now here he stood, looking down at the woman he had watched grow up.

"You look … fantastic," Tom said, smiling, every bit the role of the proud father.

Midnight did look fantastic. Her gown was fitted with the finest detailing of seed pearls, and iridescent sequins covering it. The bodice nipped in sharply at the waist, and continued snuggly to her knees where in flared. Her copper-blond hair was once again pinned up, with ringlets trickling down her back and at the side of her face. Her veil, a creation of seed pearls and sequins, came to a "V" at her forehead. She wore a pearl and diamond choker that had been a gift from Anabelle and Robert, along with a pair of pearl teardrop earrings. She looked beautiful and sexy at the same time.

At the front of the church, Rick and Joe waited, each of them cracking jokes and chuckling.

"I hate all this waiting," Joe said, under his breath.

"Me too."

"What's say we skip the reception and go straight to the honeymoon …" Joe suggested, grinning mischievously.

"Oh sure, my mum'll just kill us, that's all."

"Too right," Joe said, laughing lowly.

The music started and both men tensed. They were two men who had been in countless fights with gangs, they'd both been shot, stabbed and the like, yet the simple first strains of wedding music made both of them tense unaccountably. They both grinned at each other, knowing the other was outrageously nervous. Joe glanced over to where Taylor sat looking very reserved. He'd been surprised she'd come at all. He figured since many of his other relatives were in attendance, she thought she had to be. He thought again about everything she and Roslynn had said, and experienced a flash of doubt, but then movement at the back of the church caught his attention.

When he looked down the aisle and saw Randy looking absolutely incredible on Darrell's arm, that doubt was permanently and resoundingly extinguished. He stared at Randy, not believing that she could be even more beautiful to him than she had always been, but here she was coming toward him, and he was stunned.

Her eyes were on him, she was thinking much along the same lines. Joe looked incredibly handsome in the black tuxedo and tails he and Rick had opted for. When Darrell and Randy reached the alter, Joe stepped forward. Darrell turned to Randy and kissed her on the cheek. He turned to Joe and took Joe's extended hand. He leaned in and in an undertone said, "You better take good care of her, Sinclair." Joe looked at the younger man, and nodded slowly his eyes steady. He had every intention of taking care of Randy. His eyes went to Randy, and as Darrell stepped back she stepped forward. Joe extended his arm to her and she took it, he noticed her hand was shaking as she did.

"You look incredible," Joe whispered to her in awe.

"So do you," she whispered back, smiling shyly up at him.

They stepped aside then as the second bridge of music started. Joe looked at Rick, and saw that his friend was looking at Katherine.

As Randy had come down the aisle, Rick had looked from her to his family, his gaze coming to rest on Katherine, who had a sour look on her face. He continued to stare at her. When she finally met his gaze, he could see that she'd read his displeasure. Her face reflected surprise at his obvious discontent but it was also obvious that she didn't intend to back down. Rick shook his head slightly, pursing his lips, as if saying he didn't understand her at all. He looked up, just as Midnight and Tom Ryan entered the back of the church. Every thought about his family, his sister, everything, went straight out of his head.

He almost forgot to breath, he was so entranced by his bride. His eyes connected with hers as she started down the aisle, and their eyes stayed locked. In his look, she saw all of the love and devotion that he held for her. She also saw surprise. She thought he looked drop dead handsome in the tuxedo, and she still couldn't really believe that she was actually marrying this gorgeous man. When Midnight and Tom got to the alter, Rick stepped forward. Tom turned, raising Midnight's hand to his lips. He kissed it and smiled at her warmly. She returned his smile and winked at him.

Tom turned to Rick. Grasping his outstretched hand, he leaned in and said, "Hold on to this one tight." He said in an undertone, grinning widely at Rick. Rick chuckled lowly and nodded.

Then he turned his eyes back to Midnight's. She was watching the exchange between them with a soft smile. She took his proffered arm, squeezing it gently as she looked up at him. Suddenly she didn't feel nervous at all. She felt that this was right and what they had been destined for all along.

She had chided herself over and over again at not admitting it to herself sooner, but she knew that her independent spirit had wanted to deny needing someone as much as she needed him. Now looking up into his beautiful deep blue eyes, she knew everything was as it should be. She and Joe exchanged a quick glance and both grinned. She knew he was considering the irony of this day too. Then the priest began the ceremony and they were both caught up in his words.

Three hours later, at the reception held at the Sinclair estate, everyone waited for the entrance of the brides and grooms. Little did they know that the four were sitting in the limousine, drinking a bottle of champagne and reflecting on the day so far.

"I thought I was going to pass out, standing there forever!" Midnight said, laughing.

"Yeah, who told the guy to go on and on like that?" Rick seconded, laughing too.

"Well," Joe said, grinning, "your mum arranged the priest, talk to her."

"Great!" Rick said.

"I thought it was a nice ceremony," Randy put in with a serious face. But then she broke into a laugh as the other three stared at her openmouthed. "Okay, okay! It was a bit much!" she said then, holding her hands up in defense and laughing.

They all laughed, thinking of how often they all had wanted to tell the priest to hurry it up. When he had finally pronounced them each husband and wife, and had presented them as Mr. and Mrs. Sinclair, and Mr. and Mrs. Debenshire, they had all but run back down the aisle. After the tiring round of photographs, they had all hid out in the limousine. Joe had told the driver to drive around for a while. Meanwhile they had taken out a bottle of champagne and relaxed.

"So what do you think the odds are," Joe began slowly, looking at Rick, "that we'd get away with skipping the reception all together?" Randy and Midnight laughed. Rick shook his head.

"About nil," he said, grinning. "You know my mum, she'll hunt us down, and I don't think you or my lovely *wife* could hold her off, even with your guns ..." He had stressed the word wife, looking down at Midnight, who leaned against him, sprawled out on the seat of the limo. She had taken off her veil, and taken her hair down. It now fell in silky waves down her back. She looked momentarily taken aback.

"Wife?" she said, her voice tremulous. "Oh shit ..." she said then, a slow grin starting on her face.

"Oh, love, it will only get worse," Rick said, smiling. "Wait till it's mother of my child ..."

Midnight rolled her eyes. "Wait ... I think I want to take this back!" she said dramatically, pulling playfully at the rings on her left hand.

"Oh no you don't!" Rick said, covering her hand with his. "You're mine, there's no turning back now!"

Midnight looked at Joe, who was smiling at them. "Aren't you gonna help me?" she asked petulantly. "You are supposed to be my backup, you know!"

"Not anymore," Joe said, "not in the relationship department anyway. That's Rick's job now, just like it's Randy's job for me." He said the last, kissing the top of Randy's head. She too had removed her veil, and was sitting in the circle of Joe's arms. She turned to him, smiling.

"And I have no intention of going anywhere," she said, reaching up to touch his cheek. He leaned down and kissed her softly.

"We better get in there," Rick said after a few more minutes. The limo was sitting just outside of the gates to Joe's house.

"Hey, yeah," Midnight said, sitting up. "I haven't even *seen* your house yet. I'll need a tour, you know ..."

"Yeah, I know," Joe said, smiling. "Otherwise you'll probably get lost." He reached behind him and knocked on the glass between them and the driver, indicating they were ready to go now.

"I got lost my first day here," Randy said, laughing.

"That big, huh?" Midnight said. Then she gasped as they drove around the bend and Joe's house came into view. "Jesus Christ!" she whispered. She looked over at Joe, who was watching her for her reaction. He shrugged. She shook her head, she knew her partner was worth a lot of money, but she had never really put it into perspective until now.

As they entered the large ballroom style room in Joe's house, everyone applauded. They spent the next three hours trying to talk to as many people as possible. Joe introduced Randy to his relatives, some of whom he had never even really met himself. She was impressed with the people that made up the Sinclair family. Just about every member of Joe's family found Randy to be an enchanting girl and thought that Joseph had done well for himself. None of them seemed to take the view that Taylor had voiced. One particular uncle on Joe's father's side of the family told Randy that his brother's son was very lucky and he wished that he had been so lucky when he'd married. His wife had promptly elbowed him in the ribs, and they had laughed merrily. Randy felt much better about the whole family name thing, seeing that Taylor was apparently the exception, not the rule.

Midnight and Rick also made the rounds. Midnight met Deborah's husband and their two daughters. She decided right away that she agreed with Rick, Deborah's husband was a stuffed shirt, and she couldn't see how someone as lively as Deborah could stand his stoic manner. Their daughter's, however, made Midnight wish mightily that the baby she carried was a girl. Susan and Elizabeth were pictures of their mother. They were happy-go-lucky children, who also happened to entranced by their beautiful new aunt.

Rick was talking to one of his many relatives and happened to glance over at Midnight. A smile lit his face. She was standing with Susan on one side of her and Elizabeth on the other. Both girls were holding her hands, staring up at her adoringly. Midnight was laughing and talking to them animatedly, obviously very comfortable with children. It surprised Rick. He had never seen her deal with children, he had no idea she even liked them. His wife was certainly a mysterious package. He watched as she knelt down and hugged both girls. She closed her eyes as if making a wish. Then she opened them and looked directly at him. Seeing him watching her, she smiled and winked.

There was the time for the "fathers" of the brides to dance with their "daughters." By this time everyone knew that Darrell was Randy's older brother, and that Tom Ryan was a very close friend of Midnight's. All the same, it was very poignant to see the two men lead the two new brides out to the dance floor, both men very obviously proud of the young woman on his arm. Randy and Midnight had talked about what song they wanted to dance to with their respective escorts. They had decided on newly released ballad by Queensrÿche, called "Silent Lucidity." As the song began, both Tom and Darrell took their respective charges in their arms, surprised by the song. But as the chorus began, both women mouthed the words, looking up at the man holding them. The chorus seemed to define both Tom and Darrell's place in their lives, talking about watching over these young women and protecting them in a kind of quiet grace.

Tom smiled down at Midnight, as they continued to dance. "You look absolutely wonderful today, young lady." His eyes grew soft as he looked at her. "Certainly not the little gang member I met so long ago."

Midnight grinned at him. "Yeah, I guess not huh? Did you think we'd ever make it this far?"

"I always knew you were destined for a lot more, Midnight," he chided gently.

"Yes, you did, didn't you," she said then, a beatific smile on her face. "You were always behind me, keeping an eye on me, weren't you?"

"Yep, but you never really needed me much, you did everything for yourself. You've come a long way, Midnight."

"Yeah, but I wouldn't have, if it wasn't for you. I would have gone and killed that gang leader and probably landed in jail for it. But you changed that, you got me going the right way. That's something I don't think I've ever really thanked you for …"

"Seeing you today, as beautiful as you've become, seeing you happy, and marrying a man you so obviously love, that's enough. That's what I've always wanted for you, little one." At that moment, Tom Ryan looked every bit the proud father, and Midnight decided that he would have to play an important part in the life of the child she carried. She wanted her child to have a grandfather figure. She wanted her child to have everything she never had, a family a home life, *everything.*

Randy looked up at her big brother, once again very happy that he had come. She knew that his presence didn't mean that he accepted Joe, but it did mean that he was willing to try. She was glad.

"Have I told you today, how beautiful you look?" Darrell asked, smiling down at his sister.

"Yes," she answered, blushing.

"Well, it's still true, you look great, Randy. You look happy too," he said then, looking chagrinned. "I guess I'd have to be blind not to see that, huh?"

"I am happy, Darrell. I love him," she said softly.

"Yeah, I guess I'll have to give the guy a chance. I was just looking out for you, you know," he said looking rather sheepish.

"I know, Darrell," she said, placing her hand on his cheek. "But you have to get to know Joe; he's sweet, and caring. He needs me, Darrell, and I need him." Her voice was quiet but sure, and Darrell Curtis knew that his little sister had grown up, and that she knew what she wanted.

"So," he said, shrugging and grinning at his sister. "I'll give the guy a chance, but if he ever hurts you ..." His voice trailed off ominously.

"You'll kill him," Randy finished for him, smiling at him like a child.

"Damn right."

When the time came for the newlyweds' first dance, the dance floor cleared and Rick, Midnight, Randy, and Joe walked out. The first piano chords of the acoustic version of Def Leppard's "Hysteria" played and the guests listened intently as the words of the song surrounded them. At first, everyone was surprised that they had chosen a rock song, but everyone who knew Rick and Joe, knew they never did anything traditionally. The words of the song did seem quite fitting.

The reception went long into the night. Midnight and Joe stole off together at one point so Joe could show her the rest of the house. They ended up in his old bedroom. She looked at the picture of the Black Knights and then at him.

"I guess you've come a long way, haven't you?" she said.

Joe was sitting on the end of the bed.

"Yeah, I guess I have, but so have you," he said, looking at his partner standing in her wedding dress, in his room. He was struck again by the irony of it all. "Kinda like full circle."

She turned to him. "Yeah, that's what I was thinking too." She sat next to him, sitting shoulder to shoulder with him. "It's like, everything was always meant to be this way. Like we were supposed to meet, and work together ... you know ..."

"Yeah," he said, looking down at her. "If my parents hadn't been killed, I wouldn't have come to America, I wouldn't have worked with you, I wouldn't have gotten Randy for a secretary ..."

"I wouldn't have met Rick ..." she continued for him. "We wouldn't have ended up back here ..." She looked around the room, her gaze falling on the Black Knights jacket on the chair in the corner. She walked over to it and picked it up. She looked at it, then at him. "I still have my Vettes jacket ... somewhere ... funny that we haven't gotten rid of them ... being the sources of our pain and all ..."

"Maybe they're not though," Joe said, his eyes on her, "maybe that's just what we've always thought, but maybe being in the gang was our source of strength. It certainly was a starting point for where we are now."

Midnight looked at him, surprised by his words. "You know," she said slowly, looking again at the leather jacket she held, "I think you're right." She walked back over to him, and sitting down, holding the jacket on her lap, she bumped her shoulder against his companionably. "I'm supposed to be the one with the degree in psychology, you know," she said, grinning at him.

"Maybe you're rubbing off on me," he said, smiling back.

They sat in silence for a while. Eventually his arm went around her shoulders and she leaned against him. Both of them reflected on the day's events, and the events leading up to it. A little while later Rick stuck his head in the door, then looked back over his shoulder.

"Yep, I was right, they're in here," he said, then he pushed open the door. Randy stood behind him, smiling. "We figured this is where you two had gotten to," Rick said, grinning as he leaned against the doorjamb.

"Come on in," Joe said, motioning to his friend. Rick walked in, and stood next to Midnight. She put her hand out and he took it. Randy walked in and Joe stood and walked over to her, she looked up at him her eyes reflecting her love for him. Reaching out he pulled her to him, kissing her tenderly.

"We should get back," Joe said, after a while.

Midnight sighed loudly, throwing herself back on the bed. "No!" she said melodramatically. "You can't make me go back there!"

Rick laughed, moving to sit next to her on the bed. She moved around so that her head rested in his lap.

"Okay so maybe we can stay here for a little while," Joe said, shrugging. He sat sit on his bed then, leaning against the headboard and pulled Randy down next to him. She sat next to him, her head on his chest.

"So …" Joe said after a few minutes of silence, "where do we go from here?"

"You mean, in general?" Midnight asked, looking up at Rick then back at Joe.

"Yeah."

"Are you trying to say that life will be anticlimactic after all this?" Randy asked with a sly smile.

Joe, Midnight, and Rick laughed.

"Yeah, I guess," Joe said, leaning over to kiss Randy again.

"Well," Rick said, looking down at Midnight, "I for one intend to ask the boss about going to the academy."

"You wanna be a real cop?" Midnight asked, surprised.

"And what's wrong with that?" Rick asked, raising an eyebrow at her. "My wife happens to be a cop."

"I just … well … okay." she said, finally. Then she looked at Randy. "What about you?" she asked. "You want to stay a secretary?"

Randy was silent for a long time, she hadn't really thought much past the wedding. She nodded slowly. "I guess, for now." Then she looked at Joe. "That and take care of Joe."

"That should be a full time job in itself!" Midnight said, laughing.

"Hey!" Joe said, indignantly, grinning all the while. Midnight just laughed harder and Rick joined her. Randy was nodding with a big smile on her face. "You too?" Joe asked, a look of mock distress on his face.

There was a knock on the door. They all looked up at it guiltily; they knew they should be downstairs.

"Yeah?" Joe said finally.

The door opened and Mason stuck his head in. "Master Sinclair?"

"Master?" Midnight echoed looking at Joe, her eyes wide.

"Shut up," Joe said to her in an undertone, as she started to grin. "Yeah, Mason, what's up?"

"Mrs. Debenshire asked me to look for you, sir …" Mason said, his voice trailed off, knowing that Joe didn't like to be tracked down. He never had, not even when he was a little boy.

"Well, don't tell anybody you found us," Joe said. Then as an afterthought he said, "Hey, Mason?"

"Yes sir?"

"Bring us a bottle of champagne will you, and four glasses."

"Yes sir," Mason said dutifully and closed the door.

"Good God, Joe, you are rich aren't you?" Midnight said unable to contain her laughter anymore.

"Oh shut up, Midnight. I have news for you, little girl, you're rich now too," Joe said, nodding at Rick.

Midnight's face grew serious. She looked up at Rick and he nodded slowly, a half grin on his face. "Shit," was all she said, as she started to grin too.

After a few minutes, Mason came back bearing a tray with a bottle of Dom Perignon sitting on ice and four crystal glasses. Joe took the bottle and popped the cork as Mason stood by. They all laughed again as the champagne started to foam out. Joe good naturedly put his mouth over the top to catch it, the other three laughed. Joe poured for them. Midnight sat up, but stayed close to Rick, his arm encircled her waist.

"That's great, thanks Mason. Give us about twenty minutes and then tell them we'll be right down, okay?"

Mason inclined his head respectfully and said, "Yes sir," then he left the room.

"Well," Joe said, holding his glass up. "What should we drink to?"

Randy and Rick shrugged. Midnight sat up straighter.

"I for one know what I want to toast," she said, looking at all three of them.

"What?" Joe said, his eyes meeting hers.

"FORS," she answered. "If it wasn't for FORS none of us would be here right now." Her gazed touched on each of them. She had just realized that she loved all three of them very much, and they were like the family she'd never had. The unit she had started a little over two ago was responsible for bringing them into her life and she was grateful for it.

Joe was nodding, as were Rick and Randy. "Alright then," Joe said, holding his glass higher. His eyes touched each one of them as Midnight's had. "To FORS."

They echoed him, raising their glasses to clink together. "To FORS."

You can find more information about the author and series here:

www.sherrylhancock.com

www.facebook.com/SherrylDHancock

www.ingramcontent.com/pod-product-compliance
Lightning Source LLC
Chambersburg PA
CBHW021954190626
46807CB00005BB/2266